Favorite Harlequin His
brings you a bra...

Heirs in Waiting

*One day these Oxford gentlemen will
inherit estates, titles and wealth.*

*But for now they're forging their
own paths in life...and love!*

With great titles will come great power and
responsibility, for which they must prepare. But
waiting in the wings isn't easy for these daring
gentlemen, so they're forging ahead on their own
paths, where they'll encounter three exceptional
women who would never be found at a *ton* ball...

Let's meet them in

Book 1: *The Bluestocking Duchess*

Book 2: *The Railway Countess*

and

Book 3: *The Explorer Baroness*

Author Note

I had the privilege of living in the Magreb when my husband was assigned to the Embassy in Tunis, Tunisia. I shall always treasure the two years we spent there, immersed in a different world. The Tunisian members of the International Women's Club went out of their way to be welcoming and to showcase the beauty and richness of their history and culture.

I knew my hero, Gregory, a landed aristocrat with his roots deep in English soil, needed to be paired with a heroine entirely different from anyone he'd ever known. So, drawing on the nineteenth-century European fascination with all things Ottoman, I found Charis, born of British parents but with an Ottoman "mother of the soul," who grew up in the lands we now call the Middle East. She loves traveling with her trader father, exploring new worlds as he collects artifacts.

England is as foreign to Charis as her unusual talents and interests are to Greg, and they quickly find themselves fascinated by each other. But how can a man tied to England and a free spirit intent on wandering the world find happiness together?

I hope you will enjoy their journey.

JULIA JUSTISS

The Explorer Baroness

HARLEQUIN®
HISTORICAL™

Recycling programs for this product may not exist in your area.

ISBN-13: 978-1-335-40745-0

The Explorer Baroness

Copyright © 2021 by Janet Justiss

This edition published by arrangement with Harlequin Books S.A.

For questions and comments about the quality of this book, please contact us at CustomerService@Harlequin.com.

Harlequin Enterprises ULC
22 Adelaide St. West, 40th Floor
Toronto, Ontario M5H 4E3, Canada
www.Harlequin.com

Printed in U.S.A.

Julia Justiss wrote her first ideas for Nancy Drew stories in her third-grade notebook and has been writing ever since. After publishing poetry in college, she turned to novels. Her Regency historicals have won or placed in contests by the Romance Writers of America, *RT Book Reviews*, National Readers' Choice Awards and the Daphne du Maurier Award. She lives with her husband in Texas. For news and contests, visit juliajustiss.com.

Visit the Author Profile page
at Harlequin.com for more titles.

To my husband, Ronnie,
who has faced grave injury and chronic pain
with grace, endurance and tenacity. Your strength
and courage are part of every hero I create.

Chapter One

London May 1834

Early on a pleasant late-May morning, Gregory Lattimar, eldest son and heir of Baron Vraux, walked stiffly down the stairs from his bedchamber towards the morning room overlooking the garden at Vraux House. Though the weather had been fair enough for him to ride, cutting down the time required for the journey from the family estate in Northumberland to London, there was no avoiding the fact that it had still been a long, often bone-jarring transit.

Railways, his friend and investor Crispin D'Aubignon, Viscount Dellamont predicted, would soon criss-cross the country, both speeding long journeys and making them more comfortable. Gregory smiled as he thought of his friend, whose wedding he'd recently attended in Newcastle.

He wasn't sure he'd welcome a shortening of the route. The long journey allowed him several days of leisure between his duties overseeing Entremer and tending the family's affairs in London.

Since he'd been away from the city longer than usual, the London accounts were likely to be even more tangled than normal, he thought with a sigh. For the thousandth time, he wished that the father who, by virtue of his lack of interest and neglect, had required Gregory to take over management of the Vraux assets immediately after leaving Oxford, could at least keep in order the records of his ever-growing collection of weapons, gems and artifacts.

A wish unlikely ever to be fulfilled, he acknowledged as he reached the main floor and headed to the morning room, where an informal breakfast would be set out on the sideboard. As time went on, his father grew increasingly distant and remote, spending the whole of his day immured in his library or in the ballroom converted to hold his vast collection, having his meals delivered to that room and seldom interacting with any member of the household.

Greg sometimes wondered how the Baron could tolerate the loneliness of such an existence, but the self-imposed isolation seemed to suit him. On the occasions when Greg was compelled to invade his father's domain to receive approval for some project at Entremer, catching his father's attention became more difficult, his focus on what Greg was trying to tell him more wandering. Greg was certain his father forgot his existence before he even left the room.

The older he grew, the more easily he was able to understand and forgive his beautiful mother for coping with her spouse's disinterest by looking elsewhere for affection.

As he walked into the morning room, intent on filling a plate and ordering fresh coffee, he stopped short. 'Mama!' he exclaimed, walking across to kiss the cheek she offered. 'What a delightful surprise! What are you doing up so early?'

Despite bearing her husband one son—him—twin daughters and a second son rumoured to be fathered by another man, the lady who smiled up at him seemed hardly old enough to have grown children. The dazzling beauty that had made her the diamond of her debut season nearly thirty years ago had hardly faded. Her porcelain face remained unlined, her golden hair luminous, her blue eyes bright, and the voluptuous figure that had made men vie for her favour still inspired fools with more lust than sense to try to tempt her into affairs. Even though she'd kept the promise she made to her girls when they'd turned sixteen that she would take no more lovers.

Unfortunately, her impeccable behaviour in the years since had not been enough to redeem her reputation. Greg could not forgive the society that had dubbed her notorious, while the men with whom she'd dallied had suffered no loss of standing.

'You arrived so late last night, we hardly had time for a chat, and I knew you would be up early to start on the accounts. I wanted to have you to myself over breakfast before you disappeared to take up your duties. Fill your plate and come tell me all about the wedding. I could hardly believe it when you wrote to me that Crispin was getting married!'

'It came as a shock to me, too.' After visiting the sideboard and pouring a cup of hot coffee from the pot the footman had brought in, Greg settled at the table beside his mother. 'I'd met the girl once before—Crispin's mother might have mentioned her when she called on you.'

'Yes, the "Factory Heiress", I believe they called her?'

His mother gave a dismissive sniff. 'Cruel and condescending, the ton gossips.'

'You should know better than most,' Greg said feelingly.

'Lady Comeryn told me she was rather surprised to find Miss Cranmore quite—genteel, despite her origins in trade. Lovely, well-spoken and, despite her wealth, neither covered in jewels nor overdressed in vulgar style, unlike some cit's daughters trying to catch a titled husband. Lady Comeryn assured me then that Crispin had no serious intentions towards the girl, and was only pretending to court her so that his father would allow the family to remain in London for the Season. You know Comeryn usually keeps poor Lady Comeryn shut up in the country, the dictatorial miser!'

His mother shook her head. 'Vraux has his faults, but despite…everything that happened…he has never tried to control me, limit my funds or threaten me with banishment to Entremer.'

Though Greg wouldn't have wanted his mother to have married an arrogant, egotistical autocrat like the Earl of Comeryn, he couldn't help thinking it would have been better for them all if the Baron had paid a little *more* attention to his neglected wife.

'Yes, Dellamont told me he'd agreed to enter society so his mother might have the treat of a season, which was the last I heard of the matter before I left for Entremer. Imagine my shock to discover that Crispin not only paid attention to the heiress, he decided to marry her!'

'You must tell me all about her and the wedding.'

And so, over coffee and toast for his mother and a hot cooked breakfast for himself, Gregory related his impressions of the new bride—bright, clever, welcom ing—confirmed that his friend seemed besotted with her, and finished by revealing that not only was the bride interested in Crispin's railway projects, her engineer father had trained her to be so proficient, his friend intended to use her as his technical advisor when he evaluated potential new railway investments.

'First your former carousing partner Gifford wed your sister, now your remaining close friends Dellamont and Alex Cheverton have found brides. Which leaves you the sole bachelor of the group. Are you finding it...somewhat lonely?'

'Not especially. I would never begrudge Temper and Giff their happiness. And since we left Oxford, I haven't been able to see either Dellamont or Alex all that often, with Cheverton in Sussex running Edge Hall for the Duke of Farisdeen and Dellamont riding around England, investigating railway projects. With his new wife-advisor at his side, Dellamont is even less likely to be in London, and with Alex occupied with *his* new wife and training for his eventual duties as the next duke, he won't have much time to spare either.'

He wouldn't admit it to his mother, but he was feeling... not abandoned, precisely, but...left out. His friends all now had wives who would naturally displace him as their closest advisor and confidante, changing the dynamics of their friendship for ever, even when they could meet. Pleased as he was for Gifford, Alex and Crispin, he would miss the closeness they'd shared.

'Not that I'm hinting it's time for you to marry,' his mother added. 'Far be it for me to urge anyone into that estate! Although when you *are* ready, I urge you to choose wisely—since you will have a choice. I would earnestly wish for you to have a more fulfilling marriage than mine has been.'

His mother hadn't had much choice. Her beauty hadn't been matched by her dowry, and to settle their debts, her family had pressed her to marry the wealthiest of her many suitors.

His father. The best reason Greg could come up with was that his father had decided to marry Miss Felicity Portman because she was the most beautiful woman he'd ever seen, choosing her as the first peerless object in his collection. He'd fulfilled his obligation to beget an heir and ignored her ever since.

'Never fear, Mama. When the time comes, I'll give due regard to choosing a woman who will give me at least a fair chance of marital happiness.'

He wouldn't wound her by telling her his primary criterion for marriage was finding a woman of impeccable reputation from a family of equally stainless repute in order to redeem the rakish reputation of his own clan, dubbed 'the Vraux Miscellany' by the ever-malicious ton for their varied parentage. In particular, he intended to harness his wife's sterling contacts to try to get his exiled mother received back into society, as such a warm and loving soul deserved to be.

He looked up from those reflections to see her studying his face. 'Truly, Mama. I can't say I expect to become as besotted as Alex and Crispin seem to be with their new wives, but surely I can find a woman with whom I build a harmonious and affectionate bond?'

'That is all I wish for,' she said simply, reaching over to squeeze his hand. 'Now, before I send you off, I need to warn you the task of sorting out Vraux's papers may be more...taxing than usual.'

'I thought it might, since I've been away longer.'

'It's more than just that. Let me summon Jennie, so she can explain.'

While his mother signalled the footman stationed by the door to fetch the girl, Greg wondered what could require a housemaid's explanation. Though the rooms of his private domain would seem to any disinterested observer to be in a state of continual disarray, his father had long ago forbidden any servant to dust, rearrange or try to sort through the vast assemblage of knives, daggers, swords, jewels, miniatures and small archaeological artefacts he collected.

A few minutes later, the girl arrived, looking nervous as she made her curtsey. 'Don't worry, Jennie, no one is going to scold you,' his mother assured her. 'Just tell Mr Lattimar what happened.'

'Well, sir, you know I know better than to go into His Lordship's rooms. But as I was cleaning the hallway, I saw a paper sticking out from under the library door. I tried to pull it out, but couldn't quite get it, so I thought I'd just open the door real quiet, like, slip it out and close it again, afore His Lordship could even notice.

'But there must have been a window open in the library, cause when I opened the door, a big "whoosh" of wind sent that paper flying. That, and a whole lot more that was on his desk, and them falling knocked over a stack of those funny curved knives, and made such a clatter as to wake the dead. His Lordship right started! Then he saw me and glared and yelled for me to get all the mess out of there. So I hurried and gathered up all the papers I could, and the knives and things, and rushed them out the door, him sh-shouting at me all the while,' the girl concluded, tears in her eyes again. 'Your lady mother told me to put everything on your desk in the study. I'm awful sorry, Mr Lattimar. I didn't mean to cause a ruckus.'

'I'm just sorry he frightened you, Jennie,' Greg said. 'Thank you for leaving everything in my office. You needn't worry; I'll sort it out.'

The maid bobbed another curtsey. 'Thank you for understanding, Mr Lattimar.'

After the maid hurried out, Lady Vraux sighed. 'Poor thing was practically in hysterics afterwards, Vraux frightened her so badly. It was all I could do to persuade her not to give notice. Heaven knows what the papers concern. You know Vraux never pays a particle of attention to any of them, be they invoices, descriptions of artefacts or offers from investors to purchase some of his collection.'

'I do indeed,' Greg said with a sigh. 'I'll go and have a look and see how bad it is this time.'

'The quantity of paper was impressive. Which is why I wanted to alert you before you went in to discover the heaps on your desk and suffered palpitations of the heart.'

'Thanks for the warning. And especially for the delight of sharing my breakfast with you.'

'An even greater delight for me, darling boy. You spend so much time at Entremer, I hardly ever see you. Well, I'll leave you to sort out those papers.' After rising, she kissed his forehead and walked gracefully out, the subtle scent of her violet perfume drifting in her wake.

Greg watched her leave with a familiar mix of affection, sadness and resolve. To his shame, he hadn't always treated his mother with kindness. As a boy struggling towards manhood, he'd resented the upheaval in the house from the coming and going of the assorted men who were or had aspired to be her lovers. He'd been embarrassed and angry at the sly innuendo in remarks made about her by his schoolmates at Eton. Which had generally led to a bout of fisticuffs with the offender, often followed by punishment from the headmaster.

He had left Eton an accomplished pugilist, he thought wryly. But the mother whom he'd sometimes shunned or wounded with angry words had returned nothing but gentleness and patience.

Now, as a man grown, an observer of the love matches of his friends, his sisters and his younger brother, he understood far better the loneliness and despair that had led Lady Vraux to look outside her marriage for the love and companionship her spouse disdained to provide.

He felt an echo of that loneliness now.

Despite the disaster of his parents' marriage, his siblings had managed to wed happily. His two closest friends seemed to have found equal harmony with their brides. Perhaps he could dare hope he himself might make a marriage that offered companionship, friendship—even love.

Maybe it was time to start looking for that lady of impeccable reputation.

Two hours later, Greg surveyed the several stacks of papers on his desk, frustration and anger having driven all other thoughts from his head. The hazardous array of papers, knives and daggers he'd found when he'd walked into his office had been as large and untidy as his mother had warned. It had taken almost an hour to carefully arrange the different styles of weapon into separate piles and sort the paperwork. Some of the latter appeared to be certificates of authenticity, which he could simply file. Others were correspondence from collectors seeking to buy items from his father, which he could toss since his father never sold anything or even acknowledged such requests.

But the largest stack seemed to be invoices for his father's various purchases. An alarming number of purchases representing a rather staggering sum.

Greg's major task each time he stayed in London was to review the family's London accounts. The household expenditure was easily resolved, since his mother, along with the butler and housekeeper, kept meticulous records.

His father, however, never concerned himself with anything as mundane as accounting. Although the firms from which he acquired his objects included invoices when an ordered item was delivered, the bill was likely to land wherever Lord Vraux happened to drop it when he unwrapped his treasure. There it would languish, neglected, until on his next visit Greg invaded his father's domain to gather up all the bills he could find, pay them and file them away.

He had no idea where his father had tucked away the stack now on his desk, but most likely they had never been paid, in which case some of them were now several years in arrears.

Had the purchaser been anyone but his father, by now the vendors would have sent the bailiffs to collect the overdue debts. Greg considered his father's reputation as the richest baron in England had inspired the shopkeepers with the patience to refrain—not wishing to antagonise a client who, the invoices showed, must be one of their major purchasers.

There was no help for it; he was going to have to go

to the shops, request the assistance of the proprietors to track down the expenses and pay those still outstanding.

At least there were only a handful of providers capable of procuring the rare items his father collected. Indeed, the majority of invoices came from a single source, which would at least cut down on the number of enquiries he'd have to make.

Picking up one of those from the stack, Greg studied it again. Unlike most of the bills, the ones from this firm were handwritten on a blank sheet of fine vellum, rather than on printed forms stamped with the name and address of the shop, with only the date, goods and cost written in by hand. Nor was there a company name inscribed. Nothing but *W. Dunnfield* written in the upper-right-hand area below an engraved address:

7 King Street

Greg frowned. King Street was located in Westminster, not far from the highly fashionable—and expensive—Grosvenor Square. Not an address at which one would expect to find a tradesman.

Folding the firm's papers and putting them in his jacket pocket, he rose and walked out. He'd revive himself with a second cup of coffee, then claim his hat and cane and take a stroll through the morning sunshine to pay a call on W. Dunnfield.

Chapter Two

Later that morning, Charis Dunnfield stood in the small ground-floor parlour of her father's townhouse in King Street, rearranging items on shelves. Most of their commissions from their recent trip to Constantinople and Baghdad had already been delivered to the collectors who'd ordered them, but some dozen or so objects remained. Small daggers in their jewelled sheaths from the Ottoman Empire had become especially popular of late, and in addition to the items requested by their clients, her father had purchased a number of extra *khanjars* and *jambiyas* to have on hand, should their customers' friends or family decide they wished to purchase similar pieces.

It would take several weeks for her to use the sales proceeds already collected to order, receive and then pack the supplies necessary for their next journey, giving her father time to recover from the indisposition that had afflicted him on their journey home. Although she was always impatient to be off again, if Papa decided he needed a few additional weeks to fully recover before they set out, she could deliver the remaining items herself. Along with planning their route, resupplying their travel necessities, corresponding with clients to ascertain their current desires and with their suppliers in the Orient to determine the best source to satisfy those desires, she would have plenty to keep her busy.

The daggers secured, she returned to her desk and retrieved a strong box from a bottom drawer, where it reposed behind a secret panel. After unlocking it, she gazed admiringly at the treasures within.

Although her father appreciated the workmanship of all the items he purchased, fine jewels were his special joy. On each trip, along with the items requested by clients, he added to his private collection one or two particularly fine examples he'd not been able to resist.

Smiling, she touched a reverential fingertip to a gilded brooch set with rubies and diamonds and ran it over a Persian bracelet of pure gold in intricately carved geometric forms inset with lapis and malachite, the gems' dark hues gleaming against the brilliance of the precious metal.

She could transfer these latest acquisitions into the basement safe where her father kept the rest of his collection, but since opening it allowed him to take out and admire all his beauties, she would leave these in the strong box until he felt well enough to perform that pleasurable task himself.

After making note of which pieces still needed to be delivered, Charis re-locked the box and returned it to its hiding place. She'd just begun to log in the payments for the last items her father had delivered before taking to his bed when a knock sounded at the front door.

Absently noting the sound, she returned her attention to her work. But when that first knock was followed, after a pause, by several others, she closed the ledger with a sigh.

Since they spent so little time at the London townhouse, her father maintained only a skeleton staff here. The front door should have been answered by Jameson, their butler, footman and man-of-all-work who'd gone out this morning to make some purchases for her father. The continued knocking must mean Jameson hadn't yet returned. With their cook-housekeeper and the two maids occupied in their basement domain, she'd have to answer the door herself.

As she stood and pushed in her chair, she smiled to think how aghast Khalil Ibrahim, her father's majordomo at their house in Constantinople, would be at the thought of his mistress answering her own front door, while Alizah, the elderly Persian maid she'd inherited from her mother, would be scandalised.

Since their Ottoman servants poorly tolerated both the climate and the incomprehensible customs of chilly England, her father had left all their Constantinople staff in their pleasant walled house overlooking the Bosporus after the uproar that had ensued several years ago, when Papa had tried bringing some of them on one of their trips back to London.

Shivering, Charis pulled her shawl more tightly over her shoulders. Despite the pale sunshine that—barely—warmed the front salon, she had to agree with the assessment Khalil Ibrahim had made on his one visit to England—their island homeland was too cold, damp and cloudy for any sane person to remain there for long.

She wondered as she proceeded into the hallway who might be calling. Valuing the privacy of his home, her father never bid his customers to come and pick up their purchases, preferring to deliver them to the client's dwelling. As Father had left England at a young age, never becoming involved in English society, he had no friends or cronies here who might pay him a call. Tradesmen with household provisions to deliver or items to sell would ring at the kitchen entrance.

Charis had sent a note to her mother's aunt, Lady Sayleford, to let her know that they were back in London and that she would try to stop by. Perhaps the person seeking entrance was one of Grand-Tante's footmen, delivering a reply to her note.

Expecting to see a liveried servant, she opened the front door and stopped short, blinking in surprise. Standing on the stoop wasn't one of her cousin's employees, but a tall, commanding man dressed so impeccably he could only be an English gentleman.

And a very handsome one at that! He topped her by half a foot at least, with broad shoulders, a square-jawed face, straight, dark hair combed back off his brow and the most arresting ice-blue eyes she'd ever seen. She found herself staring before she recovered enough to ask, 'May I help you, sir?'

When he didn't immediately reply, Charis realised he'd been staring back. After spending most of her life in cities of the Ottomans and the Levant, more often than not while there she wore the loose, casual dress of the local inhabitants. Though she was forced to adopt European dress while in London, she couldn't abide the restrictive undergarments currently fashionable for ladies. As the stranger's eyes dipped lower, she was suddenly aware that she'd opted to forgo that stifling English object of feminine torment known as 'stays' and wore only a thin linen chemise under her gown.

Goodness, Alizah truly would be scandalised to know Charis had appeared before a gentleman not of her own household in this attire, she thought, pulling her shawl more closely about her shoulders.

Proving he *was* a gentleman, however, the caller immediately lifted his gaze back to her face. After setting his jaw, as if determined not to let his eyes venture lower again, he said, 'I hope so. I have...correspondence from a W. Dunnfield which lists this address, but that might be in error. Does that gentleman by chance happen to live here? If not, if you know his current direction, I would be quite grateful.'

Pulling several papers from inside his jacket, he pointed to the top one. 'My father is a collector who ordered a number of items from Mr Dunnfield. I'm afraid some—or all—of the objects he requested may not yet have been paid for.'

Charis quickly scanned the document, almost immediately identifying the purchaser. 'Your father acquired them, you said? You must be Lord Vraux's son, then.'

'Ah, so you are aware of the transactions. Mr Dunnfield still resides here, then? And yes, I am Vraux's son, Gregory Lattimar.'

'Please, come in. Father is...somewhat indisposed today, but I'll be glad to help you. I'm Charis Dunnfield. Pleased to meet you, Mr Lattimar. I serve as Mr Dunnfield's assistant, and most probably all the invoices were written by me. There are in fact a number outstanding, but let us not discuss the matter with you standing on the doorstep. If you will follow me?'

'With pleasure.'

'Leave your hat and cane there, if you like,' she said,

indicating a coat tree just inside the entrance. 'I'm sorry; our butler, Jameson, is out this morning.'

'I'm quite capable of hanging up my hat myself,' Lattimar said with a smile. And what an engaging smile he had!

Charis turned and led him down the short hallway to the salon, conscious of his tall form looming over her as he followed. A prickly feeling skittered over her skin at being overshadowed by all that vigorous maleness, particularly when she knew *he* knew she was garbed in a fashion that, by English standards, bordered on the indecent. Feeling her face flush, she made herself squelch the feeling. Since Lattimar had displayed the courtesy of ignoring her attire, she would ignore it, too.

She silently vowed that in future, she would remember not to answer the door unless she'd persuaded herself to don jump stays under her gown, the only sort of corset she could tolerate.

'Won't you take a seat?' she said, motioning him to the small sofa before the fire. 'Would you like me to ring for some tea?'

Not immediately answering, her caller was looking around curiously at the shelves that displayed both the objects still to be delivered and a portion of her father's most prized pieces. 'Mr Dunnfield is a...collector, too? I was expecting to find a shop. And no tea, thank you.'

Taking a seat behind her desk, Charis nodded. 'He began as a collector. Other Englishmen abroad, mostly diplomats, admired the things he acquired and asked him to find similar objects for them. Often after they returned to England, they would write to him requesting that he find them other pieces, or some friend or family member would want a similar one. His hobby gradually turned into something of a business, the profits of which fund our travels and his own acquisitions. Now, how can I help you? You would like to settle some of Lord Vraux's purchases?'

'I'd like to settle them all. But after belatedly discovering the invoices I've brought with me, I'm not sure these, numerous as they are, represent the whole. Or that some invoices are not duplicates. I note here,' he continued, putting some papers down on her desk and thumbing through them, 'Five invoices from different dates listing at differing prices an "Abyssinian dagger in jewelled sheath". Do these represent the same piece, perhaps at increasing prices because the original invoice wasn't paid? I cannot imagine why Vraux would need five of the same thing.'

Lord Vraux was extremely negligent about paying his bills. Was his son insinuating that her father had taken advantage of that to bill him several times for same item?

Drawing herself up stiffly, Charis said, 'I'm not sure I like your inference, sir. Unless the invoice clearly states it is a duplicate request—something very rarely done—I guarantee you that each item listed represents a different and distinctive object, even if they are similar items from the same area. The workmanship of each is considered an art, the design overseen by the person who originally commissioned the piece, and created by the skill and imagination of the individual craftsman. One could collect a score and not find two exactly the same. We are certainly not attempting to be paid over and over for same item.'

Realising he had overstepped, Lattimar said hastily, 'Excuse me, I didn't mean to offend. My father may not appear sometimes to recognise his own family, but he spends so much time studying and cataloguing his collection, I can well believe he wanted five of the same type of item—five very different, artistically crafted items.'

Mollified, Charis nodded. 'Very well. If you allow me to inspect the bills, I will identify and classify them for you.'

He pulled from his jacket another, larger sheaf of papers and placed them on the desk beside the first one, creating a stack tall enough that her eyes widened. 'Goodness, there really are quite a few!' she exclaimed. 'Lord Vraux sometimes is…tardy about settling his accounts, but I really can't imagine that many would still be outstanding. It's quite possible that a number have already been paid. I cannot be sure without checking all of these against our records.'

'I would very much appreciate it if you could do so.'

'I'm afraid that will require more than a moment. I shall have to match the acquisition dates and the general description on your invoices against the copies of the invoices and certificates of authenticity we retain after items are delivered. We keep copies,' she explained. 'In case the investor misplaces his own, or needs a duplicate to send to a prospective purchaser, if he decides to resell a piece to another collector.'

'I suspected that sorting this out wouldn't be simple. I'm sorry to put you to so much trouble.'

Still acutely conscious of the almost palpable masculine energy that seemed to emanate from him, she thought that spending additional time in his company would be no trouble. But he was altogether too appealing, and would certainly distract her from her work, should she try to complete the task with him watching her.

With her plate already full of tasks, she should dismiss him so she could finish the additional one he'd just handed her in the least amount of time.

Even though she was loath to have him quit her presence. Over their extensive travels, she'd met many charming men. But she couldn't remember one to whom she'd felt so immediate and visceral an attraction. Tempting as it was to indulge herself, nothing useful could come of it, so she might as well steel herself to send him away and get on with her work.

'Rather than have you kicking your heels here for however long it takes me to finish the task, why don't I call at Vraux House once I've had time to sort these out? I'll send you a note when all is ready, and you can reply with a time that would be convenient for you to receive me. Or if you'd prefer to dispense with another in-person meeting, I could write you a summary indicating which items still need to be paid, and you could return the amount due. I don't wish to inconvenience you.'

'Meeting you again would be no inconvenience.'

Something about the warmth and timbre of his voice had her gaze flashing up to meet his. He might be looking in her eyes rather than staring at her bosom, but she felt the heat of his attraction burn from her face all the way down her body.

An answering heat skittered to all her nerves.

Shaken by the intensity of her response, she looked away. 'Very well,' she said, working hard to keep the tremble from her voice. 'I'll look into these and send you a note when I've sorted them out.'

'I'd be very grateful. Father is obsessed by his treasures and derives considerable pleasure from them, so I must thank Mr Dunnfield for locating them. Vraux is… somewhat reclusive, and probably will not be present when you call, but I shall be very pleased to welcome you to Vraux House on his behalf.'

The sound of rapid footsteps coming down the hallway, followed by a knock at the door, forestalled her response. 'Ah, you've returned, Jameson,' she said as the butler entered.

'We have a visitor, Miss Charis? I'm sorry I wasn't here to receive him.'

The look he gave her and the slight flush on his face said he wasn't happy about her entertaining a gentleman in her current state of dress. 'No harm done, Jameson,' she said, wanting to forestall that line of enquiry. 'Lord Vraux's son, Mr Lattimar, came to enquire about some invoices. It will require some time for me to sort them out and get back to him. If you would escort him out?'

'Of course. This way, sir. By the way, I brought back the items you needed, Miss Charis.'

'Very good. I'll speak with you about them in a minute.' Rising, she extended her hand to the caller. 'Thank you for stopping by, Mr Lattimar.'

Rather than shaking it, he bent to bestow a kiss on her knuckles—setting her nerves tingling again. 'My pleasure. I'm only sorry to have made so much work for you.'

'No need for apologies. We are happy to demonstrate to our clients that all our transactions are straightforward and above board. What matters most is the beauty of the articles and artefacts we are privileged to share with other connoisseurs.' She smiled. 'If it were financially feasible, I believe Father would simply give them away to people who appreciate them as much as he does. Unfortunately, he doesn't have the resources of a pasha to present handsome gifts! I shall commence work immediately, Mr Lattimar, and hope to have answers for you very soon.'

He gave her another of those charming smiles. 'I shall very much look forward to meeting you again. Soon.' Then, with a bow, he walked out.

Watching him depart, Charis blew out a sigh. Into her mind flashed the image of a more intimate rendezvous... scented oils burning while she performed the dance of fluttering veils and ended up in his arms. But, in London as in Constantinople, such a thing was not possible unless a woman belonged to the man for whom she was dancing.

After the devastation she'd observed in her father after her mother's death, she'd vowed never to belong to any man. She intended to take the best of both cultures her upbringing had straddled: the ability to own property, manage her own money and make her own decisions, a right which even married women of the Ottoman world possessed, while she retained the European freedom of travel and independence denied her sisters in the east. But retaining that would only be possible if she *didn't* marry, since under English law, a married woman's money and property became her husband's.

As free spirited and restless as her father, she could never tolerate being pinned down in one place, restricted to managing a household, her fortune and future directed by a man.

Not even a man as sinfully attractive as Gregory Lattimar.

Chapter Three

Three days later, Gregory received the note he'd been waiting for. Miss Dunnfield wrote to say she'd completed her survey and requested that he inform her of a convenient time when she might call on him.

Immediately wouldn't be too soon, he thought, setting the note back on his desk. Instead of that impolitic reply, he took out a sheet of vellum and penned a response asking if she might be free late the following morning.

He still didn't know what to make of her.

His thoughts returned again, as they had so often the last few days, to the conflicting impressions he'd received when she'd opened the door to him at King Street garbed in that shabby, years-out-of-fashion, empire-waist gown. His first thought—that she must be a shop employee who'd bought the dress from some second-hand clothing stall—was swiftly followed by recognising that over the gown she wore an exquisite cashmere shawl of such beautiful workmanship, it would command a high price in the most fashionable London shop.

Her appearance was as arresting as her clothing was puzzling. Her pure oval of a face, possessed of a generous mouth and the most beautiful dark eyes he'd ever seen, mesmerised him. As did the luxuriant mass of dark hair which, rather than being pinned up into the elaborate knots, curls and loops currently fashionable, fell down her back in a silken waterfall, making his fingers itch to comb through it.

Then she'd shifted position, and his masculine eyes had been immediately drawn to the subtle rise of a pair of generous breasts that had most definitely not been rigidly supported by a corset. The realisation had shot such a bolt of surprise—and lust—through his brain that for several paralysed seconds, he'd stared like a green country boy seeing his first painted lady.

He'd snapped back into control, jerking his gaze to her face and firmly forbidding his eyes to stray below her neckline. Even so, he'd had to take advantage of the excuse of examining the interesting collection of objects on the shelves in the room to which she led him to get his libido and imagination fully under control.

Only then had the facts of her introduction penetrated his distracted brain. She was the daughter and assistant of the tradesman who provided his father with collectibles. But that wasn't quite accurate—Mr Dunnfield was himself a collector, who had begun his business simply as an enthusiast tracking down desirable objects for diplomats working abroad. Which meant he must also have resided abroad. As a tradesman? Or a former diplomat himself?

If the latter, he might have been born into the gentry, a junior member of some aristocratic family who, as he would inherit neither title nor money, had been obliged to seek some profession to support himself. That would better explain why his London residence was located in an exclusive area of Westminster.

And what about his daughter? She'd evidently travelled, or lived, in the Near East with him. She'd given the same last name as her father, so he assumed she was unmarried. Yet the languid, almost dance-like movements of her hands and fingers as she'd pointed out an item on the invoice, the exotic grace with which she'd moved, revived the lust he'd been trying to control and made him long to pull her into his arms and run his fingers through that glorious hair while he filled his nostrils with the jasmine scent of her perfume.

He felt shaken again, just remembering it.

It had taken every bit of his considerable resolve to force himself to concentrate on the business that had brought him to her door—sorting out his father's invoices. But he wouldn't be hypocrite enough to deny he hadn't been delighted when the complexity of doing so meant she'd be obliged to meet him again.

He'd left her still consumed with curiosity about the puzzle she represented. A happy thought had occurred as he'd headed back towards Brook Street. Her possessing the same last name as the trader might mean she was his daughter-*in-law*, rather than his daughter, despite the fact that she'd referred to Mr Dunnfield simply as 'Father'. Since she served as his chief assistant and there'd been no mention of a husband, perhaps a widowed daughter-in-law?

Her having been married might explain her sensual allure. And a widow might well be amenable to a discreet affair before she set off on her journeys again.

But he was getting ahead of himself.

He could have delayed until he'd received the note on his desk, then during their upcoming interview discreetly tried to ascertain her true status. If he confirmed his impression that she was available and equally attracted to him, delicately hint at a possible liaison.

But he'd been too impatient to wait. Instead, deciding on the moment, after leaving King Street he'd switched directions and proceeded not home but to his club. Several long-time members would be holding court there, as they always did. One in particular, garrulous old Lord Hipplewyte, liked nothing better than to indulge in gossip.

The surname 'Dunnfield' hadn't meant anything to him, but Greg didn't pretend to know the family names of every member of the ton. But since Hipplewyte had been a part of society for going on forty years, if William Dunnfield did have some connection to the gentry, the Baron likely would know.

What he'd discovered was only partially illuminating and had left him no less intrigued. Whatever transpired between them, though, he was incredibly impatient to meet Charis Dunnfield again tomorrow.

Late the following morning, too impatient to look over accounts, Greg wandered into the morning room, halting on the threshold when he spied his mother on the sofa. 'Good morning, darling,' she said, coming over to kiss his cheek. 'You seem…distracted. Is something wrong?'

Cursing the mischance of encountering his far too perceptive mother, he gave her a smile. Not that he worried she might, like the mothers of many of his acquaintances, pounce on the knowledge that he was interested in a woman to push him towards fulfilling his duty to marry. Even so, he'd rather not have her discover his attraction to Charis Dunnfield, especially as he didn't yet know what, if anything, he could do about it. 'Nothing of importance, Mama.'

'Are you sure?' She angled her head, turning her discerning eye upon him. 'You seem unusually…restless.'

The problem with having a mother who lavished on her children all the love and attention her spouse disdained was that she knew him far too well. There was no point trying to deny his agitation; that would only fuel both her curiosity and her concern.

'Later this morning I am supposed to meet the representative of the company who issued the bulk of those invoices Jennie left on my desk. I'm hopeful of finishing up the matter this morning…and only hope it won't cost a fortune to do so.'

'I'd be surprised if even a large amount would risk Vraux outrunning his income. But I see that you are worried. I can certainly cut back on household expenses, if that would help.'

His mother had so few indulgences, he certainly didn't want his agitation to prompt her to curtail acquiring the new gowns that she so enjoyed purchasing. 'I don't think that will be necessary, Mama. Can't have you falling out of fashion!'

'Ah, but no one outside the family would notice,' she said, her smile bittersweet.

The fact that her social contacts were so limited that her statement was correct fuelled his simmering anger and regret—stiffening his resolve to try to change that. Sooner rather than later.

'Would you mind if I sit in on the interview?' she asked. 'Vraux doesn't often show me the pieces on which he lavishes so much attention. I'd be curious to know exactly what he's been collecting.'

Curious to know about the items whose company he preferred over that of his wife, Greg thought.

Distracted by sadness and sympathy, he replied without thinking, 'Of course, if you like.'

Not until the words left his lips did he remember why having her attend his meeting with Charis Dunnfield would be a very bad idea. He could hardly make euphemistic enquiries about the lady's willingness or availability to indulge in a discreet affair with his mother listening in.

But having invited her participation, it would raise even more questions if he were to withdraw his permission now.

'Unless you'd rather not have me there?' she said, instinctively attuned to his silence. 'Since I'm just a silly woman who couldn't comprehend acquisitions anyway,' she added, a bitter note in her voice.

Dismayed that she might think herself unwanted by him too, he said, 'Nonsense! You're a better hand at finance than I am. If I appear…unsettled, it's because the person who will be calling has…a rather unusual background. I'm not quite sure how I should treat her.'

'Her?' his mother said, her eyebrows winging upward. 'Now I'm even more intrigued!'

Greg exhaled an annoyed breath. He might as well tell her what he knew. She might even be able to advise him how to proceed. He certainly didn't want to insult a virginal maiden by hinting he'd be amenable to an affair, if the lady turned out to be 'Miss' rather than 'Mrs' Dunnfield.

And yet…there'd been the dance-like grace of her movements. The freedom and confidence with which she'd received him, displaying none of the shyness or hesitance he would have expected in an unmarried girl whose father had sheltered her from the world.

Surely such behaviour couldn't be that of an innocent maiden? Or maybe he was letting his own erotic desires run away with his imagination.

'William Dunnfield is the trader on the majority of the invoices. The person calling will be his daughter, Charis Dunnfield. She was so…unusual that when I dined at my club, I asked Lord Hipplewyte if he knew anything of the family. He didn't at first recognise the surname, but at length he recalled that the late Viscount Hasterley's youngest son William, something of a black sheep, ran away to India when he was just sixteen. Apparently it caused quite a scandal. After kicking about the Orient for a number of years, reputedly earning a fortune in India, he set himself up as a trader, using his mother's maiden name as his surname to avoid having the taint of commerce embarrass the family.'

'Viscount Hasterley? Why, yes, I did know him! That is, I knew the present Viscount, who at the time had not yet inherited and was styled simply "Mr Hasterley". One of the prizes on the Marriage Mart during my season. I do recall there was some contretemps about his younger brother.'

'Hipplewyte said William married the daughter of a British diplomat serving in Tehran, has lived almost exclusively in Armenia, Persia and the Levant, and that his business is reputed to be moderately successful. He didn't, however, know anything about any offspring. Since she referred to Mr Dunnfield as "Father", my first assumption was that she must be his daughter. Although it would be odd for a maiden lady to conduct business, and she seemed so capable and…experienced.

I now wonder whether she is perhaps his daughter-in-law instead.'

Which was as much as he intended to tell his mother about his reaction to the girl.

Lady Vraux nodded. 'Hence your dilemma. You don't know whether to treat her like a sheltered maid…or a worldly woman.'

He should have known his mother, wise in the ways of sensual attraction, would need only the sparse bit of information he'd imparted to guess the whole. As aware as he'd been of her intrigues all his adult life, he felt his face heat at the idea that his mother might sense his erotic interest in this woman.

'That's the gist of it,' he said tersely.

Her smile widened. 'This should be interesting.'

A short time later, at precisely the hour he'd indicated on his note, the butler knocked on the door of the morning room, the place he and his mother had decided would be the most appropriate to receive this particular caller. Using the salon would imply they were entertaining a person of rank, but conveying her to his study would indicate they were treating her as merely a tradesperson.

With not even his mother knowing exactly how to place her, they'd chosen to remain in the informal family room. And Gregory was still not sure whether or not it had been a colossal mistake to allow his mother to be present.

Trying to quell his nervous agitation, which he was uneasily certain his mother sensed, he sucked in a breath as he waited for Charis Dunnfield to enter. A little shock went through him as he spied her lovely face—along with a pang of disappointment when he realised that today she was garbed in a respectable if somewhat worn spencer, her hair braided and pinned discreetly under a small hat.

No threadbare gown to offer beguiling hints of her body, and all those glorious tresses hidden from view.

'Good morning,' he said, bowing to her curtsey. 'Thank you for calling. Mama, may I present Charis Dunnfield. My mother, Lady Vraux.'

'Mr Lattimar—and Lady Vraux.' As she rose from her curtsey to glance at his mother, her eyes widened and she made a gesture with her hands that must be a sort of obeisance. 'I'm honoured to meet you, *khoshgelam*! Now I understand why Lord Vraux began collecting jewels! Only the finest of gems are worthy to grace the neck and arms of such a beautiful one!'

'If only that were true,' his mother murmured. 'I'm honoured to meet you, too—is it *Miss* Dunnfield?' At the visitor's affirmative nod, which put a dagger through the heart of Greg's amorous imaginings, his mother waved towards the sofa. 'Won't you have a seat, Miss Dunnfield?'

'Yes, but you must excuse me. I didn't mean to be impolite,' the caller replied, turning back to Greg as she took the place on the sofa beside his mother, while he prudently chose an adjacent armchair. 'It's just that I've seldom seen a truly beautiful woman in London. In the Ottoman lands, where incomparable beauty is foremost among the requirements men of importance have when choosing wives, almost all of the harem ladies are astoundingly lovely.'

His mother chuckled at that, while Greg, stupefied, wasn't sure what to say. All the erotic images that had circulated, especially among men in society, since the publication of *One Thousand and One Nights* and the engravings of Ingres' famed portrait *La Grand Odalisque*, stirred in his brain.

Harem.

Beautiful women chosen to please their lord.

Had *she* been part of all that?

While he remained speechless, his mother asked the question it would have been shockingly impolite for him to voice, even had his wits not been scattered.

'Are you well acquainted with harems, then?'

'Naturally. Oh, not with what you probably are thinking! All those silly portraits by European painters who have never seen the inside of one! Though Islam permits a man to have four wives as long as he treats them all equally, most men do not avail themselves of the permission. It would be horridly expensive, for one.

'"Harem" is merely the term for where women of a family reside apart from the men, like the *zenana* of the Moslem ladies of India. Females in those lands are much more secluded than European women. A girl remains within the walls of her father's house until she marries, then within the walls of her husband's. I've been privileged to become friends with several important ladies, including a dear friend of my late mother who looks upon me almost as a daughter of her own. The "daughter of her soul", she calls me. But pardon me, you are wanting to hear about Lord Vraux's invoices, not listen to me natter on about my life in Anatolia.'

'But you are mistaken,' his mother said, echoing his own feelings. 'It's fascinating to hear about a land so different from our own. I would love to learn more! But did I understand you no longer have your own mother with you?'

Sadness dimmed her bright eyes. 'No, alas. Mama

died when I was barely in my teens. I think that's why Father took up trading. He couldn't bear to stay in the house he'd bought for her. He had contacts in many lands, from Persia to Mesopotamia to Anatolia, and began to travel back and forth, at first just visiting, and later looking for pieces in which to invest. So it has been just he and I on our adventures.'

'He hasn't tried to find you a husband? Here in London, or abroad?'

She laughed. 'Goodness, no! We are old travelling companions now, and no one knows his needs and wishes better than I. Besides, I've become too important to the trading business for him to marry me off.'

Thanks to his mother for once again asking what he dearly wanted to know but would have been most improper for him to ask. Though it did make matters disappointingly complicated.

Not that he'd truly entertained much hope that she was in fact a widowed Mrs Dunnfield.

No man of honour would make a disreputable proposal to an innocent. Yet how could an innocent seem... so exotic?

Even now, her jasmine perfume teased his nose and he was having to battle to keep the image of *La Grande Odalisque* from creeping back into his consciousness.

He'd simply have to banish that picture from his brain and convince himself henceforth to think of *Miss* Dunnfield as a gently born, innocent maiden.

'I would love to hear more about your adventures,' his mother was saying.

'Perhaps I could call on you some other time. We should be in London for a month or so before we leave on our next journey. But now, no more delaying Mr Lattimar, who I know must be impatient to settle this business so he may move on to other important tasks.'

Greg made a noncommittal murmur. In truth, he'd utterly forgotten about the invoices. He'd listened with as much fascination as his mother. He, too, wanted to know more about Miss Dunnfield. Know *everything*.

Even if she weren't available for amorous adventures. He'd never met a woman remotely like her. And despite the presence of his mother as chaperone and Miss Dunnfield's maiden state, his attraction to her was as strong as ever.

'Let me explain the accounts,' she was saying, taking papers out of her reticule and spreading them out on her lap. 'I've checked all the invoices you left against our own records. You'll be relieved to know that most of the older ones have already been settled. The total outstanding remains substantial, but not shockingly so. As you can see here—' she pointed to a summary sheet '—I've listed all the invoices chronologically, indicated the date of payment, if it was in fact paid, and left the ones still outstanding blank.

'On the next page—' she moved aside the first sheet, exposing a second '—I've listed just those invoices still outstanding, with the total here.' She pointed to the column at the bottom of the page. 'You are welcome to keep these; I made a copy for our own records,' she concluded, handing him the documents. 'There's no hurry in settling them. My father knows Lord Vraux always honours his obligations.'

'Eventually,' Greg said drily. 'Nonetheless, I wish to settle them immediately. I will visit my bank and have a draft prepared today. Perhaps I could call later today or tomorrow and bring it to you?'

She looked up at him then. Some wordless current pulsed between them, the same shock of connection underlaid by a powerful sensual attraction that had struck him in her salon three days ago. A sense of belonging and a desire so powerful, it took a moment for him to pull free of its hold and get his paralyzed brain working again.

'You could bring it by King Street if you wish,' she murmured, her eyes still on his. She paused, as if about to say she'd be as eager to see him again as he was to see her. Especially with no inconvenient chaperone to oversee them.

But that was ridiculous. Having confirmed she was a virtuous maiden, there was nothing he could say or do with her that couldn't be said or done in front of his mother or a roomful of observers.

It was just her unusual background and the whole *aura* about her that made it so difficult for him to fall into the proper patterns of behaviour towards unmarried women. Behaviour that was normally so second nature, he adhered to its rules without thought.

Common sense warred with that nagging desire. He suspected the rules of conduct towards maidens in Constantinople were, if anything, stricter than those governing the treatment of English virgins. Such innocents were walled up in their father's houses until they married, she'd said.

So why was he floundering in indecision, struggling to rein in his jumbled thoughts and chaotic desires, even as he knew what the outcome of meeting her must be?

At least he'd be able to see her one more time. By then, he'd have had time to sort out his confusion and be able to proceed with both honour and confidence.

While he dithered, Miss Dunnfield was already standing, expressing again her pleasure at meeting his mother, thanking him for his attention and repeating there was no need to inconvenience himself rushing to settle the account.

'Nonetheless, you can expect to see me again, probably tomorrow,' he said as, with no excuse to prolong the meeting, he walked her to the door.

Pausing on the threshold, she gave him a look that suggested that she, too, felt the heady attraction he sensed between them. 'I will look forward to it.'

'As will I.'

He stood on the doorstep for a moment, watching her walk away—with that swaying, dance-like grace that sent his pulse rate surging.

How *was* he to treat her going forward? Though cold logic said 'like any other maiden', she was most assuredly *not* like any other maiden.

He turned back to find his mother watching him. 'What an exceptional young woman! No wonder you had no idea how to treat her.' She paused a moment, looking thoughtful. 'If she truly is the niece of Viscount Hasterley, she comes from good family, even if her father is something of a tradesman. I would imagine that family would like to see her respectably married rather than touring the world with her disreputable father.'

Before Greg could consider the implications, his mother laughed. 'Gracious, I should like to see the effect if she *were* introduced to society. Such potent allure! The men would be falling over themselves, trying to win her favour!'

A corrosive surge of jealousy blasted through him at the thought. He had seen her first. He wouldn't allow anyone else to claim her.

And then felt appalled. *Claim* her? The only way he might claim a well-born virgin was to marry her. And much as Miss Dunnfield fascinated and aroused him, she was about as far as he could imagine from the type of woman he needed to wed.

An impeccably behaved, well-connected maiden. Not an adventuress from the Ottoman East.

But then, in response to his mother's enquiries, Miss Dunnfield had expressed neither any inclination for marriage, nor indicated that her family had any plans for her to make a London debut. On the contrary, she'd informed them that she and her father intended to leave soon on another journey.

She was her father's companion, too important to his business to marry and leave him.

With them soon to set off again, Greg might well never see her again after he delivered that bank draft. Which, since her presence seemed so quickly to paralyse his brain and touch some chord buried so deep in his soul he'd not previously been aware of it, was probably a good thing.

Which made the inexplicable sense of loss he felt at the prospect of her exiting his life the day after tomorrow both illogical and ridiculous.

Chapter Four

⧼⧽

The next afternoon, Charis hurried up the front steps of the King Street townhouse, shivering. The two layers of chemises and the detested stays she'd added under her gown had been donned as much for warmth as for modesty. She'd worn over the gown her thickest pelisse and gloves, her Kashmiri shawl draped over her shoulders and the stoutest boots she possessed, but the chill wind blowing under scudding grey clouds still seemed to penetrate to the marrow.

She was blowing on her cold fingers when Jameson opened the door. 'Frozen, Miss Charis?' he asked after one look at her. 'I'll have some tea sent up immediately.'

'You're a treasure, Jameson.'

'Did everything go…successfully?'

'Yes, no problems at all.'

The man's face relaxed. 'Glad to hear it. You…won't have to make any further excursions?'

'There are still a few more items to be delivered,' Charis admitted. 'All the clients I called upon this afternoon had written at least twice to express their eagerness to take possession of their treasures, so it was essential that

I deliver those pieces. Perhaps the others will be patient enough to wait until Father can call on them himself. And you really needn't worry that we don't have a footman who can accompany me. Having dealt with us for many years, most of the customers already know me. I was everywhere treated great respect, all the gentlemen expressing appreciation for the background information I provided them about their purchases.'

The butler nodded as he walked her into the front salon and took her pelisse and bonnet. 'I'll have Jane put these in your room, Miss Charis. And I built up the fire, knowing you'd appreciate some extra warmth after your outing.'

Charis went immediately to the hearth, lifting her fingers to the low flame. 'As I said, you truly are a treasure! Many thanks for your thoughtfulness.'

Jameson bowed. 'I'll have that tea up in a trice, Miss Charis.'

As the butler exited, she turned her back to the fire, basking in the welcome blast of heat. Dear Jameson. He had been her father's valet during Dunnfield's first year at university—before, lured by the mystique of the East and chafing at the restrictions imposed on the behaviour of a noble's younger son, he'd turned his back on it all and run away. In later years, after having acquired more wealth and having inherited the townhouse from his mother, her father had tracked down his former servant and set him up as butler in charge of this establishment—an elevation in service rank Jameson had never ceased to appreciate.

Not least, she thought with a smile, because he oversaw a reduced staff for an employer who was gone more often than he was present and paid him a handsome sum while leaving him a great deal more leisure than would normally be enjoyed by a man with a butler's responsibilities.

Jameson was as protective of her father as Alizah, her mother's former nurse, was of her.

But when she recalled the reason behind Jameson's solicitude, her smile faded. It wasn't that she minded delivering the orders. On the contrary, she often knew more about the background of the pieces than her father and loved to explain to the appreciative connoisseurs where their treasures had come from, how they were constructed and the special techniques used by master craftsmen that made them exceptional.

She'd learned those details at the feet of a master, her father having started to bring her along on the deliveries when she'd been barely in her teens. They both enjoyed the calls, viewing the turning over of their purchases to owners who truly appreciated their beauty as the culmination of the long process of seeking out and acquiring such treasures.

She hadn't been at all worried that some investor would try to take advantage of her. She was much more concerned about her father's lingering illness that had forced her to make the calls without him.

After receiving several more pleading notes this morning, she'd gone to his chamber, explaining though she'd hoped they might make the calls together, she thought it necessary to deliver some items immediately. Patting her hand, he'd agreed that it wasn't fair to let their faithful clients wait any longer and had urged her to go at once.

Though he'd smiled and made no complaint about the state of his health, he continued to look disturbingly wan and tired. It wasn't that she'd never seen him ill before.

The rigours of travel across barren lands, the sometimes uncertain quality of food or water, had occasionally led to bouts of sickness. But he normally recovered quickly. Never before had he lingered on like this, leaving his bed only to recline in an armchair before the blazing hearth, swathed in blankets.

Never before had he failed to rally enough to dine with her in the evening. When she joined him now, both of them taking their supper on trays in his chamber, he barely picked at his food and drank only a sip of wine. As soon as she finished her own repast he retired back to his bed with apologies, his face grey and drawn, as if even that slight exertion was too much for him.

She was beginning to fear they would have to delay their departure much longer than she'd originally planned. In the meantime, she should probably contact the rest of their clients and arrange to deliver the remaining items herself.

She pushed to the back of her mind the insupportable thought that Father's illness might drag on, stranding them in England for the foreseeable future.

At least the late May weather was giving way to summer, she tried to cheer herself. What passed for summer in England, anyway. Surely there would soon be weeks, rather than occasional days of sunshine, and warmth enough that she could dispense with a pelisse when walking in Hyde Park.

Though she would probably avoid walking in that fashionable locale in her current wardrobe unless she was prepared to elicit stares at her exceedingly *un*fashionable garments. The collectors upon whom she'd called were older men so keenly interested in their purchases that they'd spared hardly a glance for her apparel, but commenting upon the appearance of the people passing by them doubtless made up much of conversation of the ton visiting the park. If she wanted to stroll in any fashionable area and retain her preferred public role as an invisible observer—how marvellously the *feradge* of Constantinople that enveloped a woman from head to foot and the *yasmak* that covered all but her eyes achieved that aim—she would have to acquire garments more *à la mode* than the ones she currently owned.

That conclusion produced a sigh of irritation. Her outdated, high-waisted gowns and pelisses were uncomfortable enough. The latest styles for ladies—with their voluminous skirts, waists made as narrow as possible by means of boned stays and tight lacing and the sleeves so wide, it was impossible to do anything useful while wearing them—were as impractical as they were uncomfortable.

That was probably the point, she reflected. Like the quantity of jewels worn by an Ottoman lady, the fashions were designed to show that the wearer was so wealthy, she had no need to perform any domestic tasks herself.

It made Charis faint, just imagining being caged inside one of those gowns. So she wouldn't purchase any, she decided. She would put off any house calls, which meant she'd continue to make deliveries while garbed in outdoor dress. If the weather continued cool, she could conceal her outdated gowns beneath a voluminous cloak.

She would need to visit Grand-Tante, who had replied to her note expressing her delight that Charis was presently in London and begging her to call as soon as convenient. That formidable arbiter of society was likely to be pained at seeing her great niece so poorly dressed, but with feminine fashions certain to have changed by the time Charis was next in London, it was a waste of blunt to purchase a gown she would never wear again after calling on her great-aunt.

Rather than peruse fashion magazines, she'd spend the afternoon double-checking the addresses for the pieces still to be delivered, read through the post looking for replies from the suppliers she'd written to, check on the provisions already delivered and put on hold acquiring any perishables. No sense having those delivered now when she wasn't sure when they would be able to depart.

Reluctantly abandoning her position near the hearth, she was heading to her desk to flip through the post Jameson had left for her when the butler shouldered open the salon door, bearing a tray with a cup and a steaming pot. 'Here you are, Miss Charis. This will warm you right up.'

'*Degerli biri!* Thank you!'

'Will there be anything else?' he asked, setting the tray down on her desk.

'Tell Mrs Davenport I'll be down in the kitchen later to check the dry goods our supplier delivered. Since it appears our stay in London will be...somewhat longer than anticipated, we need to find an out-of-the-way place to store them for the time being.'

'Very good, miss.'

After the butler bowed himself out, Charis poured herself a cup, clasping the warm porcelain in her hands and breathing deep the steaming vapor. She must see about brewing Father some tisanes while she was in the kitchen with Mrs Davenport. Before going down, she'd pull out her journal and look up some of the recipes Bayan Zehra had given her—then ask the cook where she might obtain some of more exotic spices required to prepare them.

* * *

The tea had finally succeeded in warming her from the inside out when Jameson reappeared. 'Mr Lattimar is here to see you, Miss Charis.'

A rush of sensual awareness and anticipation heated her more effectively than the tea. 'Good. Show him in, please,' she said, rising and turning towards the door.

Fruitless as it was to indulge her desire for his company, as nothing could come of their attraction, she was still glad to be wearing stays. Had Jameson deemed her not respectably garbed, the ever-protective butler would probably have told Lattimar that his mistress was not receiving.

She thought perhaps her memory, which dwelled far too often his image, might have embellished Lattimar's attractiveness, but as he walked in and bowed to her, that overwhelming awareness of his handsome form and potent maleness washed over her again. She barely restrained herself from making him an awed obeisance, as she had to the beauty of his mother.

'Good day, Miss Dunnfield. I've brought your draft, as promised.'

Recovering herself, she replied, 'A gentleman true to his word is as appreciated as one of Father's treasures. Thank you,' she said, accepting the draft he handed her and putting it in the desk drawer.

With his errand dispatched, there was no reason for her to invite him to remain. But she couldn't seem to make herself utter the appropriate politenesses that would dismiss him.

He made no move to leave either, lingering as if hoping to prolong the meeting. While the attraction between them sizzled, subtle but ever-present, like the soft buzzing of the bees over the jasmine in her garden by the Bosporus.

What harm would there be in simply enjoying his company, just once more?

Her resolve to be sensible and send him away crumbling, she said, 'As you can see, I was just having tea. Would you like a cup?'

'Thank you, I would enjoy that.'

Turning to Jameson, who'd been hovering at the door, obviously expecting to show the caller back out, she said, 'Bring another cup for Mr Lattimar, won't you? And see if there are any of Mrs Thompson's lemon tarts left from dinner last night.'

Jameson gave Lattimar a measuring glance, as if assessing whether he trusted him to remain alone with his mistress. The baron's son must have passed muster, for after a moment the butler nodded. 'At once, Miss Charis.'

'Please, have a seat,' she said, prudent enough to motion him to the armchair in front of the hearth while she took a seat on the sofa.

'You put the draft away without even looking at it,' he observed. 'Do you trust all your clients that much?'

She laughed. 'Actually, we do, since we've dealt with most of them for years. I assure you though, I will examine it in detail—later.'

'Ah, you are prudent as well as lovely.'

'And you are honest as well as handsome. Trustworthy too. Have you always overseen finances for your father?'

'Since I left Oxford some years ago. Vraux...concerns himself with little beyond his treasures. Like many collectors, I imagine.'

She noted he didn't refer to his sire as 'Father' or 'Papa'—and she didn't think he used the man's name just for formality's sake. Though many of their clients were absorbed by their collections, she didn't know any beside Lord Vraux who seemed to ignore everything around them save for their acquisitions.

Still, there was no need to remind the man's son of that hurtful truth—a truth of which he was undoubtedly aware. 'Many collectors focus much of their attention on their collections,' she replied carefully. 'Who could wonder at it—' she gestured towards the shelves displaying some of her father's prize pieces '—when the objects are so worthy of admiration?'

'Objects of beauty are always worthy of admiration,' he said, his warm gaze telling her he wasn't referring to the collectables on display.

'Indeed they are,' she replied, meeting his eyes with a frankness that told him she found his physical attributes as pleasing as he apparently found hers.

For a moment, neither spoke, both held in thrall by the force of the connection between them.

Lattimar looked away first, which was fortunate, for Charis wasn't sure she could have. How could someone she'd met only twice exert such a hold over her? Forcing herself to concentrate on conversation, rather than the pull she felt to him, she said, 'Are you always in London, then, overseeing the family's affairs?'

'No, I'm actually seldom in London. Our family's principal estate, Entremer, is in Northumberland. It's a vast property, with a large number of tenant farms, mostly sheep and cattle with a small amount of corn, as well as some mining interests. There's always something that needs tending. We've several smaller properties scattered here and there in other counties that require periodic visits, so I spend the majority of my time in the country, usually at Entremer.'

'So you are able to travel, then. How refreshing! I do so dislike being trapped in one place.'

'I don't get to destinations as exotic as yours, but I do enjoy riding through the ever-changing beauties of the English countryside. There's a vast variety, from the dense city of London to the marshy coasts, to the seaside bluffs outside Eastbourne to the wilds of the high moorland.'

'It sounds lovely. I haven't seen much of England. Father isn't close to any of his family, so we never visit them, not even those who might be in London when we're in residence. Not that we ever remain here long. The only family I generally call on is a relative of my mother's, whom we've always referred to as Grand-Tante.'

Conversation halted for a moment as Jameson brought in a cup for Lattimar and a plate of lemon tarts, moved the tea service to the piecrust table between the chair on which she sat and the sofa, then bowed himself out.

As Charis poured a cup for Lattimar and another for herself, the fascinated gaze he fixed on her made her suddenly self-conscious. Bayam Zehra had so effectively drilled into her the technique of artfully moving her hands and fingers while serving tea that the mannered gestures were now automatic.

'The movements of thy hands should embody grace and loveliness, making the ceremony of offering refreshment a pleasure to behold,' she heard her mentor whisper as she handed Mr Lattimar his cup and passed him the plate of sweets.

'I hope you enjoy the tarts. We have lemons and oranges growing in our garden in Constantinople. Father misses being able to pick the fresh fruits. I try to remind him of those happy days by baking them into his sweets.'

Still watching her hands as she moved them back to her own cup, he remained silent for another moment after she took a sip of her tea. Then he shook his head as if breaking a spell.

'You told my mother your primary residence is in Constantinople,' he said at last. 'Alas, I've never voyaged beyond England, despite the freedom of travel we've been permitted since the wars finally ended.'

'Ah, but you have so many responsibilities to discharge here.'

'True. You speak of your home with such affection. I've only heard vague tales of the Ottoman lands. Won't you tell me something about your house and the city?'

Knowing when she bid Lattimar goodbye this time she was unlikely to see him again, she was happy to seize this excuse to prolong his visit and the guilty pleasure of his company. Happy, too, to describe to him the places she loved and missed.

'Our house is in Pera, the European section a short distance outside the city—only adherents of the Muslim faith are allowed to reside within the walls of Constantinople itself. Most of the European and diplomatic community have their dwellings there, and the views from the heights are tremendous. The Bosporus at our feet, the outline of the Topkapi Palace, the Sublime Porte and the Seraglio, the domes and minarets of St Sophia and the other mosques above the city walls, the mountains in the distance...'

'It sounds beautiful. And what is your house like? I understand they are very different from European dwellings.'

'They are. The house itself follows the old Roman plan. You can see nothing of it from the street but solid, windowless walls with a great iron-studded entrance door. Once admitted, you pass through a small vestibule into a central courtyard, around which all the rooms are arranged on two floors, with pillars supporting balconies on the upper level. At the centre of the courtyard is a large pool with several fountains, surrounded by pots of verbena and lemon trees, while jasmine twines up trellises between the pillars. Ah, the soft sound of water splashing, cooling the stone floors even in the heat of summer! The heady perfume when both the jasmine and the lemons are in bloom…'

The remembered scents making her homesick again, it was a moment before she could continue. 'The rooms opening off the courtyard are illumined by large windows on the outer walls, the frames latticed to allow the occupants to look out while no one outside may see within. Behind the house, sheltered from prying eyes by another high wall, is the garden, paved pathways bordered by beds of roses, jasmine and verbena interspersed with fruit trees, fountains and a gazebo at the end where one can rest in the heat of the day.'

She smiled, seeing it again in her mind's eye. 'It's not just the pleasing array of scents, shapes and patterns—in the tile of the floors, the rugs and tapestries, the glitter of mosaics. Even the light itself is different from England's. Soft, golden in the morning, dazzling at midday when it glitters on the domes and the walls of the buildings. Rose and orange and gold in the setting sun. And above it all, a sky so clear and piercingly blue, my Persian nurse used to say one could see all the way up to paradise! I think it's the light I miss most here. There's so little sun, and it's so…grey.'

'I'm afraid London is often like this. With the smoke and soot, grey even when the sun is shining.'

By now, he'd finished his tea, and the pot was empty. There really was no excuse to put off his departure any longer. Which was fortunate, because she was far more tempted than she should have been to coax him to remain, to further plumb the sense of connectedness his appreciation of her beloved home had only deepened.

But to what end? She didn't want a suitor. And despite the sensual attraction between them, she couldn't risk taking a lover. Better to end this interlude now, before the erotic spell he seemed to cast over her prompted her to do something more rash than beguile him with the motion of her hands.

So she made herself smile, collect his empty cup and stand, signalling an end to their meeting. 'Thank you for being so diligent about settling Lord Vraux's accounts. I expect he will contact us when he wishes to purchase more objects.'

Looking as reluctant as she felt, he rose as well. 'I'm certain he will. When do you plan to depart? I'll try to impress upon him the urgency of making a list of the items he desires before you leave again.'

'Within the month, if Father has recovered. The… indisposition which laid him low during the journey has lingered longer than expected,' she confessed, that frisson of concern tightening her chest again. 'Which is why he did not come down to greet you. He would certainly have offered you that courtesy, had he been feeling more like himself. Of course, Lord Vraux is always free to write to us in Constantinople, if he has not determined what he is seeking before we leave.'

'I hope for your sake that Mr Dunnfield recovers soon. It must make you anxious to have him ill.'

'It does,' she admitted. 'He is so very seldom indisposed, seeing him like that is...unsettling. Well, thank you again for delivering the draft so quickly and in person. It wasn't really necessary for you to inconvenience yourself.'

Although I am so glad you did.

'It was necessary...for me,' he murmured, gazing at her.

Charis drew in a breath as that sharp, powerful connection once again surged between them. It took several moments before she could summon enough wit to say, 'I suppose this will be goodbye, then, Mr Lattimar.'

'Regretfully, I suppose it will. Good luck on your travels.'

'Good luck to you sorting out your father's affairs, and your family's.'

He laughed. 'Thank you. I'll need it.'

She should walk him to the door and call for Jameson, who was doubtless loitering nearby, waiting to escort him out. But she couldn't pull her gaze from that handsome face: the noble forehead with the dark hair brushing his brow, those remarkable blue eyes the colour of deepwater ice. The sensual shape of his lips...

She couldn't bear to send him away for good without touching them.

Quickly, before the voice of prudence could forbid her, she rose on tiptoe. 'Goodbye, Mr Lattimar,' she murmured—and kissed him.

But the moment her lips brushed his, he responded

to her impulsive gesture with a much deeper kiss of his own. Any idea of drawing quickly away dissolved in a firestorm of sensation.

For a dizzying few minutes, the kiss went on, his mouth pressed urgently against hers, his tongue tracing her lips, sending rivulets of fire streaming from her mouth to every nerve of her body.

Finally, he broke the kiss and stepped back, gasping, looking as astounded and shaken as she felt.

Driven by a belated instinct for self-preservation, she backed to the doorway. 'J-Jameson will see you out,' she stuttered, then turned and practically ran for the stairs, taking them up to her room as fast as her feet would carry her.

She told herself she fled from embarrassment at her shockingly wanton behaviour. But in truth, she knew she'd needed to remove herself before she did something even more forbidden.

Raised in the lands of the East, she'd grown up believing that physical pleasure was a normal and natural need of both men *and* women. There were even learned texts describing the techniques to arouse and satisfy lovers. Rather than repulse Lattimar, she'd been tempted to draw him to the sofa, coax his hands to caress her body...

Upon reaching the safety of her room, she closed the door and leaned on it, still panting, her aroused senses furious that she would never see him again.

While her rational mind thanked a merciful God.

Chapter Five

∞

In the afternoon of the following day, garbed in the newest of her outdated gowns, Charis paused outside the door of Grand-Tante's imposing townhouse on Grosvenor Square. The large square boasted a fine park at its centre where residents could stroll, she noted approvingly, unlike the situation of many of the houses in the city, jammed together along narrow streets that blocked what little sunlight they received and possessed little or nothing by way of a garden.

As she waited for the butler to answer the door, her spirits rose with anticipation at seeing Mama's aunt again. Lady Sayleford had always been so kind to her, never reprimanding her for any deficiency in her English manners and always so welcoming on her infrequent visits.

Sighing, she hoped Grand-Tante would be forgiving enough not to be too pained at her outdated attire. In any event, the visit would relieve some of the loneliness she'd been feeling as their time in London dragged on and would allow her to put aside for a while her unease over her father's ill health, which still showed no signs of improving.

Though she should hardly be surprised. How could anyone's health improve in a city that was so cold and damp?

The visit would also help her put out of mind her inexplicable—and inexcusable—lapse of propriety during the meeting yesterday with Mr Lattimar, she thought, feeling her face warm at the memory.

Not, alas, because of the shame she couldn't persuade herself to feel. But at remembering the desire he seemed to arouse so easily.

Though she knew—in theory, having never experienced it herself—all about what happened during the pleasuring between husband and wife, she'd never before realised just how powerful the desire for that pleasure could become. How difficult to resist its siren call.

And Lattimar's kiss had given her only a taste of it. The prospect of sampling all of it, everything, almost tempted her to reconsider her decision to avoid marriage.

Almost. But the price of a husband, even one as attractive as Gregory Lattimar, would be her freedom. Marry an Englishman, and she'd be stuck in this cold, grey dampness for ever. With no control over her wealth and no recourse to court if someone should wrong her, not even the ability to divorce her husband if he mistreated her.

Not that she expected Mr Lattimar would ever mistreat a woman, she thought as the butler answered the door, bowing her in. On the contrary, she was certain he would please his fortunate lady quite wonderfully.

Pulling her mind from contemplating the enticing Lattimar—it would not do for highly perceptive Grand-

Tante to realise she'd been distracted by a gentleman, especially an English one—she followed the butler to the front parlour.

'Charis, my dear!' Grand-Tante said, rising to greet her. 'What a delight to see you again. Though I'm afraid I cannot extend that appreciation to your gown,' she added, her welcoming smile turning to a frown.

'Je m'excuse, Grand-Tante,' Charis said ruefully, coming over to accept the hug Lady Sayleford gave her. 'I must apologise for my attire.'

'Goodness, child, you look like a rag-picker's daughter, not the offspring of a prosperous antiquities trader! Here, sit by me on the sofa where I will have less of a view of it. Harris, would you bring us tea, please?'

'It's years out of date, I admit,' Charis said, taking the place indicated. 'But you know I can't abide English fashions. They grow more impractical and uncomfortable every year, which even you must allow! After all, you admitted as much when I coaxed you to try on the loose robes and embroidered gowns I brought you from Constantinople on my last visit.'

Once the butler bowed himself out, Lady Sayleford leaned close to Charis, her voice lowered conspiratorially. 'I wouldn't admit it to anyone but you, but I do enjoy them. I even wear them, to the horror of my maid, when I'm not in London. How lovely to go about without a corset! But enough of clothing. How are you? You look lovelier than ever, despite that wretched gown. Tell me everything!'

'First, let me give you this. Just a little trinket, a token of my great love for you.'

From her reticule, Charis extracted a small velvet box and offered it to her great-aunt, who opened it to reveal a pair of delicate gold filigree earrings, their intricate geometric pattern inset with jasper and onyx.

'These are exquisite!'

'They don't boast diamonds the size of walnuts or rubies large as acorns, but I thought the unusual style and design would appeal to you.' Charis laughed. 'Not that I could afford diamonds the size of walnuts or rubies as large as acorns anyway.'

'Setting them with stones any larger would ruin the effect. I'm so touched that you were thinking of me. Here, help me put them on.'

After Charis assisted her to remove the diamond drops she wore and put on the new earrings, Lady Sayleford leaned back, regarding Charis with a smile. 'How like your dear mother you've become.'

'Now you are being kind. You still keep her miniature—' Charis pointed to a small portrait in a gilded frame on the bookcase '—so you know very well I'm not nearly as lovely as she was.'

'With those marvellous eyes, that perfect skin and that lustrous hair? You are quite beautiful, my dear. Even more so because of the particular grace with which you carry yourself. Your upbringing in Persia and Anatolia, I expect.'

'My training by Bayam Zehra: "a lady should walk as if dancing, her movements a delight to gaze upon". I understand English maidens are forced to walk with a book balanced on their heads. The Bayam made me walk back and forth, back and forth, until she deemed my stride fluid enough.'

'Your tutor was skilled, for your movements certainly are a delight to observe. So, what is news? How long will we keep you in London this time?'

'We had a very successful buying trip, obtaining excellent examples of the artefacts our clients desired, as well as having good visits with Father's old friends in Tehran and Baghdad. Nearly all the objects have been delivered now. I had hoped to be off again by the end of the month. Now I'm not so sure.'

Angling her head, Grand-Tante studied her. 'Something is worrying you. What is it, my dear?'

'I should have known I wouldn't be able to hide anything from you,' Charis said wryly. 'It's Father. He fell ill on our journey to London. It's been more than a month now and he's still not much improved. Lethargic, with no appetite and none of his usual energy. It seems to sap all the strength he possesses just to go from his bed to his chair and back.'

'Shall I send my physician?'

'Goodness, no! I'd not have him treated by one of your English quacks who would probably insist on bleeding him, or some such nonsense. I've brewed some tisanes and will keep on feeding him nourishing broths. I do wish I could obtain more fresh fruit and vegetables for him. The market nearest our house seems always in short supply.'

'I shall overlook your slur on English physicians. The supply of fruits and vegetables will increase as spring goes on, but in the interim I'll order some to be sent in from the glasshouse at my estate. My gardener keeps me in lemons, limes and pineapples and there should be some cherries soon, as well as apples that were put away last autumn.'

'That would be wonderful! Thank you!'

'Of course, child. Now, we must do something to amuse you while you wait for your father to improve.

I've always regretted that he never attempted to reconcile with the family that rejected him. It leaves you with no one in the city to visit save me.'

'I do have the collectors to call on.'

Lady Sayleford wrinkled her nose. 'Old men waxing eloquent about their treasures, no doubt.'

Charis smiled. 'I enjoy waxing eloquent about their treasures, too.'

'But that's hardly lively enough company for a young person! You need to be able to spend time in a group of convivial people closer to your own age. Ladies and gentlemen with whom you could sing, perform on the piano, play cards or ride in the park.'

'I do read to Father in the evenings, so I'm not wholly without entertainment.'

'Yes, I know how much you both enjoy reading. All well and good to improve the mind, but a young lady should have exercise for the body as well. Dancing, while conversing with handsome young men she can flirt with.'

The image of one handsome young man flashed into her mind. She could easily envision enjoying dancing and flirting with Gregory Lattimar. Though after her scandalous behaviour in kissing him, he'd probably flee in the opposite direction if saw her. Or treat her with the insulting familiarity her wanton behaviour merited.

No, better not to see Gregory Lattimar again.

She looked up from her reverie to see Grand-Tante watching her closely. 'Ah, you are lonely!' her great-aunt cried, reading Charis's expression only too accurately. 'I knew you must be. That decides it; I shall put together a small gathering for you. Dinner, cards and a bit of dancing.'

'But I wouldn't know what to converse about with

young English people my age. And if I'm lonely, only think of poor Father, accustomed to crossing seas and deserts, always on the move, always meeting people, now stuck alone in his room. How could I go out and amuse myself, leaving him deserted?'

'I'm sure he can spare you for an evening. Indeed, I expect if you tell him of my plans he will insist that you go out. After all, you will then have tales to relate to him when you return—about the so odd English society.'

'Perhaps, but frankly I have nothing to wear that would not shame you.' A sudden suspicion struck, and she bent a sharp glance on her aunt. 'Or is that in fact your object, dreaming up this entertainment just to induce me to purchase some more fashionable gowns?'

Smiling, but making no reply, Lady Sayleford said, 'I shall take you to my own dressmaker. I'm sure she can come up with something you can tolerate that will be stylish and attractive without making you feel you've been trussed up like a duck for roasting. Nor do I expect you will find all English society dull, as you seem to think it.'

'You are not dull, certainly. But all I know about is the world to the East, in which I doubt few fashionable members of society will have any interest. Unless…unless you promise to invite some diplomats or perhaps some collectors.' Feeling a spark of enthusiasm, she continued, 'It would be a joy to compare with someone the beauties of Tehran or Baghdad, or to discuss the merits of onyx versus malachite with a connoisseur who knows what he's talking about.'

'True. Very well, I shall invite a few people with whom you will have interests in common. I've not entertained in some time and owe invitations to a number of friends, so the party will end up being somewhat larger than I initially described. But I promise you need converse only to those with whom you feel comfortable. There will be dancing, though, and you must promise me you will take a break from your collectors and diplomats long enough to take the floor with some of the younger gentlemen.'

'I could always dance with the diplomats and collectors.'

Grand-Tante laughed. 'If you prefer. Although if you neglect this opportunity to dazzle some handsome young gentlemen, I shall be much disappointed. We will dine together first, just the two of us *en famille*, so you will have a chance to gird yourself for the festivities to come. So, do we have a bargain?'

Charis nodded. 'I have to admit, I have missed being around other people. At home in Constantinople or when travelling, we are never alone. There isn't the great divide you have here between master and servant, the staff remaining below stairs except when required to perform some task, the family isolated in their own area above. My maid Alizah is always in attendance, along with most of the female servants, and there's a stream of visitors to the house, balls and receptions to attend in the diplomatic and trading communities and visits to Bayam Zehra and the harems of other ladies, and one always travels with a large cortege. It will be nice to be in company again. Worth, I suppose, the discomfort of a new gown.'

'A handsome admission!' Grand-Tante said with a laugh. 'What an unusual girl you are, to be sure. I don't believe I've ever heard a female complain about having to purchase new gowns. I promise they will not be all that uncomfortable, and you will look delightful.'

Picturing ballooning sleeves, a tightly pinched-in waist and skirts heavy enough to trip over, Charis sighed. But since wearing a new gown would obviously give pleasure to this lady whom she loved dearly, surely she could tolerate it for an evening?

'Since I must purchase a gown, I shall order a riding habit as well. If we are to be marooned in London longer than expected, I should like to be able to ride, and the only English-style habit I possess is so old, I'm afraid it might disintegrate if I attempted gallop in it.'

'I'm sure Madame Therese would be delighted to make a habit for you. Excellent! I'll send word to the stables to have my carriage made ready. As soon as we finish tea, I'll bear you off to the dressmaker—before you can change your mind.'

'Very well, I surrender,' Charis said, smiling as she took another sip of tea. It would be interesting to attend a London ton event, something she'd never done before. Father had no interest in the entertainments of the season, his sole outings while in London his meetings with their clients and other collectors. In any event, they didn't normally linger in the city once they'd delivered their commissions and restocked the supplies necessary for the next voyage.

'I shall try not to embarrass you,' Charis said, feeling her face flush as she recalled her inappropriate conduct with a certain gentleman. 'I understand the rules governing the behaviour of unmarried females in society are very strict. I doubt I have a sufficient grasp of all the subtle nuances.'

'Fortunately, you don't need to worry about being perfectly conventional,' Grand-Tante said. 'It will be known that you have lived almost exclusively in Anatolia and

the Levant, far from normal English society. Any ir-
regularities in your behaviour will be attributed to that.'

Boldly kissing a gentleman to whom you were neither
affianced nor related was an 'irregularity' that wouldn't
pass muster in any society, Charis thought wryly. The
denizens of the Ottoman lands might consider the taking of pleasure a normal, enjoyable part of life, but the
rules governing the behaviour of unmarried maidens
there were even stricter.

But then, she'd never previously had any urge to flout
those rules—until she'd met Gregory Lattimar.

Who, fortunately, was unlikely to attend Grand-
Tante's entertainment. Should she encounter him again,
she wasn't sure what would be more agitating—her need
to apologise for her behaviour, or her desire to repeat it.

Though it would be helpful to be forewarned, she
didn't dare ask Grand-Tante to confirm Lattimar
wouldn't be among the attendees. That enquiry would
raise far too many questions she didn't want to answer.

She would look forward to enjoying the evening by
confining herself to conversing with knowledgeable investors and trading stories with former ambassadors delighted to compare their experiences of the East.

The following day, Gregory encountered his mother
just as he was about to leave the breakfast room. 'Up
again so early?' he asked, smiling as he waved her to a
seat and poured her a cup of coffee. 'Do you have some
commission for me? I shall be out most of day with the
solicitors, going over figures from our southern properties.'

'I know, which is why I rose early to catch you before
you departed,' she said, kissing his cheek before taking

the chair opposite. 'I know you are planning to leave London soon, and wanted to ask if it were possible for you to delay your departure a bit longer.'

In truth, he should leave tomorrow after that consultation with the solicitors. But he'd thus far made no plans to depart. He knew he was lingering in case his father suddenly decided which objects he required W. Dunnfield to obtain for him, giving him an excuse to call again on his daughter.

He'd debated calling again without an excuse so he might apologise. So unprepared had he been for her unexpected kiss, which had unleashed a desire he'd been struggling to control almost since the instant they'd met, he'd responded to her initially chaste salute with a full-out sensual assault that had sent her fleeing the room.

Of course, it was shocking that she'd kissed him to begin with, initially confusing him again about just how knowing she might be. But the kiss itself—a little awkward, very obviously inexperienced—had quickly proven that, alluring though she might be, she was also an innocent. Despite her forwardness in initiating the contact, he was certain she was not a wanton.

An innocent, yet bold enough to kiss him. Once again, she presented a puzzle he longed to solve. Too bad her kiss hadn't proved she was an experienced player of passion's game. He might then have called again immediately with a proposition that could please them both.

Recalling how her response had progressed swiftly from startled to ardent, he knew he could give her pleasure. But that was not a possible solution to the dilemma of his attraction. Despite Charis having invited his kiss, her maiden status forbade him to follow through on their mutual attraction unless he was prepared to offer marriage as the price to claim what he was certain would be a sublime, sensual experience for them both.

If not for his family's circumstances…if not for the mother to whom he owed so much…he might have been rash enough to pay that price. Never before had he felt so strongly connected both physically and mentally to any woman.

But Charis Dunnfield wasn't the sort of wife he needed, and that was that. She might not even still be in England. And were he to take the plunge and wed her, he wouldn't be happy about her periodically running off with her father to search out treasures for collectors. Nor could he see her being content to remain permanently in England.

No, it was impossible.

Despite that truth, he decided to talk with Vraux again today and see if his father had made a list of the objects he wanted to acquire next. Though the problem of his attraction had no acceptable solution, he might at least see her one more time.

If the Dunnfields hadn't already departed the city.

Suddenly Greg realised he'd been standing there, lost in thought, while his mother studied him with concern. 'Sorry, Mama! Wool-gathering, I'm afraid.'

'Considering all that is left to be accomplished before you can leave London?'

Seizing that convenient fig leaf to cover what he'd really been thinking about, he nodded. 'There is always so much. What is it you wanted to ask of me?'

'An invitation came in the post yesterday. Lady Sayleford is having a soiree. That in itself is unusual, for she seldom entertains. She has invited us both. I would truly love to go—if you are free to escort me.'

Gregory felt both grateful and torn. Lady Sayleford, grandest of society's grand dames, related by blood or political connection to almost everyone who was anyone in the aristocracy, was one of the very few hostesses who still invited his mother to her parties. Although even her influence wasn't enough to persuade other prominent women to extend the olive branch to his infamous mother. If he married a well-connected female who could add her persuasion to that of a society leader like Lady Sayleford, it might just be enough to end that exclusion.

Being present at the fete would allow him to fend off any feckless fools who tried to follow his mother about, drawn by the allure of her beauty and scandalous reputation like mariners bewitched by the song of the sirens. 'When is the event?'

'Two days from now. So attending it wouldn't delay your departure all that much.'

Greg nodded. 'In any event, I hadn't yet set a firm date for leaving. It will partly depend on the reports I'm reviewing today. I might need to ride to one of the estates to the south before I return to Entremer.'

His mother made no comment, though she did give him a speculative glance. He'd already remained in London a week longer than he usually stayed. But he wasn't about to add another word, lest his perspicacious mother suspect there was another reason he was marking time in London when neither of his closest friends was currently in residence to make such an extended stay more understandable.

Better leave before she decided to query him further. 'Go ahead, send an acceptance for us both. If there's enough time, buy a fetching new gown to wear. Despite having paid off Vraux's forgotten invoices, we're not forced to out-run the bailiff yet.'

That earned him a smile. 'You're sure? I would like that.'

After rising, he went over to kiss her cheek. 'When your mother is the most beautiful woman in London, she needs to dress the part. Dazzle them.'

Smiling back, tears sheening her eyes, she said, 'Then for you, I will.'

Chapter Six

Two evenings later, Greg walked up the stairway of Lady Sayleford's grand townhouse, his mother on his arm. He was already tense as he waited with other guests to go through the receiving line, conscious of the curious looks given his mother, how few met her eye and nodded, how many ignored her completely. His ire smouldering, he tried to scan the ballroom beyond to see if there were any gentlemen present who might cause problems.

Meanwhile, his mother, like the lady she was, exchanged a few pleasant words with those who acknowledged her and gracefully ignored those who snubbed her. Greg didn't think he could have been so charitable.

While he debated strategies for detaching any gentleman who tried to make his mother too much the subject of gallantry, setting off another round of malicious rumours that were not her fault, the line slowly moved to the ballroom entrance. As the butler intoned their names, Greg stepped forward with his mother, who gave her hostess a deep curtsey, thanking her again for inviting them.

Lady Sayleford, Greg was gratified to note, made a

point of kissing his mother on both cheeks before expressing in a carrying voice how pleased she was that Lady Vraux had chosen to grace her ballroom with her enchanting presence.

Responding to Greg's look of gratitude with a tiny smile, she inclined her head towards the room full of guests. 'Would you be kind enough to seek out my young relation? The connection is distant, her late mother being my favourite niece. She and her father do not reside in London, so she is seldom in the city and knows almost no one here. I would be most grateful, Mr Lattimar, if you would promise to coax her to dance later.'

'We would be happy to talk with her,' his mother replied, while Greg gave his hostess a nod, mentally preparing himself to partner an awkward country bumpkin who probably danced poorly and had even less conversation.

'Ah, here she is now,' Lady Sayleford said, as a young woman turned from the elderly gentleman with whom she was conversing and walked towards them. Only to stop short, her eyes widening in surprise, as Greg froze in place, shock, delight, desire and confusion robbing him of speech.

'Miss Dunnfield is a relation of yours?' his mother asked. 'Indeed, we've already had the pleasure of meeting her. A lovely young woman! Vraux is a long-time client of her father's business. She recently helped us unravel a little problem about his receipts.'

Greg found his gaze riveted on Miss Dunnfield's face, her skin under the glow of candlelight as luminous as pearls, her great dark eyes dazzling. Her hair was swept up onto her head in an intricate arrangement of braids, rather than in the exaggerated loops and curls currently fashionable. As his gaze travelled downwards, he noted that her gown was also subtly different, the sleeves the correct shape but not as wide, the waistline more natural, the skirts a bit less voluminous than current fashion dictated. But he could only commend the low neckline that revealed a glorious view of her neck and shoulders before dipping down discreetly to hint at the swell of her breasts.

He'd still not recovered his powers of speech when, with that particular gliding motion unique to her, she resumed walking towards them to halt beside Lady Sayleford. 'Lady Vraux! What a pleasure to see you again! And you too, Mr Lattimar.'

While they exchanged bows and curtseys, his mother murmured, 'We are delighted as well.'

'Lady Vraux, I believe one of your good friends has already arrived,' Lady Sayleford said, pointing towards the distant corner. 'Lady Ragsdale?'

'Why, yes, that is Elizabeth! I must go and greet her. Gregory, I will leave you to entertain Miss Dunnfield. I'm sure she will enjoy your escort much more than mine.'

After another round of curtseys, Greg found himself with Charis Dunnfield's hand on his arm, his feet moving automatically as he walked her away, his senses too overwhelmed by her nearness to register anything else.

'This is an unexpected pleasure,' he said, finally getting his mouth in working order. 'You mentioned that your mother had a relation here, but I had no idea that relative was the undisputed leader of London society!'

'I hadn't realised it either until I viewed the turnout of fashionables tonight. She has always been just Grand-Tante to me, dearest of my mother's relatives and for that reason, after I lost Mama, especially dear to me. I hope you were not...disturbed that she more or less forced me on you.'

'Not at all! As I said, it's my pleasure.'

She looked up at him, anxiety in her dark eyes. 'She had no idea we were already acquainted. After my... rather outrageous behaviour at our last meeting, I was afraid I'd given you distaste of me. It was...not well done of me.'

'Perhaps,' he acknowledged. 'But my response was not well done of me, either. Sending you fleeing in horror! Perhaps we can both say we were...unexpectedly overcome, and leave it at that?'

She looked away and blew out a breath, and he realised she'd been just as agitated and uncertain as he was about how to behave if they met again. 'You are most kind. Many gentlemen would interpret my behaviour in...much less generous terms. Though in honest truth, I wasn't fleeing in horror. Only in prudence.'

She glanced back up, the look in her eyes and her frank admission a confirmation that she felt as strongly as he did the potent connection between them. But the uncertainty in that gaze reinforced the impression he'd formed after her kiss. That, despite her bold move, she was an innocent. A woman with a deep capacity for passion, a desire about which she was unashamed, but one she knew would be dangerous to indulge.

Could he allow the strong connection between them while protecting both her honour and his?

Shaking his mind free of that question to which he still had no answer, he said, 'How is your father? Recovered enough for you to begin planning your departure?'

She frowned. 'Still not that well. Lady Sayleford has

tried to help, having fruits and vegetables sent in from her country estate so our cook can have fresh ingredients to prepare meals that tempt him. I only wish Grand-Tante could order up some sun.' She gave a little smile. 'Powerful as she is in society, not even she can do that.'

'Unfortunately, there are limits even to her influence,' Greg replied, a touch of bitterness in his tone as he watched his mother walk back towards her hostess after having greeted Lady Ragsdale. Watched as most of the guests turned their heads away so as not to acknowledge her.

Having followed the direction of his gaze, after a moment Miss Dunnfield wrinkled her forehead, looking puzzled. 'Why are those people so discourteous to your lady mother? She is an invited guest, one Grand-Tante greeted warmly.'

'Has Lady Sayleford told you anything about my family?' When she shook her head, Greg sighed. 'You know Vraux. How single-mindedly devoted he is to his collections. He's been that way as long as I can remember.'

'He neglects your mother, then.'

'Yes. Mama's debt-ridden family more or less forced her to marry Vraux, who'd agreed to settle all their obligations. It was to be a marriage of convenience on both sides—but Mama had no idea when they wed how little Vraux would contribute to the relationship. By the time I was born, she'd given up hope for her marriage. Still outstandingly beautiful, able to attract any man she wanted, ignored by my father, she fell in love with a handsome young baronet. He loved her too, enough to defy his family and accept being ostracised by society for wedding a divorced woman—only my father refused to divorce her.'

Miss Dunnfield frowned. 'But why not, if he had no

desire for her himself? Such a matter would be easily settled in Anatolia.'

Greg shook his head. 'Who knows? The best I can determine, he considered her the first jewel of his collection. And as you know, he never sells any of his treasures, no matter how much other collectors offer him. In despair and pressed by his family, the baronet ended up marrying someone else, unaware that the woman he loved was carrying his child—my brother Christopher.

'That indiscretion might have been papered over, as Vraux didn't repudiate the boy, but after losing her one true love Mama became…completely careless about her behaviour. She was seduced by a rich, well-born scoundrel who delighted in persuading her into scandalous rendezvous, then boasting of them to his friends. By the time she was delivered of his twins, she'd repudiated him, but by then it was too late. Her misbehaviour had been too flagrant for most of the ton to forgive—although her former lover continues to be everywhere received.'

'Infamous of him!' Miss Dunnfield said angrily. 'But so it is with society. Even in the Ottoman world, women are considered temptresses who must be hidden away from susceptible men. How proud I am that Grand-Tante stood by Lady Vraux.'

'I'm very grateful. And guilty. Despite the sins laid at her door by society, she was a loving mother to all her children. A mother that I, resentful of the infamy she'd attracted when I was growing up, often didn't treat with the courtesy she deserved. Now that I have a more adult understanding of her circumstances, I'm trying to make up for that.'

Miss Dunnfield angled her head at him thoughtfully.

'From what I observed of you together, if she ever blamed you for disdaining her, you have been forgiven.'

Greg smiled wryly. 'She never gave any indication that my slights hurt her, though they must have. Which is why I try to support her as much as I can now—escorting her tonight, when I usually avoid ton events.'

Miss Dunnfield patted his arm approvingly. 'That's well done of you. There is a saying in the East: "heaven lies beneath a mother's feet". The mother of a sultan or a pasha is one of the most important people in his household, her son's supporter and often his counsellor. It does you honour to treasure your lady mother. And I am honoured that you confided the truth of her circumstances to me.'

Miss Dunnfield gave an unexpected laugh. 'In addition to which, Lady Vraux's unfortunate story serves as a pointed reminder of the fate of a woman society judges to be wanton. Which makes me even more grateful for your discretion in overlooking my…lapse.'

Greg smiled at her. 'It was my lapse as well.'

'Yes, but if anyone should learn of it, I alone would be thought culpable. I do assure you, it was a *singular* lapse. Save for the…attraction that made it impossible to resist kissing you, my conduct around gentlemen has always been irreproachable. It has to be, given the freedom I'm allowed as I as travel about with my father, often dealing with customers on my own. It's vital to avoid arousing unsavoury rumours that might harm Father's business and to forestall pursuit by unscrupulous men who might believe me an easy conquest.'

Before he could assure her he would never insult her by thinking of her as 'easy', two gentlemen approached them. Lord Stansberry and Mr Hornsford, whom he recognised vaguely, younger men who'd entered university just as he was leaving.

'Lattimar, you must present us,' Stansberry said.

Greg studied the two for a moment—and didn't like what he saw. Their avid eyes inspected Miss Dunnfield with a barely concealed sensual interest that immediately raised his protective instincts. But with a refusal likely to provoke an incident he'd rather avoid, he said reluctantly, 'Miss Dunnfield, allow me to present Lord Stansberry and Mr Jeremy Hornsford.'

They bowed to her curtsey. 'How lovely you are,' Stansberry said. 'A true ornament to the festivities.'

'Divine,' said Hornsford, casting a lascivious glance up and down her figure. 'As appealing as a portrait by Ingres.'

Miss Dunnfield's polite smile faded. 'That's hardly a compliment, sir. The artist painted a European woman set in his imaginary vision of a place about which he knew nothing.'

'You do live most of the year in Constantinople, don't you?' Stansberry asked.

'The land of harems and dancing girls?' Hornsford suggested. 'Your grace would rival any of them.'

Infuriated to observe his mother's prediction about the attention Miss Dunnfield's allure would arouse playing out right under his eyes—but in a most unsavoury way—Greg said bitingly, 'Would you like to repeat that remark about her kinswoman to Lady Sayleford? Or have me repeat it to her for you?'

'She…she is related to Lady Sayleford?' Hornsford asked, blanching, while Stansberry sent Greg a resentful glance.

'That wouldn't be sporting of you, Lattimar. Especially since you're monopolising the lady. Shows you've already thrown your hat into the ring.'

'You'd better make sure I don't throw down the gauntlet. Miss Dunnfield's father is a close associate of Vraux's. She's considered a part of my family, almost like a sister.' Only the depth of his anger could have allowed him to spit out a falsehood like that without choking. 'I would have you treat her with the same respect you would expect me to show to your sister.'

Turning to Miss Dunnfield, he said, 'Shall we get some refreshments?'

Not waiting for a reply from Stansberry or from the lady, Greg put her hand on his arm and led her off towards the refreshment room.

Hornsford and Stansberry were prudent enough not to follow, but as they crossed the ballroom Greg noted with concern that other men were watching Miss Dunnfield with the same sort of heightened interest. His keen ear caught bits and pieces of the whispers...

'...*denizen of Constantinople...*'

'...*actually lived in a harem...*'

Miss Dunnfield must have heard them, too, but she walked with her head high, giving no indication that anything had occurred to embarrass or alarm her. He couldn't tell from her calm, proud bearing whether or not the men's inappropriate remarks had distressed her.

Was he being hypocritical to be furious with them? After all, upon learning of Miss Dunnfield's visits to a harem, he too had immediately thought of erotic tales and the Ingres portrait. He'd wondered about her character and her availability. The exotic way she moved and her striking differentness was bound to excite speculation, even among gentlemen too polite to give voice to it.

No, he wasn't being unreasonable to expect gentlemen to act like gentlemen, he decided. He might have begun by entertaining similar thoughts, but he'd refrained from voicing or acting upon them until he'd learned the truth about her maiden status—and then had vowed to treat her with the respect she deserved.

That kiss had been a momentary aberration.

Wanting to divert her thoughts if she *had* been upset by the remarks, after procuring her a glass of wine Greg said, 'Who was the older gentleman with whom you were conversing when we arrived? Another collector like Vraux?'

'Yes. I told Grand-Tante I'd only agree to attend an evening gathering if she promised to include some people with whom I'd have something in common. In addition to conversing about the sources for the finest rubies with Lord Mulbaron, I had a lovely chat in Farsi with the former ambassador to Persia, comparing our favourite parts of Tehran. Two other of Father's collector friends are present, one who specialises in jewels and another who collects *shamshirs*—the curved swords of Persia.' She sighed. 'Although I did promise Grand-Tante I would dance when the music begins.'

'Do you not enjoy dancing?' he asked, forbidding his mind to jump to the image of dancing girls Hornsford's unsavoury remark had aroused.

'I don't know many of the English dances. And I'm well aware that the way I was trained to walk makes me…distinctive in this country. The Scheherazade effect, I imagine. From the covert—and some not so covert— looks I've been receiving tonight, along with the remarks by your friends Lord Stansberry and Mr Hornsford, my background seems to be firing many gentlemen's heated imaginings about residents of the Ottoman empire.'

'Please, Stansberry and Hornsford are acquaintances only, certainly not friends. Still, I apologise for any... speculation that makes you uncomfortable. But if you don't mind my asking—you said you were *trained* to move in the unique way you do?'

She nodded. 'After my mother's death, her dear friend Bayam Zehra felt it her duty to take Mama's place and school me in the skills she believed necessary to guarantee my successful marriage. Since I didn't possess outstanding beauty, it was doubly important I make up for it by being graceful in all my movements—from greeting guests, to serving coffee, to dancing. To possess the most pleasing laugh, the sweetest of singing voices, to read and tell stories with great eloquence. So that when I entertained my husband, he would be so captivated, he would forget about my lack of beauty and end up devoted.'

Greg listened to her explanation, slightly astounded. 'Your mother's friend thought *you* unattractive? Was she blind?'

Miss Dunnfield smiled. 'She didn't think me *un*attractive. She just recognised that I don't possess the sort of outstanding beauty, like that of your mother, which is highly prized by prospective husbands in Anatolia. So, I had hours of practice lifting my arms and turning my hands and fingers just so when serving tea, walking with a dance-like sway to my steps, singing and reading in a beguiling and pleasing voice. Although Bayam Zehra was a stern taskmaster, I'm afraid I've been a sad disappointment to her.'

'A disappointment? You are both lovely and a knowledgeable collector, a true assistant to your father. How could she find you a disappointment?'

'It's those accomplishments that cause her to despair. I've reached this great age, you see, and am still unmarried. She finds it incomprehensible that I prefer travelling the world with Father to remaining in a fine home with children to spoil and a husband to indulge me with furs and jewels.'

'I suppose many English mothers would agree with her view of a woman's role,' Greg allowed. 'Still, I can't get my mind around the idea that she did not consider you beautiful.'

'That's kind of you, but only consider your mother. Mine was equally dazzling, with skin like alabaster, eyes whose brilliance rivalled gemstones, hair like satin, a voice and a laugh that would make one think of the angels in paradise. Do you really think a gentleman would notice any other woman, if she or your Mama walked into the room?'

She laughed. 'There's an old superstition among the Ottomans—one must never praise the beauty of a child, lest you bring the evil eye upon him. When describing the youngster, one always shakes one's head over his supposed defects, even when there are none. Bayam Zehra could look at me and say, "Oh, poor thing,"' and truly mean it.'

Another dandy, whom Greg recognised as the younger brother of a fellow student from Oxford, walked over to halt beside them. After nodding to Greg, he said, 'Introduce me, won't you, Lattimar? I'm eager to hear Miss Dunnfield's tales of the Arabian nights,' he concluded.

Irritated anew, Greg said, 'She has none to tell you. Take yourself off.'

The man looked as if he meant to argue the point, but as Greg continued to fix him with a hostile gaze he shrugged and walked away.

Miss Dunnfield sighed. 'I should have anticipated something of this nature when I agreed to attend this entertainment. I'm afraid I didn't sufficiently think over the implications. It's one thing to talk with diplomats who have lived and travelled in foreign lands. Far too many other men need only hear I resided in Constantinople to think of harems and odalisques. I appreciate your attempts to shield me, especially after I gave you good reason to believe that description might be true, but you needn't hang about me all evening. I can deal with those attentions quite well enough.'

'Are you sure? I don't wish to leave you unprotected from the impudence of ill-informed reprobates.'

'I can hold my own, I assure you. Once, when Father's sudden illness during a desert crossing required us to claim the hospitality of a Sharif for a good deal longer than anticipated, I had to beguile him into deciding that he didn't really want to marry me after all. If I could disarm his ardour, I think I can handle overly forward London gentlemen.'

Greg chuckled. 'I wish I had seen that!'

'Oh, it was a masterful performance,' she agreed, smiling. 'I shall need nothing as inventive in London. Now that I know Lady Sayleford possesses such influence, I need only mention she is my aunt, and I'll be as safe from unwanted attention as if I were surrounded by a squadron of palace janissaries. No gentleman who wishes to remain in the ton's good graces will dare treat me disrespectfully, regardless of his suspicions about my virtue.'

Having finished her wine, she was handing her glass over to a servant when the orchestra began tuning up. 'Oh, dear,' she murmured. 'The dancing will soon begin. I must hurry to a place against the wall and find some diplomat to talk with.'

'It sounds like it will be a waltz. Surely you've danced that at embassy balls?'

'True, I do know how to waltz.'

Quickly, before better judgement could prevent him, Greg said, 'Then won't you honour me? I did promise your great-aunt I would entice you to dance.'

She looked up at him, uncertain. Reluctant, as if knowing as well as he did that, with the strong sensual attraction simmering between them, it was unwise to indulge in a dance that would place her in his arms, the whole length of their bodies nearly touching as they whirled about the floor.

While he waited, knowing it would be better for her to refuse, hoping she wouldn't, she slowly nodded. As if she were as unable to resist this opportunity to be close to him as was he.

His heart rate soaring, Greg offered her his arm and walked her out to the dance floor. He couldn't marry her. He couldn't even kiss her again. But for a few marvellous minutes, he could hold her in his arms for the duration of a waltz.

They took their places, the music began and he swept her into rhythm. Her satin hair tickled his chin while her jasmine scent engulfed his senses, making him think of hot climes, trickling fountains and velvet black nights under a brilliant canopy of stars.

He imagined her voice in his ears, recounting tales of her travels and experiences. Envisioned drinking the coffee she made for him with those graceful, artful gestures. And at the end of her last tale, pulling her into his arms to make love to her all through the night.

The waltz had been a mistake, he realised, striving to drive those beguiling images from his brain. As soon as it ended, he must move away from the seduction of her touch, the intoxication of her scent.

But despite those good intentions, when the music stopped, he simply drifted with her to a halt. One hand clasping hers, his other at her waist, he stood gazing into her eyes, the intensity of the bond between them making him oblivious to everything around him, as if there were no one in the ballroom but the two of them.

The heat of the candles and the murmuring of other voices suddenly penetrated, shocking him into realising the other dancers were staring at them. His heart stuttering back into rhythm, he forced himself to release her.

As curious glances followed their departure from the floor, he told himself to hand her off to some safe gentleman and escape before the madness she inspired in him made them even more a subject of gossip.

'I shall turn you over to a diplomat now,' he said as they reached the clusters of guests ranged around the edges of the ballroom. 'Which gentleman would you prefer?'

Her hand on his arm trembled, as if she had been as deeply under the spell of the dance as he had. But in a voice that wobbled, then steadied as she gave him an ambassador's name, he understood that she was as determined as he was to resist the enchantment that had possessed them on the dance floor.

'You are sure you can handle everything on your

own?' he asked, half-hoping she would confess herself uncertain and give him a good excuse to remain.

'Absolutely,' she replied, her voice steady now.

She was being as steadfast in her resistance to any further missteps as he must be. 'I shall let you go, then. I dare not monopolise you—that would lead to speculation about serious intentions neither of us possess.'

'We wouldn't want to encourage that,' she agreed as he led her to the gentleman she indicated, who was chatting with a group at the other side of the room. 'Although I'm not much concerned about gossip. With luck, within the month Father and I will be on our way out of England, any such speculation the *on dit* of the moment and as soon forgotten. When returning to London, we normally stay only long enough to distribute our purchases and restock our supplies, so I don't anticipate attending any society events in future. I shall take care to have Father avoid a recurrence of illness that might strand us in England.'

By now, they'd reached the diplomat, who turned to greet her with delight. 'You see, you leave me in good hands. And how are you this evening, Effendi?' Giving Greg a curtsey, to which he bowed, and avoiding his gaze, she turned back to the diplomat and asked him a question in some language Greg didn't understand.

He'd been dismissed. He needed to search out his mother anyway, make certain the lascivious-minded gentlemen who'd been sniffing around Miss Dunnfield didn't transfer their attentions to Lady Vraux. And for the rest of the evening, avoid the temptation of approaching Charis Dunnfield again.

His future would be lived out in chilly northern counties under cloudy English skies. It was pointless to indulge in dreaming about nights that were never going to happen under spangled stars beside trickling fountains.

Chapter Seven

Three days later, Charis came down the stairs from the salon at Vraux House after paying a visit to Lady Vraux. She'd liked the lady upon their first meeting, even more so after her sympathy had been aroused by the circumstances her son had confided to her. When, after encountering the baron's wife in the lady's withdrawing room at her great-aunt's entertainment, Lady Vraux had invited her to call, she'd been happy to agree.

As she hadn't made a secret of her presence in the house, she wasn't sure whether to be relieved or sorry not to have encountered her hostess's son. Meeting him would only have disturbed her, however, and she didn't need such disturbances.

Though she'd been surprised by his appearance at her great-aunt's entertainment, on that occasion she'd been as relieved as she was wary. He, at least, knew the truth of her circumstances, and though they'd shared that potent kiss, he'd been gentleman enough not to insinuate anything from it—unlike some of the 'gentlemen' who'd tried to claim introductions to her.

Rather than deal in veiled innuendo, he'd asked about

her upbringing, seemed to enjoy her stories and repaid her confidences by confiding the circumstances of his own family. Though the sensual connection remained strong—as did the memory of their erotic kiss—she genuinely liked the handsome, courteous and surprisingly knowledgeable Gregory Lattimar.

But liking was as far as she could allow her emotions to go. Their waltz might have been magical, but it had also been a mistake. She didn't need English magic to divert her from her true path. Magic that tried to beguile her into imagining that she belonged in his arms or walking by his side.

She'd badly needed the dose of reality of speaking Arabic with a former Baghdad diplomat to remind her of place and purpose.

Still, as she descended the final few steps, she had to admit she was a *tiny* bit disappointed not to have encountered Lattimar. She reached the hall, wondering what could have happened to the butler for whom her hostess had rung to bring her bonnet and pelisse, when she saw Overton, the butler, nip down the hallway, not towards her but towards the front door. A shock of nervousness and anticipation zipped through her when she heard Lattimar's voice from beyond the door, responding to the butler's greeting.

Conflicting impulses held her immobile. The instinct to duck into an anteroom and avoid him warred with a stronger desire to walk forward to meet him. Deciding after a moment's indecision that it would be silly to hide herself away, she raised her chin, straightened her back and remained where she was, ready to greet him politely, like a sensible woman.

Despite her intention to appear calm, she could feel

her heartbeat accelerate. She had to take a deep breath to still the flutters in her belly while she waited for him to notice her. Vain as it was, she was glad she was wearing one of the attractive new gowns Lady Sayleford had talked her into buying. Which, true to Grand-Tante's promise, managed to minimise the most outlandish elements of sleeves and skirts while providing a bodice with stays barren of boning, so she was even able to breathe comfortably.

As comfortably as she could when the sight of his commanding form and handsome face made her catch her breath.

Lattimar handed his hat and cane to the butler before he turned and spied her. 'Miss Dunnfield?' he said, his eyes widening in surprise.

Charis smiled. 'I'm not an apparition, though I imagine you are wondering at my sudden appearance in your hall. I've just had a very pleasant visit with your mother. I encountered her in the ladies' withdrawing room at Lady Sayleford's entertainment and she invited me to call.'

For another moment he stood simply staring, as if befuddled as to what to do next. 'Would…would you like some tea?'

'Thank you, I've just had some with your mother.'

'Ah, yes, I imagine she would have ordered some.'

Silence fell between them. She should ask the butler to fetch her belongings, bid farewell to Lattimar and take her leave. But she couldn't quite get her lips to form the words.

While she struggled, Lattimar said, 'Are you…quite pressed for time? I've had a chance to talk with Vraux. I have some idea about what he might want you to ob-

tain for him on your next journey if you have a moment
to discuss that?'

She should refuse, or at least invite him to call at
King Street. Where in her domain, surrounded by objects about which she could talk with him, she might
better resist him.

Although she hadn't done such a good job of resisting
him the last time he'd called there. But how many more
times could she expect to meet him? Being a guest in
his house, where servants or his mother might walk in
at any moment, would restrain her alarming tendency to
lapse into inappropriate behaviour with him.

Besides, this conversation would be all about business.
Though she'd be willing to bet the notion of discussing
his father's potential purchases hadn't come into his head
until he'd seen her standing at the bottom of his staircase.

'Of course, Mr Lattimar, I can spare half an hour,'
she replied, keenly aware of the butler hovering beside
him. 'Lord Vraux has been a loyal supporter of my father's trade for many years. He would certainly want
to know about His Lordship's requirements before we
leave London.'

'Excellent. If you are sure you don't want more tea?'
After she shook her head, he continued, 'Thank you, that
will be all, Overton. I'll ring when Miss Dunnfield is
ready for her pelisse. Won't you follow me to the breakfast room?' He waved an arm to usher her forward.

Hesitating, the butler gave her a look. He was probably
thinking that she'd just paid a social call on his mistress,
and that a respectable young unmarried lady was not entertained by a single gentleman without a chaperone. But
he'd also ushered her in a week ago as little more than
a tradesman's daughter, a female whose behaviour was

not nearly as restricted. In any event, he had little choice but to nod, bow and walk away.

'I think I've scandalised your butler,' Charis said as she walked into the morning room. 'I almost felt I should reassure him I wouldn't try to seduce you in your own breakfast room.'

'More's the pity,' Lattimar said with a smile.

Giving him a reproving glance, she continued, 'I don't think he knows quite how to treat me. I seem to have that effect on English people. I believe it's what prompted your mother to invite me to call.'

'How so?' he asked, angling his head enquiringly as he motioned to the sofa and took a seat on the adjacent armchair.

'That requires a bit of explanation. After talking with the diplomat at Lady Sayleford's soiree, I went up to the ladies' withdrawing room. Rumour about the "unusual newcomer" had spread through the ballroom over the course of the evening, no doubt along with speculation about my exotic upbringing and what that might mean about my character. The matrons to whom I'd been introduced earlier turned disapproving and the unmarried maidens, who'd initially been friendly, became frostier and more distant as the evening went on.'

'Probably because they noticed that the gentlemen found you fascinating.'

Charis grimaced. 'Ah, yes, the gentlemen. The ladies might have deserted me, but after I finished speaking with the diplomat, I was besieged by men asking questions about my life in Constantinople, full of innuendo about Scheherazade and exotic odalisques, until I was quite near losing my patience. Rather than respond rudely, I took refuge in the ladies' withdrawing room.

The three maidens who were in the room as I entered took one look at me, exchanged glances and exited as quickly as possible.'

Charis laughed. 'I'm not sure whether they were scandalised by my exotic presence or worried that my peculiar reputation might sully theirs if they were known to associate with me. Just after they left, your mother came in. As we chatted, two other groups of matrons walked in, saw us, turned around and walked back out. We agreed then and there that two females whose mere presence had the power to send proper ladies fleeing should get to know each other better.'

Lattimar smiled. 'And did you?'

'Yes. Lady Vraux possesses such sunny spirit, cheerful and engaging despite the sad events of her life. I can see why you are so fond of her and so resentful of her banishment. She seemed genuinely interested in finding out more about my growing up and my life in Constantinople, Baghdad and Tehran. And she was far more knowledgeable about the customs of those lands than I expected! She told me your sister Temperance, who had always wanted to explore abroad, purchased all the travel accounts she could find about foreign lands and shared with her what she'd read. She said Temperance's twin Prudence married a former soldier who, like Father, acquires antiquities and collectables for English investors.'

'Yes, Pru married Johnnie Trethwell. Did you ever meet him on your travels?'

Charis paused a moment, running the name through her memory. 'No, I don't think so.'

'Not surprising. Johnnie served in India before he was mustered out after being injured in an ambush. He met my sister while he was recuperating with his aunt in Bath.'

Lattimar laughed. 'It was ironic. Temper was the sister who longed for adventure and wanted to travel the world, Pru the twin who craved a safe, quiet life in rural England. Temper is now married to an earl, helping promote his career in Parliament, while Pru is the one travelling throughout India and Punjab. Vraux commissions Johnnie to obtain antique weapons from his sources on the Indian subcontinent, but he prefers jewels and daggers that come from Ottoman lands.'

'Do you really have a list of what he wants us to find for him?'

Lattimar gave her a guilty look. 'Well, no. I just… couldn't resist seizing the opportunity to talk with you again.'

'I didn't think so.' Feeling her face warm at the admission, Charis said, 'I couldn't resist the chance to talk with you again, either. Even if I did scandalise the butler.' She sighed. 'Now I must decide if I wish to continue scandalising society.'

'Indeed? In what way?'

'I called on Grand-Tante the day after her entertainment to thank her for going to so much trouble for me. To apologise, too, for causing such a stir. When I told her I hoped the misfortune of being related to such a peculiar young woman wouldn't tarnish her sterling character, she just laughed. She said she'd already accepted several more invitations for us both.

'Thinking she wasn't aware of some of the…comments made about me, I was about to explain in plain language what had occurred when she patted my hand and told me she was quite aware of just what sort of stir

I'd caused. That it wasn't such a bad thing to shake society out of its complacency from time to time. She wants me to continue to go to entertainments with her—after assuring me of what I already knew: that no one would dare to snub any female she sponsored.'

'Are you going to do it?'

'I haven't decided yet. I told her frankly that if I do agree, I couldn't promise to be meek or apologetic if someone challenged or misrepresented my background. As I told you, the way I move is so automatic, I couldn't change it even if I wanted to now. I told her that if young men were going to trail after me, hinting about sensual delights, I might get annoyed enough to play rather outrageously into their fantasies. She said if any man was boorish enough to act with such a lack of decorum, I might respond to his misapprehensions as I liked.

'It's my understanding that young English women are usually introduced into society for the purpose of finding a husband. Since Grand-Tante doesn't have to worry about my odd behaviour chasing away proper suitors, I got the impression she'd find it quite amusing to watch me overturn society's expectations.'

'Watch you face down the disapproving and verbally slash the importunate to ribbons?'

'Exactly.'

'So...are you going to?'

'I am tempted. As she pointed out, I have few other options for diversion. Besides, Father did find my account of the evening vastly entertaining, so attending events would be not just for my own enjoyment. I do so like to amuse him.'

Her smile at that admission faded to a frown. 'He's

still not well enough to begin preparations for our departure.'

Lattimar's smile faded too. 'I know you must find that upsetting. If there is anything we can do to assist him…'

His concern touching on a worry that was steadily growing stronger, she had to blink back tears. 'I don't think there is anything, but thank you.'

'If you do decide to launch your attack on society, let me know. I can arrange to get myself invited to whatever events you attend and can help support you—and be on hand if the blade you are using to slash the importunate is not quite sharp enough to repel all offenders.'

A little flare of relief and excitement lifted her spirits. 'You would do that? It would be amazingly kind! Though I'd hate to take up your time. You told me you don't usually attend society events.'

Lattimar sighed. 'I haven't before now, but I'm going to need to start, little as I expect to enjoy it. I'd intended to return immediately to Entremer, but I've recently been thinking about how the rest of my friends have already married and several have babes on the way. I probably should stay in London and make the effort to find a wife. As your mother-of-the-soul Bayam Zehra would tell me, as heir to the title, it's my duty to marry and produce heirs.'

'She would definitely approve. Of course you must do your duty. And when you do, you should choose a wife from an important family who can add her influence to Grand-Tante's and help restore your mother to society. A wife who will also please you, of course.'

Lattimar angled a surprised look at her. 'How perceptive you are! That's exactly the sort of wife I've decided I must seek.'

She nodded approvingly. 'Honouring your lady mother is your most important duty, along with producing an heir to your title. Have you any such lady in mind yet?'

He smiled ruefully. 'No, alas. As I told you, I've seldom spent any time in society where I might encounter such a paragon.'

'But you should, and soon. Your mother is still beautiful, but beauty doesn't last for ever. Once it fades, she may decide it's too late to re-join society. She, who has always been feted for her loveliness, would not want to return as a withered old crone! She must be reinstated while she is young enough to still be admired, to enjoy company, dinners and dancing.'

'She does enjoy all of that. And buying new gowns to wear to such events.'

'So she should.' Pondering the matter, Charis frowned. 'Normally, a mother would be her son's greatest ally in the search for a bride, observing all the available young ladies, determining candidates who might be suitable, creating opportunities for a chosen few to display their talents and deciding who was most worthy of him.'

Lattimar listened with growing incredulity. 'Is that how things are done in Constantinople?'

'Not quite. The search is usually more formal than that. Mothers do control the process—since gentlemen are never allowed inside the harem where they might meet and evaluate eligible maidens. Usually official matchmakers do much of investigating. They meet with mothers and observe daughters at the hammam—the baths where women gather to bathe, chat and conduct business. Then call at the harem, where the young lady in question must demonstrate her skill in making cof-

fee, serving tea, dancing, singing and story telling.' She
paused. 'I don't suppose you have matchmakers here?'

Lattimar grinned. 'Not official ones. Though we have
plenty of mothers of eligible daughters who are eager to
make the most advantageous marriage for their daughters. Mothers of *sons* might observe eligible maidens
and mention those they find exceptional, but they seldom try to push their son into marrying any particular
girl. He'd be more likely to rebel against her interference
than take her advice.'

'How strange!' Charis said, shaking her head. 'This
I don't understand, for his mother could only have his
best interests at heart.'

A sudden thought struck, igniting her enthusiasm.
There might be a way to express her gratitude for his
friendship—while preventing herself from falling any
deeper under his spell.

'Since Grand-Tante is so eager for me to attend entertainments, perhaps I shall go and serve as your
gorucu—your official matchmaker! I could observe all
the unmarried maidens, evaluate them and recommend
those I think are sufficiently skilled and from families
influential enough to assist your mother's return to society. I've already set up the orders for the supplies we'll
need for our next journey, so I've nothing more pressing
to do while I wait for Father to recover. I might as well
make myself useful. What do you think?'

Lattimar stared at her for a moment. 'You are serious, aren't you?'

'Of course. I wouldn't jest about something as important as your marriage and assisting your mother.'

'You, as matchmaker.' Lattimar shook his head,
chuckling. 'I suppose it would be amusing, if nothing

else. As long as you'd not be offended if didn't take your advice.'

'Even if it were best for you…and your mother? But you are right; it is just as important that the lady please you, and you alone must be the judge of that.'

While he stared thoughtfully into the distance, obviously considering it, she thought it would be the best for her too. Much as her inclination pulled her to him, that could not be. The most effective way to prevent herself from doing something foolish would be to lead him into the arms of a woman who would appreciate him as she did, but who was the proper English maiden he needed to oversee his house, bear his children and reinstate his mother.

Thereby safeguarding the honour of them both.

Looking back at her, he shook his head and laughed again. 'Very well, I'll give your recommendations serious consideration. So, how do we begin this escapade? You'll let me know which invitations Lady Sayleford has accepted, so I may secure invitations for myself?'

'That would probably be easiest. I'll call again on Grand-Tante, let her know I've decided to go into society with her, then send you word of which entertainments we will attend. In the interim, if you do get a list from Lord Vraux of items he'd like Father to seek out, feel free to call at King Street. Otherwise, I suppose I shall see you next…at some social event. Now, I must return home before Father begins to worry about my absence.'

She rose, obliging him to stand up also.

'I'm so glad I happened to return before you left.'

'So am I. Perhaps before Father and I leave England, I will have the pleasure of recommending to you the beautiful, talented lady who will become your wife.'

He fixed that intense gaze on her, opening his lips as if to speak, then closing them. 'Perhaps,' he said, looking away from her.

Forbidding herself to be disappointed that lady could not be her, Charis walked out beside her host.

They exchanged idle pleasantries while she waited for Overton to bring her outer garments. After an exchange of bows and curtseys, she walked out, descended the entry stairs and set off towards King Street, still thoughtful.

She liked Gregory Lattimar—far too much. She certainly desired him. But she couldn't claim him. She just needed to convince herself that the wisest way to express her affection and respect would be to find him a wife who would honour his mother and be worthy of him.

Chapter Eight

Three nights later, her heart swelling with a delight she told herself not to feel, Charis curtseyed to Gregory Lattimar as he came to greet her at the side of Mrs Worthington-Carver's salon. She'd taken up a place where she could quietly observe the throng while Lady Sayleford walked around the room, chatting with friends.

'So you were able to get an invitation,' she said in relief. 'I was beginning to think you hadn't secured one.'

'The unmarried eldest son of the richest baron in England? I could finagle an invitation to any event short of a royal reception,' he teased.

'I'm glad to see you. Though your presence isn't absolutely essential for our purposes.' *Other than to add to my enjoyment,* she added silently. 'I'd be able to observe the candidates' musical performances and watch them dance with others, if not with you. Gathering essential details to add to the information I've been able to obtain from Lady Sayleford about their backgrounds.'

'You talked about them to Lady Sayleford? Did she not think it odd that you were asking for information about young ladies with whom you were not even acquainted?'

'Oh, no. I told her why I wanted it.'

'Heaven preserve me!' Lattimar muttered, his face flushing. 'Why did you do that?'

'Why should I not? It would be silly not to take advantage of the knowledge of the most knowledgeable lady in society. True, I had no idea just how influential Grand-Tante is until the event she hosted a few days ago, but after my observations on that occasion and talking about her with your mother, I now know she is one of the most highly respected ladies in London society. Certainly the most well-informed. Your mother says she is related to half the ton, friends to the rest and knows everything about everyone. Famed for her discretion and her sage advice, she is entrusted with many secrets and confidences.'

'I can't imagine what she thinks of me, to allow you to undertake this "matchmaking" project.'

'What could she think, but that you are being very sensible? When I told her what I intended, she quite approved. Far too many young men in London waste their time dangling after females with only pretty faces to recommend them, she said. Of course, beauty is important, but for long-term contentment in marriage, a wife must possess suitable temperament, skills and talents. She agreed that having an advisor making observations and judgements so as to recommend suitable brides was a very wise idea. And your mother may be able to help, too. After all, who knows best what will make her son happy than his mother?'

'Perhaps in this instance. I am fortunate to possess a doting mother, but not all gentlemen do. Some aristocratic mothers hardly see their offspring.'

'Truly?' Charis said, surprised. 'Ottoman ladies are

never parted from their children. Even sons remain with their mothers for the whole of their childhood. Why would a mother not want to keep her precious children close?'

She shook her head. 'I don't understand this English system. In any event, Lady Sayleford was happy to provide information about the young ladies present tonight. All are acceptable by birth and dowry. But as you observed, being possessed of a large fortune yourself, the dowry a lady brings to the union is less important than character and talents of the lady herself.'

'So you've picked out some promising candidates for me?'

'Several. As the musical performances will begin shortly, we should station ourselves where we can watch.'

'Are you going to tell me their names?'

She gave him a mischievous grin. 'I don't think so. I don't want you to be influenced for or against any young lady until I have a chance to observe them.'

'And what will you be looking for as you *observe* them?' he asked, his tone curious.

'Traits both obvious and subtle. Appearance first; one hopes for great beauty, but as that quality seems rather rare here in London, I shall not rule out those who are merely pretty. You enjoy music, don't you?'

'Very much.'

'Then it will be essential that the lady play expertly and sing with a pleasing voice. You enjoy dancing as well?'

When Lattimar nodded, Charis continued, 'After the musical performances, I'll observe the maidens' skill on the dance floor. She would need to be able to converse intelligently while she dances, too.'

'That would be desirable.'

Suspicious of the twinkle in his eyes and the amusement in his tone, she shook her head at him. 'You mustn't mock. The process is quite serious.'

His expression sobered. 'I can see that you are serious about it. I'll try to treat your endeavour with the respect it deserves.'

'As you should. We should take our seats. The performances are about to begin.'

'Will you be performing?'

Charis shook her head. 'I know few English songs and the music I enjoy is not likely to be to the taste of this audience. Besides, I'm here to evaluate other maidens, not to be on display myself. Shall we join Lady Sayleford?'

'You'll allow me to sit with you? Assuming I can withstand the scorn of your great-aunt.'

She gave him a darkling look. 'Far from being scornful, she finds this approach for choosing a bride sensible. And I'd be happy to have your escort. Though I mustn't keep you near me too long. We wouldn't want society to think you were courting *me*.'

'Would it not make other maidens try harder to capture my attention—and a chance to snag my wealth and position—if they thought I was already courting someone?'

'Not if the someone was me!' she said bluntly. 'Were they—or their mothers—to believe you were pursuing a female so odd and woefully ignorant of the ways of society, they might question your intelligence or your judgement.'

'The maidens might have their doubts, but my fat pockets and eventual title would overcome any reservations their mothers might entertain.'

Charis shook her head. 'What a cynical appraisal! You can't really believe that you would be sought after solely for your wealth and position?'

'You think they would give equal weight to my handsome form and sterling character?'

'They couldn't help admiring the handsome form. I'm beginning to wonder about the sterling character, however,' she added tartly.

Laughing, he guided her to a chair where they would have a good view of the piano and the performers. 'Will this serve as an adequate observation post?'

'Yes, this will do nicely.'

They took their seats, Charis relaxing and allowing herself to enjoy Lattimar's nearness, his leg nearly brushing her skirts, his shoulder just inches from her own, intensifying the ever-present sensual awareness that hummed through her. Glancing covertly at his profile, she thought if she lifted her chin and leaned up just a bit, she could kiss his cheek.

Fortunately, the music room was full of guests. With a handsome face added to his wealth and lineage, Lattimar would be the focus of many appraising female gazes. Her consciousness of all those observing eyes would keep her desire to kiss him in check.

Having committed herself now to finding him another lady, she could simply enjoy his presence and his company, knowing she would be sending him away before he claimed too much of her interest and affection.

Lady Sayleford returned from her visiting to take the seat Charis had saved for her, giving Lattimar a pleasant nod. Behind her back, he mimed wiping his brow with relief, making her smile in spite of herself.

'Behave now,' she murmured to him. 'The entertainment is beginning.'

The first performer curtseyed to the guests, took her seat at the piano and began playing. Charis focused intently on the young lady, wanting to evaluate not just her level of skill, but also the grace of her movements while she performed, an ideal candidate being a delight to both the eye and the ear.

'What did you think?' Lattimar murmured to her after the maiden ended, the guests applauding politely.

'She seemed skilled, although I am not familiar enough with classical European music to be a truly qualified judge. Father and I have attended musical evenings at some of the embassies, but we never hear it while travelling. Her piano playing seemed accurate but there was a sharp edge to her singing voice that I could not admire. Did you not notice?'

'Yes, I suppose some of the high notes were a bit… piercing. So, she is crossed off your list?'

'Yes. Her movements were not very graceful either. Did you note how stiff her curtsey was? Not the gentle, fluid dip and rise one would prefer.'

'I hadn't really noticed. You are very exacting!'

'Of course. When one is contemplating acquiring a companion to last a lifetime, nothing but the best will do.'

He smiled. 'I suppose so. Do you play the pianoforte yourself?'

'I do, but not well, sadly. Mama had begun to teach me, but I'd not acquired much skill before she died. She herself played gloriously. Father had the piano put in a storage room when we went on our first journey shortly after her death and never got it out again. He…has never really got over losing her. I suspected that having me play might be a sad reminder, so I never asked him to take it out again. Nor was there anyone who could teach me. Bayam Zehra took over my training after Mama died, but her skill is with stringed instruments. I'm most proficient at playing those.'

'You must play for me some time. I would love to hear some traditional Ottoman music.'

Charis shook her head doubtfully. 'I'm not sure you would enjoy it. It's quite a different sound from European instrumentals.'

'I'd like to try it. Do you have an instrument in London?'

'Yes, we always carry a *tambur* and a *kemenche* in our travelling baggage. Father likes to hear me play on our evenings alone. On our journeys, I often entertain our hosts when we stay with friends, or the other guests and diplomats when we visit embassies. But hush, the next performer is about to begin.'

Three more young women played and sang, only one of them skilled and graceful enough to make it onto Charis's list. The amateur performances ended, the guests rose to proceed from the music room to the ballroom, where professional musicians were tuning up to play for the dancing to follow.

With Lady Sayleford at her side, Charis walked with Lattimar to the ballroom. 'You may dance with whomever you choose, of course, but if possible, secure dances with these four,' Charis said, naming the candidates one after another. 'In particular, search out Lady Amelia Carthorpe.'

'Ah. She was the lovely brunette who played with

superior technique and sang with a particularly pleasing voice.'

'Exactly.'

'Obtaining a place on your list, while the others fell short?'

'As you may remember, we already eliminated the first. The performance of the second was workmanlike, but she clearly had no love for the music or flair for performance. The third—the comely brunette—was quite acceptable.'

'And the final performer was rather dreadful. Whatever possessed her mother to allow her to play? I felt sorry for the poor girl.'

'Her mother has a tin ear and performs dreadfully herself,' Lady Sayleford interjected. 'But she is blessed with an outstanding dowry which, along with her good looks, will outweigh her inferior musical talent. Now, if you young people will excuse me, I shall seek out the card room.'

'Of course. You'll come fetch me when you are ready to leave?'

Lady Sayleford nodded. 'Unless you decide to try your hand at cards first.'

'Not likely. I understand society plays for much higher stakes than I would care to risk!' Charis said with a laugh.

'The stakes are high in every game,' Lady Sayleford said with a glance towards Lattimar.

The stakes of that game were too high indeed, Charis thought with a sigh. Shaking herself free of the melancholy that thought evoked, she curtseyed to her great-aunt, who nodded to acknowledge the gesture and Lattimar's bow before walking towards the card room.

'What will you do while I'm dancing?' Lattimar asked.

'Sit quietly in this corner. There are no collectors or diplomats here tonight, alas. Besides, my duty is to observe you with the ladies.'

'If I dutifully stand up with every lady you've suggested, will you dance with me later?'

Perhaps a waltz, like the one they'd shared before…? A little thrill ran through her as she remembered the heady delight of being held in his arms, his hands on her, his body a hair's breadth away… But that was the sort of temptation she needed to avoid.

'Dancing together doesn't move us closer to our goal,' she said prosaically. 'The point of this evening is to evaluate potential marriage partners for you. Anything else is a waste of time.'

'Something delightful is never a waste of time,' Lattimar replied, his voice low, his gaze fixed on her, re-firing the heat of the simmering connection between them.

Despite knowing she should avoid dancing with him, she felt her resistance waver. She deserved some reward for being wise enough to direct her efforts towards finding him a more suitable bride, didn't she? Once she discovered that paragon, she would have no further chance to dance with him.

That truth was enough to make her good intentions crumble. 'Very well. But you must dance with all four of them.'

'Excellent,' Lattimar said with a grin. 'I wasn't going to dance with any of them unless you agreed to dance with me, too. And you needn't tell me again,' he added, holding up a hand to forestall her response, 'That dancing with you serves no purpose. Can one not dance with a friend, just for the pleasure of it?'

It would certainly be a pleasure. As long as she kept reminding herself that they were and must remain just friends. 'Yes, friends. But first, the others. We can hardly progress towards our goal unless you develop a closer acquaintance with the ladies.'

Lattimar sighed. 'This might be an exercise in boredom.'

'If the ladies have no conversation, I'll know to cross them off the list.'

'You have an answer for everything,' he complained.

'Of course. The first set is about to begin. Time to do your duty.'

'Very well, fair taskmaster.'

She watched him walk over to the first maiden she'd named, bow and, after exchanging a few words, offer the lady his arm. They were walking onto the floor when Lady Sayleford appeared beside her.

'Back so soon? Was there no one of interest in the card room, Grand-Tante?'

'No one of sufficient talent. I enjoy a lively game, but there's no challenge in plucking pigeons. Why don't you dance? You can observe Lattimar's partners just as well from the dance floor.'

Charis shook her head. 'If there were anyone here from the diplomatic world who knew me, I might. But with gossip about me already circulating, I'd rather not accept the hand of some unknown gentleman. I know no one would dare *behave* with less than propriety— not with you right here in the ballroom! But it is quite tiresome to reply politely to comments full of ignorance and innuendo. Honestly, I must warn you again there's a good chance I will lose my temper and do or say something outrageous.'

'I stand forewarned,' Lady Sayleford said, smiling. 'You don't have that problem with Lattimar? I heard you accept his offer of a dance.'

'No. Despite some early...misapprehension, he has been the perfect gentleman throughout.'

Lady Sayleford focused her insightful gaze on Charis. 'You find it so easy to turn him over to another?'

Charis sighed. 'Grand-Tante, Lattimar is an English gentleman who will inherit land and title. His life is here in England, as it must be. I won't deny I find him vastly appealing, but I could never bear to be tied to one place. I love travelling with Father and have no desire to marry.'

Especially not a man who was so vastly appealing that, if she weren't very careful, he might steal her heart. And nothing but heart*ache* could come from that.

'What will you do when your father retires and no longer travels?'

Charis shrugged. 'Father may eventually give up his business, but he'll never stop travelling. If collecting becomes too strenuous, we'll go by easy stages between our house in Constantinople and visits to friends in Baghdad, Tehran and Damascus.'

'Not to be morbid, but in the way of nature, you will outlive him. If you don't marry, what will you do then for companionship?'

'Perhaps I'll continue Father's business. Hire an indigent and terribly handsome secretary to assist me...and maybe to give me pleasure in my old age.'

'Naughty child,' Lady Sayleford said, batting her on the arm with her fan. 'But if you eschew marriage, what of children?'

'I've watched how Bayam Zehra cossets her children, who are her chief delight. That's the sort of love and attention a child should have, and I don't know that I have it in me to provide it. I'm too restless, too eager to explore new places, discover new treasures.'

'You might find it different if the child were your own. Certainly your mother doted on you.'

'She did,' Charis agreed, her eyes misting. It wasn't only her father who had never quite recovered from her mother's death. Another reason to avoid marriage—and the possibility of losing a child she did come to dote on.

A movement from across the room caught her eye. 'Isn't that Lady Richardson beckoning to you, Grand-Tante? Please, go speak with her. I shall be fine here in my corner.'

'If you are sure? I wouldn't want you to feel neglected.'

'Not a bit of it. I have my task, you know.'

Shaking her head at that, Lady Sayleford walked off to chat with her friend.

Though she'd thought her little corner rather obscure, several gentlemen did seek her out and ask for dances she had no problem refusing. The first suggested she tell him all the secrets of Constantinople while they waltzed. Another annoyed her by pressing his attentions on her while she was trying to observe Lattimar's dance with the promising Lady Amelia. Her patience already sorely tried, it was all she could do to politely refuse the third, who said that a lady who moved as she did must dance divinely.

Fortunately, before anyone else could approach her, Lattimar walked over. 'I've done my duty and come to claim my reward. You must dance with me as you promised.'

'Thank goodness,' she responded, offering him her hand with more enthusiasm than was wise—especially when she realised the dance the musicians were beginning was another waltz.

He frowned as he led her onto the floor. 'I saw Northurst, Kleymer and Innisfield approach you. Were they bothering you?'

'You had time while dancing to notice who approached me?' she asked, surprised.

'I am always aware of where you are and who approaches you.'

His concern sent a wave of warmth through her. 'Protecting me?'

'Of course. Didn't we agree to protect each other?'

'We did. But you needn't be alarmed. They were harmless, if exceedingly annoying. God grant me patience! But enough of that. Tell me if you found any of your partners particularly pleasing.'

'Miss Westmorton danced well enough, but had no conversation at all, answering my questions with monosyllables. Miss Barborough gushed at everything I said. Miss Staplewood stepped on my toes.'

Charis nodded. 'And what of the attractive Lady Amelia?'

'Lady Amelia, who glanced appraisingly at every gentleman we passed and informed me her Mama would only allow her to dance with men who already possess, or will soon inherit, great wealth?'

'Oh, dear. Although I confess I am glad she gave you a distaste of her. I disliked the way she danced, nodding and smiling at other gentlemen, holding herself as proudly as a queen, as if you ought to feel privileged to partner her. Giving no sign at all that she appreciated your attention or was interested in pleasing *you*. If she values herself so high, let the highest bidder have her. As we have already said, beauty alone is not enough to make a wife pleasing over the long term.'

'So have you crossed off your list all the ladies here tonight?'

'Sadly, yes. But do not despair. There will be other entertainments, and surely many more attractive single females in London.'

'I'm dancing with one now. The most attractive of the evening.'

Discussing his prospects had distracted her, but now she could no longer ignore the warmth of his hands on her, the heady scent of shaving soap and virile male. She yearned to lean into him and move to the music with her body pressed against his, inhaling the essence, strength and pure delight of hm.

Once again, waltzing had been a bad idea, even though, anticipating her response, she was more armoured against it now.

Stop fighting and enjoy it, a little voice said. *A handful of dances, a few conversations, is all you will ever have of him. Why deny yourself that pleasure?*

So she would enjoy it. 'If you don't mind, could we stop talking and just dance?'

'As you command.'

As if intuitively aware of her thoughts, he pulled her closer. Charis gave herself to the music flowing over her, the swaying movements of the dance that brushed her body against his at every sweeping turn. The sweet pressure of his hand at her waist, at her shoulder. The delight of gazing up at that strong jaw, those diamond ice-blue eyes. Being so near him, being held by him was a sensual delight, like a honeyed sweetmeat she could eat every day yet never have her fill.

Alas, it was a sensual delight and a treat destined to be enjoyed by some other lady. Even if she should waver about her own requirements, she was certainly not the bride he needed. Not only was she afflicted with a wanderlust, but his marrying an outsider whose gliding walk and exotic upbringing would always arouse speculation would hardly help him refurbish his family's image of propriety. Nor would she ever possess the influence that could bring Lady Vraux back into society.

She would enjoy this treat while it lasted. Until she found him a more suitable wife.

Which she must do soon. Before the idea of giving up the sweet and returning to plain, ordinary fare became even more unappealing.

When the dance finally ended, he once again released her very slowly—although this time, they did not linger on the floor to provide speculation for onlookers.

Perhaps he, too, had become more armoured against enchantment.

'That was the most enjoyable part of the evening,' he said as they reached the side of the ballroom.

'Truly a pleasure,' she admitted. 'But only a diversion. We didn't advance very far towards our goal tonight, though I suppose eliminating the unworthy is progress. I told Lady Sayleford I didn't want to attend anything as large as a ball, so we are to attend Mrs Gardner-Rice's dinner and rout party in three days. If I see you there, we can try again.'

'Yes, to the entertainment. In the meantime, I have

talked with Vraux, who said he was contemplating adding some gems to his collection. Could I call some convenient afternoon and talk with you about them? I'm afraid I don't know much about jewels. Perhaps you could show me some from your father's collection, so I can better understand and advise you about what Vraux is seeking. Of course, he ought to consult you himself, but I could never persuade him to make the call.

'I know,' he continued, holding up a hand to forestall her, 'You would be kind enough to call at Vraux House. But much as it pains me to admit it, Vraux might well consent to receive you and then, when you arrive, deny he ever agreed. Or just take it in his head at that particular moment to refuse to see anyone. It would be safer for me to do the groundwork.'

'Very well, call at King Street if you prefer. I have some errands tomorrow morning, but I'm free any afternoon,' she said, warmed despite herself at the idea of being able to see him again without having to wait three days.

'I have a consultation with the solicitors tomorrow. Would the day after be convenient?'

'That would be fine.'

'I'll escort you to Lady Sayleford, then.' But before offering his arm, he took her hand—and kissed it, sending such a shiver of delight up her arm she scarcely heard him as he continued, 'Thank you for this evening—and your efforts on my behalf. I appreciate them, even if it appears I sometimes treat them with too much levity.'

'You are welcome,' she replied, placing her still-tingling hand on his arm. 'It would make me very happy when I leave England to know you were settled with a properly lovely, skilful and appreciative wife.'

His brow creased in a sort of frown before he smiled, the expression coming and going so swiftly she wasn't sure what had caused it. Before she could decide whether or not she dared ask him, he'd halted with her beside Lady Sayleford.

'Thank you for lending me your niece this evening,' he said, bowing to her great-aunt. 'Lady Sayleford, Miss Dunnfield, I hope to see you both again soon.'

As she watched him walk away, Charis wondered if she'd spoken the truth. Would it make her happy to see him settled with a wife? Or sad and regretful that she could not occupy that place?

Regret, when she recalled the pleasure his mouth could offer. But she knew herself well enough to know she would never be happy permanently marooned in England and, after pleasure faded, she would end up making him unhappy, too. He deserved better than that.

She just needed to keep her mind focused on her nobler purpose. And pray that Father improved soon, before maintaining that focus grew too difficult.

Chapter Nine

In the afternoon two days later, Gregory presented himself at King Street. As he knocked on the door, he told himself not to think about the kiss that had ended their last meeting here…even as a simmering excitement deep in his gut urged him to repeat it. But that wouldn't be fair to her, or safe…since he wasn't sure, if he let himself embrace her again, that he'd be able to stop at just a kiss.

Instead, he'd take advantage of the need to discuss his father's potential commission, admire her expertise and simply enjoy spending time in her unusual and energising presence.

The butler answered his knock, giving him a look so forbidding, Greg wondered uneasily if he'd witnessed that forbidden kiss. He had probably seen his mistress quit her guest's presence at a run, and was accurately blaming the person responsible for her speedy retreat.

Nonetheless, Jameson bowed and stood aside to let Greg enter. 'Miss Charis will receive you in the salon,' he said, his tone heavy with disapproval as he motioned Greg to follow him.

But despite the butler's reluctance, when Greg walked

into the room, the leap of his heart made him forget everything but the delight of seeing her again. As always when he first saw her, those luminous dark eyes held him captive, mesmerising in the pale glow of her face. Only later did he realise she'd worn another new gown which, like the one at the musicale, paid homage to current fashion without exactly following it.

Also as before, it took a moment before his dazzled brain could get his tongue working. In the meantime, smiling, she waved him in and instructed the butler to bring tea. 'Please, have a seat. I'm so excited to hear what your father is seeking. Talking about it will make heading out on our next journey seem more imminent.'

The smile he returned was a bit more restrained. She was anxious to leave London; he didn't want to think about the prospect.

'Is your father better, then?'

She frowned. 'I'd like to tell myself he is, but in truth, he is probably much the same. But,' she added, visibly trying to cheer herself, 'Only now am I able to get a sufficient of quantity of vegetables and spices necessary to create his favourite dishes.' She laughed. 'And having a time of persuading Cook to prepare such un-English dishes. I'm sure that once he is well-fed, with all the rest I've insisted on, he'll soon begin returning to his usual self.'

'If there is anything I can obtain to help speed his recovery, I'd be happy to assist.' Not that he'd be happy to speed her departure, but he would like to remove that worried frown from her brow.

'Your family's estate is in Northumberland, you said. I understand some of best lamb comes from there. I'm not sure that what is available in London markets is quite up to our usual standards.'

'I'll write to Entremer and have some sent down. Though we mostly raise the animals for their wool, we do pride ourselves on the quality of our meat.'

'Thank you! I would appreciate that.'

Pleased to have been able to offer something that brightened the eyes concern had dimmed, he watched as she took a case from her desk and placed it on a side table she'd arranged in front of the sofa. 'I've assembled an assortment of Father's favourite gems. We can look at them while we have tea.'

A knock at the door announced the butler's arrival with the tea tray, which he placed on the piecrust table between the sofa and chair.

'Thank you, Jameson, that will be all for now.'

'I could send Jane up to serve while you discuss the gem stones with Mr Lattimar.'

Miss Dunnfield shook her head. 'You know Mrs Davenport can't spare her from her work. If I'd known we would be remaining in London this long, I would have had you engage extra staff. Mr Lattimar can look over the gems while I pour.'

The butler bowed, but the look he sent Greg was still suspicious. 'If you say so, miss. I'll be working in the hallway. If you need anything, just call out rather than ring.'

'I'll come fetch you when Mr Lattimar is ready to leave.'

Giving Greg one more darkling look, the butler walked out.

'If it were up to Jameson, he probably would have told me you weren't at home,' Greg said ruefully. 'He's not forgiven me for sending you fleeing the last time I called.'

Her eyes widened. 'I hadn't thought of that, but you are right. He probably did hear me running up the stairs while he was escorting you out. I wondered why he wanted to foist Jane on me,' she said as she poured them each a cup.

'Aside from the fact that he is so very English. He doesn't approve of me, an unmarried lady, receiving or calling on clients without a maid tagging along, though I'd already started doing so even before Father's illness. Sometimes Father has happened to be out when clients called, understandably anxious to take possession of their purchases or to have some detail about one explained. Since we didn't want to make them wait until Father returned, I would see them.'

'Would an unmarried woman have so much freedom in Constantinople?' Greg asked after taking a sip. 'I thought ladies there were much more restricted, single or married.'

'They are and they aren't. It's true that European ladies move about more widely, able to travel into the city or around the countryside, much as they do in their home countries, although those of greater importance are always accompanied by a large entourage. Ottoman ladies live in the harem apart from men, but by donning the proper garb that renders them anonymous, they are free to go wherever they like in the city. Most often, they will go to the hammam or to visit the harem of friends. Sometimes such guests remain for days. If a husband sees the slippers of a visiting lady outside the door of the harem quarters, he will not venture within to seek his wife. Nor does he have the right to make the visitor leave until she and her hostess are ready.'

'Truly?' he asked, considerably surprised. 'I thought men had complete control over their female relations.'

'As I'm sure is true in England, not all men treat the women of their family with respect and allow them the rights accorded them by custom.'

Thinking of his reclusive father's refusal to grant his mother a divorce to marry the man she loved, Greg had to agree. 'You would be correct. But a woman could not, as you are doing, openly receive a gentleman or call on one?'

'Not openly, no. But there are lots of scandalous tales of ladies going out heavily veiled to visit the hammam or the harem of friend, only to slip out a back entrance and go secretly to meet a lover. The lady is taking a great risk, of course, but if the friend or her servants remain silent, it would be almost impossible for her to be discovered. A man is not allowed to approach or speak with a woman on the street, even his own wife. Wearing a *feradge*, an enveloping cloak that covers all her clothing, and a *yasmak*, a fine muslin veiling all of her face except for her eyes, a woman walking about is almost impossible to identify.'

While she paused to drink her tea, Greg said, 'Did you dress like that when you went out?'

'Since I straddled both worlds, if wanted to visit Bayam Zehra or shop at the markets without fuss, I would go out in Ottoman attire, so I might walk around without the tiresome escort most Europeans took with them—a show designed to demonstrate their wealth and status. If I wanted to meet clients, I would receive them at our home wearing European attire—something that would be impossible for an Ottoman lady. Outside the cities, women in the desert regions are much more casual about veiling, which can interfere with their daily chores of drawing water and caring for animals, while Berber women don't veil at all.'

'What a fascinating life you've led! No wonder you find rounds of parties dull and gossip boring.'

'We all have worlds to which we belong,' she said, raising her gaze to meet his. Was she subtly underscoring the fact that they occupied very different ones?

Before he could decide whether that was in fact her meaning, she looked away and set down her cup. 'Now, for a treat much more enthralling than tea. Let me show you these.'

Opening the box on the table before him, she said, 'The most valuable diamonds and rubies come from India. Those gems, along with ropes of pearls, are the jewels most highly sought-after by ladies of the Ottoman world. This—' she tapped the piece with a fingertip '—is a broach of rubies and pearls Father obtained on our last trip. Note the luminosity the finest pearls possess! Note the brilliance of the ruby, the beautiful workmanship of the gold setting.' Moving on from the broach, she said, 'This small rope of pearls with a diamond clasp was a favourite piece from a previous trip.'

'They are both exquisite,' Greg said admiringly. 'Are those the sort of gems your Bayam Zehra thinks a husband should spoil you with?'

She laughed. 'Exactly. They are rather irresistible, aren't they? Costly as they were, I wouldn't have tried to dissuade Father from purchasing them even if I could. Bayam Zehra says a wise woman never hesitates to add such valuables to her collection, an Ottoman woman's jewellery being both her dowry before marriage and protection against want afterwards.'

'Circumstances would have to be dire to force a woman to part with something as beautiful as these,' Greg said, wishing he could put the rope of pearls around her neck and admire the sheen of the gem against the softness of her skin. He wasn't sure which would be more luminous.

'Circumstances are almost always dire when they do,' Miss Dunnfield agreed. 'It was one such sad case that prompted Father to add gemstones to his business…and my mother's close friendship with Bayam Zehra that ended up with me becoming his assistant.'

'Indeed? How did that happen?'

'You truly wish to know? You've listened very kindly to my stories, but I don't want to bore you with more tales of the East.'

'They're not at all boring. Fascinating, rather,' he said, meaning every word.

'Well, if you really want to hear the story…'

'I do. Won't you tell me?'

'Very well. First, let me refill your cup.'

'Please,' he said, offering it to her. *Refill it as often as you like*, he thought. Now that he knew she'd been made to practise the graceful, balletic movement of hands and fingers as she poured, he loved watching her, the gestures as fascinating as her stories.

After pouring more tea for them both, she began, 'Bayam Zehra's husband is a Pasha who holds a position of high authority in government, which means she knows all the important women in the city. She's also a very wealthy woman in her own right. As such, she is sometimes discreetly contacted by ladies who have been widowed, or whose husbands have suffered a reversal of fortune and are in need of additional funds.

'Once when my mother was visiting, she found her friend in a fury. The Bayam told her she'd just learned that a highly respected older lady whose husband and son had died was being forced to sell some of her gems, but the dealer had offered her only a fraction of what they were worth. Mama agreed it was reprehensible for such a woman to be taken advantage of. She related the story to Father and asked him if he could find a buyer for the gems who would offer a fair price. He'd already begun trading in other antiquities and as it happened, had recently been contacted by a client interested in acquiring gems. The Bayam called on the lady, who agreed to let Mama show the gems to Father, who then promised the lady a much higher price for them.

'It wasn't long before the ladies of the city learned that if any of them needed to sell jewellery, Bayam Zehra knew a dealer who could offer them the best price. At first, she would have Mama accompany her to the harem of the lady with jewels to sell, but after a time, she sent Mama to the harem to speak with the seller directly, Mama being fluent in all the languages spoken in Constantinople.'

'The go-between for the go-between. How did you become involved?'

'I'm getting to that. Mama often took me with her on those visits, as the ladies of the harem love children, and I am as fluent in their language as Mama was. I was only thirteen when Mama died, but by then I was as known and trusted within the city as she and Bayam Zehra. Since Father could never have called on ladies, after Mama's death, I became the link between Bayam Zehra, the seller and my father.

'I still am. Although I've become something of an expert in daggers and architectural artefacts after working with Father, he can deal with men directly to obtain those. But he cannot approach ladies with jewels to sell. So you can see—' she held up pearls reverently, their subtle gleam as lovely as the brighter shine of the silver teapot '—why I remain indispensable to Father's business.'

'So you are able to help these ladies make the best of a sad necessity. I can see you thrive on it.'

'Not on the circumstances that sometimes force some dear creature to part with her treasures. But undertaking the role has allowed me to meet many women, from the widows of pashas who staff the emperor's administrative departments, to wives of dealers and tradesmen, to the daughters of sheikhs. As etiquette dictates, all offer hospitality to a visitor and with a little prompting, all are willing to talk about their lives and their families. Their love for their children, their mourning for their lost loves. If I were a poet, what tales I could pen!'

'You are certainly an eloquent story teller.'

'It's the stories that are marvellous, not my telling of them,' she said, waving a dismissive hand. 'Although Bayam Zehra would be pleased to have you compliment my skill.'

Story telling—a skill to captivate her eventual husband with and make him devoted to her for life, he recalled her saying. How could any man possess her loveliness and not become besotted?

His gaze lingered on those plump, soft lips. The desire he was holding in check intensified, the urge to kiss her again nearly overwhelming. *She'd run away from him after that last kiss not in horror, but in prudence.* Gazing into her eyes, he saw an answering desire that said she wanted another kiss as much as he did.

She lifted her head, her eyes never leaving his. He found himself leaning downwards, eager for another taste of her...

A loud scraping of feet in the hallway had him jerking back upright.

After a short knock, Jameson walked in, giving Gregory another suspicious look. 'I thought I'd see if you were finished with tea, Miss Charis. I know you like to have space to spread items out on the table when you're showing them to *collectors*,' he added, emphasising the term, as if to reinforce that he'd allowed Greg to enter the house only because he was a client whose purchases would add to the Dunnfield family coffers.

'Yes, thank you, Jameson, you may take the tray,' she replied, only the heightened colour in her cheeks betraying how close they'd come to committing another indiscretion.

He should be thankful to have been prevented. Instead, he wished the butler could have delayed his appearance for another five or ten minutes. Or an hour...

After Jameson exited with the tea try, she continued, 'Let me show you several other pieces.'

Removing the top tray from the box, she took out several more items from the lower layer, handling them with reverence, her hands and fingers moving with the same grace she used to serve tea. A necklace of rubies caught the light, flashing red hues as vivid as the fire in the hearth. Another gleamed with a glitter of diamonds. Several others were made up of assorted sizes of pearls.

After laying them on the table in front of him, she said, 'Go ahead, pick them up and examine them if you like.'

Gingerly, he lifted one after another. He slipped pearls with the touch of cool silk through his fingers, held bracelets and necklaces of brilliant gem stones up to the light and marvelled at the deep blue of lapis and the rich green of malachite showcased in intricately wrought settings of gold.

'They are wonderful, masterful,' he said, carefully placing the last piece back on the tray. 'How difficult it must be for the owners to part with them.'

'You mustn't imagine all of them came from broken-hearted widows. Father deals with jewel traders as well. Who, as the experience with Bayam Zehra showed, usually buy at bargain prices and then sell again much higher. Depending on the jewel and how good a deal Father can strike, he will purchase objects from traders as well.'

Walking back to her desk, she pulled a sheet of paper from the drawer and brought it back to him. 'I've made sketches illustrating the loveliest necklaces, broaches, rings and bracelets in Father's collection. The drawings will show the typical patterns and designs, but you will have to describe the richness of the colours to Lord Vraux.

'Ladies from the highest born to the most lowly wear as many jewels as they can afford, with rings on every finger, six or seven bracelets on each wrist, so one finds a larger variety of those smaller items for sale. Since a lady possesses more of them, if she must part with some jewellery, she prefers to sell a ring or a bracelet and hold on to her more valuable gems.'

'So I should tell Vraux you are more likely to be able to obtain a variety of rings and bracelets than an assortment of necklaces.'

'Yes. Nonetheless, we almost always find a few exquisite larger pieces. Show the sketches to your father and determine which designs he finds most interesting. Let us know what he prefers and approximately how much he wants to invest in purchasing them, and when we journey back to Constantinople, we will contact our sources in Baghdad and search for them.'

Greg took the sketch, letting his fingers touch hers, and felt a spark leap from her hand to his.

Her eyes widened, telling him she felt it too. Gazing once again at those compelling eyes, those beckoning lips, he felt his control slipping.

He'd better leave before temptation overwhelmed him—and he did something that would make the butler refuse to admit him the next time he stood on her doorstep.

'I could gaze on such beauty for ever,' he said, hoping she understood he was not referring just to the jewels. 'But I imagine you need to lock those away. I'll take the sketches and describe your father's treasures to Vraux. Perhaps I'll have a list for you by the time we meet at the next entertainment—which is to be what?'

'Mrs Gardner-Rice's dinner and dance will be next. Lady Sayleford promised to lend her influence to several friends who have granddaughters to present. She agreed to attend if she could bring me with her, after promising those friends I was not in the market for a husband, so would not be in competition with their granddaughters for the attention of the bachelors invited to the event.'

Greg chuckled. 'Obviously the friends haven't met

you, or they would probably have refused that condition. You garner attention from bachelors whether you are in the market for a husband or not.' Recalling the fascination she elicited, he felt a flash of jealousy, which made him doubly glad she truly was not trolling for a mate.

Charis shrugged. 'Having already deflected enough impudent comments, I certainly hope not to receive any notice. But since these debs *are* looking to capture the eye of some eligible gentlemen, they will be delighted to have *you* attend.'

Greg sighed. 'Yes, I suppose so.'

She chuckled. 'They probably imagine you come supplied with diamond necklaces and pearl bracelets to deck out your bride.'

He would love to adorn *her* with them, he thought. Love to see her in the Ottoman dress she'd once described, her hair in braided tresses down her back, her feet bare, her arms and hands adorned with rings whose sparkling gems would make her graceful movements even more arresting.

'You needn't worry about wasting your time on someone ineligible. Lady Sayleford will have me well-informed about the background of every young lady at the event, so I will tell you which ones to approach. I'll watch them closely all evening. Hopefully this time, we will find one or two who possess the beauty, wit and graceful manners to make them worthy of further pursuit.'

None will hold a candle to you, he thought. But that was like the proverbial comparing of apples and oranges. Or rather, fine English apples compared with apricots grown by trickling fountains under a hot Ottoman sun.

Both might possess grace, beauty and allure. But they were incomparably different.

He already suspected he wasn't going to be able to concentrate on finding the English apple he needed until the sweet, alluring apricot was no longer within reach.

Although he knew it was time to leave, he still felt a flash of disappointment when she stood, signalling an end to their meeting. 'Shall I see you at Mrs Gardner-Rice's house in two days, then?'

'I wouldn't miss it.'

She walked him to the door, calling out, 'Jameson, Mr Lattimar is leaving, if you would fetch his hat and cane.'

'At once, Miss Charis,' came the answer from somewhere in the hallway.

Greg grinned. 'He can't wait to see the back of me.'

'He's just being protective. Especially as Father is unable to join me to receive clients, as he normally would.'

A pang went through him at that assessment, though it shouldn't have. Still, he couldn't prevent himself from asking, 'Is that all I am...a client?'

'A client, but also, I hope, a friend.' After a brief hesitation, she offered him her hand.

He might want more, but he would settle for friend. Wishing it were her lips, he quickly dropped a kiss on her knuckles—before the butler arrived and observed a gesture that would probably deepen his disapproval.

'Thank you for sharing your treasures. I understand better now why Vraux is so keen on acquiring some.'

'Their intrinsic worth,' she said softly, gazing at his face—making him imagine she wasn't only referring to the gems.

'Their intrinsic worth,' he agreed, gazing back, knowing he, at least, meant much more.

The butler arrived to present him with his hat and cane, Miss Dunnfield gave him smile and a nod, and there was nothing to do but follow Jameson out.

And prepare to wait two more days until he could see her again.

Chapter Ten

Two nights later, Greg presented himself at the town-house of Mrs Gardner-Rice in Upper Brook Street. A note from Miss Dunnfield, whose great-aunt had obtained details about the event, informed him there would be thirty sitting down to dinner, the meal to be followed by a dance to which another fifty had been invited. Six of the guests were young ladies in their first season, with approximately twelve of the guests eligible bachelors, like him. The rest of the party would be made up of the parents of young ladies and friends of the hostess.

All of the debutantes, Miss Dunnfield wrote, met her basic criteria of being well-born and connected to families of sufficient influence to make whichever one pleased him, if any of them did, well-positioned to be an effective advocate for his mother's cause.

He'd shaken his head as he read the note. As amused as he was by her efforts, he couldn't help but be appreciative of the trouble she was taking and how seriously she regarded her mission. He ought to reward those efforts by trying to resist his fascination with Charis Dunnfield and concentrate on giving the girls with whom he chatted or danced real consideration as potential wives.

Aside from Lady Marry-the-Wealthiest-Candidate Amelia, it hadn't required much effort on his part thus far to charm his partners. The allure of wedding a wealthy would-be baron had been all the cachet he needed, each girl with whom he'd danced or chatted thus far quite obviously eager to engage his interest. He had to take care to walk the fine line between being polite and responding with enough enthusiasm to make the ladies believe he intended to pursue them.

None so far had inspired him with that desire. But marry he must, so he ought to be more grateful that Miss Dunnfield was beating the bushes to flush out as many potential candidates as possible.

Despite that resolve, as he handed his hat and cane to the footman and proceeded up the stairs to the dining room, he hoped his hostess had seated him close enough to Miss Dunnfield at the dinner table that he'd be able to converse with her.

Unfortunately, that hope was not realised. His hostess had interspersed the single gentlemen between the debutantes at her end of the table, awarding to Lady Sayleford, as co-hostess, the seat of honour at the opposite end of the table. She'd placed Miss Dunnfield beside her great-aunt, safely distanced from the bachelors and surrounded by older guests. Apparently, despite her great-aunt's assurance that her relation was not entering the Marriage Mart, the hostess was taking no chances on the possibility that the society doyenne's unusual charge might distract attention from the proper English young ladies for whom she and her friends were seeking husbands.

The arrangement was effective, the other single gentlemen being polite enough not to offend their hostess by neglecting the fair ladies beside whom they were seated. But Greg noticed that from time to time every one of them let his attention stray to the opposite end of the table, where Miss Dunnfield carried on an animated conversation with her great-aunt and the two gentlemen on either side of that lady.

Trying not to feel jealous of those lucky two, he struggled through the meal trying to converse with his dinner partner, who, though quite lovely to gaze upon, was either too nervous or too slow-witted to add more than an occasional 'Yes, indeed,' or 'Oh, quite,' to his monologue.

When at last the interminable dinner concluded, he rose with the gentlemen while the ladies exited. He was looking forward to a brandy to reward him for that long exercise in patience Giving her the benefit of the doubt, poor Lady Katherine might well have been intimidated at dining under the eyes of two such important society hostesses and nervous about trying to impress the single gentleman. But he wouldn't need Miss Dunnfield's evaluation to eliminate her from the list of potential brides. If Lady Katherine's lack of conversation was habitual, he didn't want to spend the rest of his life seated across the breakfast table from someone incapable of producing at least a modicum of amusing or intelligent chat.

Much as he enjoyed the brandy—and the absence of his monosyllabic dinner partner—he was impatient for the dancing to begin. He intended to claim at least one waltz and a good deal more conversation with Miss Dunnfield. She'd want to present him with her evaluation of the debs here tonight, a process he intended to drag out as long as possible and then try to extend further by persuading her to talk of something else.

Preoccupied by his own thoughts, he was paying little attention to the chatter around him—until Miss Dunnfield's name on another man's lips recalled his wandering mind.

'What did you think of her?' he heard Lord Trevethen ask Thomas Lynch.

'There's certainly something exotic about the way she looks. Her gowns are stylish—yet *different* too. And the way she moves...' Lynch whistled. 'I'm going to snag a dance. A waltz if I can get one.'

'Did she really live in the East?' Trevethen asked.

'I have it on good authority that she lived in a *harem*.'

A pause in conversation along the table left the word reverberating in the sudden quiet. A bevy of masculine heads, of older men as well as the younger ones, looked towards Lynch.

Noting the extra attention, he waggled his eyebrows. 'I wonder what she learned there.'

Several men sniggered. His anger rising, Greg said, 'You do know she is the great-niece of Lady Sayleford?'

Lynch shook his head. 'More's the pity. One can get away with flirting under Lady Sayleford's nose, but attempting to arrange a rendezvous to discover the full range of La Dunnfield's talents will be more difficult. Especially if she's residing with the old dragon.'

'You think you could discover the full range of her talents?' Trevethen asked.

'Possibly. Despite the Grand Dame's sponsorship, her birth is questionable. Her father's some sort of trader. If she weren't a distant relation of the countess, I doubt she'd even be received. I asked Lady Gardner-Rice outright—discreetly, of course—and Lady G was emphatic in assuring me the girl's not looking for a husband. Wise of the chit. With her chequered background, she'd find it difficult to bring a well-born gentleman up to snuff. So what else could she be looking about society for?'

'Looking like she does,' Trevethen said, 'I think you know.'

'And I could be just the man to fulfil her *needs*. Discreetly, of course,' Lynch said, making the other gentlemen laugh.

Greg had to bite his tongue to refrain from delivering a stinging rebuke. But intervening here and now would not be effective. The men would just assume, as had Stansberry the other night, that he had amorous designs on her himself and was trying to discourage potential competition. Which would in turn only further pique the men's prurient interest.

He felt a sudden, unexpected surge of sympathy for his mother. Any woman who didn't adhere to society's strict standards about proper appearance and behaviour was presumed to be of questionable character, and thus fair game, unworthy of claiming the protection a gentleman owed to a lady.

Scowling, Greg vowed that when not actually dancing with each of the young ladies to whom, unfortunately, he was already promised, he would hover near Miss Dunnfield. Just in case she experienced any difficulties discouraging the attentions of these so-called gentlemen, none of whom, he was certain, had gentlemanly intentions.

How he wished he could punch the lascivious grins off the faces of Lynch and Trevethen.

At last, the ritual of brandy and cigars over, the gentlemen rose to re-join the ladies, who after retiring to refresh themselves would be heading to the ballroom. Greg could already hear the sounds of the small orchestra beginning to tune up. He would try to catch her and warn her to avoid the two before the first sets were made up.

He strode past the other men into the ballroom, spotting Miss Dunnfield with Lady Sayleford in a small knot of guests who'd arrived for the dancing, and headed straight for her. She nodded as he halted beside her but, being in conversation with an older gentleman who hadn't been present at dinner, didn't greet him.

When the man paused for breath, she turned to him and curtseyed. 'Lord Rollesbury, are you acquainted with Mr Lattimar?'

'I've not had that pleasure. I'm seldom in England, you know.'

'Then may I present Mr Lattimar, eldest son of Lord Vraux. Mr Lattimar, Lord Rollesbury, of the diplomatic service.'

After what he'd just overheard at table, Greg shouldn't resent her bright tone or obvious pleasure in finding someone to talk to with whom she had something in common. Nonetheless, he felt an instinctive antagonism. Rollesbury was older—Greg judged him to be in perhaps in his early forties—and though his manner towards Miss Dunnfield was perfectly respectful, Greg sensed an undercurrent of more personal interest.

'You are Felicity Portman's son?' Lord Rollesbury was saying to him. 'I remember her from when I first came up to London after university. You and your siblings must have been almost grown by then, but she was still the most stunning woman in the room. I had the pleasure of dancing with her at several parties. I hope Lady Vraux is well, Mr Lattimar.'

Greg might be wary of the man's interest in Miss Dunnfield, but he couldn't help but appreciate the courtesy and genuine admiration with which Rollesbury spoke about his mother. 'She's very well, thank you. And still as beautiful.'

'I am sorry to miss the delight of seeing her here tonight.'

Rollesbury truly must not be often in London, Greg thought, for he made that remark without a particle of irony. Apparently he didn't know Lady Vraux was seldom invited to society parties, and never to events at which unmarried young ladies were being feted.

'You are in the diplomatic service, Miss Dunnfield said?'

'Yes, I've spent my career posted in various nations throughout Europe. I haven't had the opportunity of serving in lands farther east, about which Miss Dunnfield has been telling me such fascinating tales,' Rollesbury said, smiling at her.

He *was* interested in her, Greg thought, eyeing the man narrowly.

'It's good to see you out in society again,' Lady Sayleford said. 'I know the loss of your dear wife was a terrible blow.'

An expression of sorrow passed briefly over Rollesbury's face before he summoned a determined smile. 'It was. I very much appreciated the kind note you sent me at the time.'

'She was a charming lady and is sadly missed. The dancing is about to begin. Mr Lattimar, I believe you are engaged? You must go and claim your partner.'

Damn and drat. He'd not have a chance to exchange a private word with Miss Dunnfield after all. 'Yes, I must,' he replied, biting his tongue to avoid adding *Unfortunately.*

'Perhaps we can talk again later, Lord Rollesbury. I'm sure my mother would be pleased to hear your latest news.'

Rollesbury nodded. 'I'd be happy to send my respects to her.' Turning to Miss Dunnfield, he asked, 'Do you dance, Miss Dunnfield?'

'Actually, I prefer not to.'

'You'd rather repair to the card room?'

'Not really. I enjoy watching the dancers. They are so graceful, are they not?'

'Would you mind if I stay with you?'

'If you like. Although with so many lovely ladies here, if you enjoy dancing, please do claim a partner. Lady Sayleford will keep me entertained.'

'As you entertain me, my dear,' Lady Sayleford said in a dry tone, the significance of which, though lost on Lord Rollesbury, was perfectly comprehensible to him.

There was no help for it, Greg had to bow and walk away, reluctant as he was to leave her with the baron. Despite Miss Dunnfield having indicated on several occasions that she had no desire to marry, learning that Lord Rollesbury was not only a diplomat, with whom she was bound to have much in common, but also a widower, made him uneasy.

Still, since he couldn't remain to guard her, he ought to be grateful for the diplomat's presence. Unlike the men about whom he'd been unable to warn her, Rollesbury had accorded her the same courtesy he'd showed her great-aunt. Greg suspected he wouldn't tolerate her being shown any disrespect, and would make short work of dismissing Lynch, Trevethen or any other gentleman who didn't treat her as the lady she was.

But if someone could tempt Miss Dunnfield into contemplating marriage, it would probably be someone like Rollesbury. A diplomat, older, respected and respectful, who'd had a broader experience of life and could offer the enticing prospect of carrying her off to explore new lands.

But now he was being ridiculous. She loved her father and was essential to his trading enterprise. She wouldn't just traipse off into the sunset with some diplomat and leave her father in the lurch, without the go-between he needed to conduct business with the ladies of the Ottoman Empire and further east.

Besides, it was none of his concern if she did take it into her head to marry. He had no claim on her, nor any right to speak for or against marital candidates. Even though she was exercising that right for him, he thought, amusement at her serious pursuit of that mission chasing away his unease for a moment.

Reaching the young lady to whom he had promised this dance, he bowed to her curtsey, thanked her mother for allowing him the privilege of dancing with her and walked her onto the floor. To honour his bargain with Miss Dunnfield—and reassured that she had someone to look out for her—he did his level best to keep his attention focused on his partner, who mercifully was a much better conversationalist than his dinner partner.

Still, he couldn't deny his relief when the dance ended. Miss Ludlowe was pretty, pleasant and a spirited conversationalist. Though her face was winsome and her figure admirable, he felt not a spark of sensual interest.

Thank heaven Miss Dunnfield had agreed that no matter how talented a lady was otherwise, she must first and foremost please him.

Miss Ludlowe hadn't inspired him with the distaste for the unlamented Lady Amelia, but he felt no desire whatsoever to prolong his time in her company.

He escorted her back to her chaperone, and with a sigh, walked off to find the lady from whom he had claimed the next dance.

At length he finished his final obligation—thank heavens he hadn't promised Miss Dunnfield to dance *every* dance with someone else—and made his way back to her side. Where he found the diplomat still lingering.

'We've been comparing festival processions we've observed in different countries,' Miss Dunnfield said when he joined them. 'Lord Rollesbury was describing some of the events that take place at the Palio in Siena. Bareback riders in mediaeval dress—what a thrilling spectacle it must be!'

'Often dangerous, too. But you mentioned you had observed a unique event in Constantinople?'

'Yes, a procession in honour of the sultan that featured individuals from all walks of life, from officials reciting verses from the Koran to bakers' apprentices throwing fresh-baked loaves to the crowd. The spectacle lasted for hours! Of course, we ladies were quite comfortable, as we observed it all seated on cushions in one of the latticed window alcoves, with servant girls bringing us sherbets and sweetmeats.'

'Your description of refreshments makes my mouth water,' Greg said, having waited impatiently to get a word in. 'You declined a dance, but you did promise you would let me take you in for a beverage. Shall we go now?'

'I've made myself thirsty too,' she admitted, her eyes dancing with amusement at his abrupt intervention. 'Yes, I would like a glass of wine. If you will excuse me, Lord Rollesbury?'

'That was a fine bit of kidnapping,' she murmured as they walked off.

'I thought you might want rescuing. Rollesbury seemed to have monopolised you the entire evening.'

'It's been interesting to compare notes. He served in Italy, Russia and France and knows most of the ambassadors from those countries who were assigned to the Sublime Porte, the government of the Ottoman Empire. It was pleasant to talk of mutual acquaintances, discover where they are now posted and what they are doing. But I'm sure refreshment was not the main reason you carried me off. Despite talking with Rollesbury, I was still able to watch all your partners closely, as well as observing them at dinner. Are you ready for my evaluation?'

Ever serious about her task, he thought with a smile, for the first time this evening beginning to enjoy the event. 'I've formed some opinions, but I'm always interested in hearing yours.'

'Lady Katherine Seaton seemed hardly able to add a word to conversation during dinner. Though she danced well enough, her lack of confidence in that regard is enough to eliminate her. Are you agreeable to crossing her off the list?'

'Absolutely. I've never had to talk so much through a meal in my life. My throat will be sore for days.'

Though she shook her head reprovingly, she couldn't suppress a smile. 'Very well, moving on. Miss Upgate was the prettiest of the lot and danced very gracefully. But one could not avoid hearing her conversation at dinner. She has an unfortunate, penetrating voice with a sharp edge to it, like the screech of sharpening a sword on a whetstone. How unpleasant it would be to spend a lifetime listening to that! Shall we eliminate her?'

At his nod, she continued, 'Miss Honington was also quite pretty. But her movements are less than graceful and she smiles so continuously, one begins to wonder if she is vacuous rather than amused. I'd not have you matched with a woman whom your guests might take to be a lackwit.'

'She didn't impress me either.'

'And the last, Miss Ludlowe. You seemed to enjoy your dance with her.'

'She was the most spirited of the lot. A good conversationalist, with a lively wit.'

Miss Dunnfield frowned. 'Her wit might be lively, but did you not notice her laugh? And she laughed often, a sort of *ha-ha-ha-ha* with the rising pitch of a monkey's squeal. Not at all the gentle, pleasing sound one would want in a wife.'

Retrieving from memory the sound of the girl's laughter, Greg had to laugh himself. 'I didn't particularly notice it at the time, not being seated that close to her at dinner, but now that I think about it, her laugh was rather…unusual.'

'I can't imagine how you could have avoided noticing! Anyway, it's been overall a most disappointing evening. But Lady Sayleford assures me we've thus far met only a fraction of the debs being presented this year, so we need not despair yet.'

She looked up suddenly and, following the direction

of her gaze, he saw Lynch and Trevethen approaching. At the heightened sensual interest in their eyes, Greg immediately stiffened.

'Lattimar, Miss Dunnfield,' Lynch said, stopping to bow beside her. 'Such tales I've been hearing of your life! I understand you've lived mostly in Constantinople. Where females are trained in…many pleasing arts.'

A flare of anger flashed in her eyes, but before Greg could intervene, she put a hand on his wrist and gave him a tiny shake of her head, warning him to silence.

'Indeed, gentlemen,' she murmured in a voice he'd never heard her use before. Smoky, intimate, overlaid with sensual tones that sent a rush of sensation shivering across his skin.

By their widened eyes and sudden intake of breath, he knew the two men felt the force of it, too.

What in the world was she doing, *encouraging* their insulting presumptions? he wondered indignantly.

Not only had her tone changed, she angled her head coyly, giving the men a glance, accompanied by much batting of her eyelashes, that Greg could only describe as provocative.

'You've doubtless heard a great deal about the *particular* talents of Ottoman ladies,' she breathed, in that come-take-me voice.

The two men nodded, their gazes fixed on her with the fascination of cobras bewitched by a snake charmer.

Leaning closer, she murmured, 'Would you like to know the secret of their most important skill, the one most essential to…*pleasing* their masters?'

'W-with breathless anticipation,' Lynch stuttered, while Trevethen looked incapable of speech.

She made one of those graceful circular gestures with

her hand, as if about to present them with something. *'Coffee,'* she whispered. 'Most important of all skills is to properly make the master's coffee. It's quite an art to prepare Turkish coffee with just the right consistency and foam.'

'That's it?' Lynch said. *'Coffee?'*

'Sadly, I can convey only one secret at a time.' Touching Greg's sleeve, she said in her normal voice, 'Would you escort me back to Lady Sayleford? I think I've had all the *entertainment* I can stand for one evening. I should like to go home.'

'Willingly.'

'Wretch,' he said as he led her out. 'You had them almost panting.' *And me too*, he added silently.

'They were already panting before I said a word,' she said angrily. 'I admit, it wasn't well done of me. I shall confess my bad behaviour to Lady Sayleford before the aggrieved spread their tales. But honestly, I've had *enough* of the innuendo and titillation. I'd rather prick their pretentions with a sharp *kilij* but, however justified an Ottoman lady might find that act, I doubt a constable would agree they deserved stabbing. Though such a dire response might finally dissuade others from approaching me.'

Before he could respond, they reached Lady Sayleford. 'I'm weary, Grand-Tante. Would I be taking you away from friends too early if we leave now?'

'I'm ready whenever you are, child. I hope you are appreciating my great-niece's efforts on your behalf, Mr Lattimar.'

'She is most diligent.'

Lady Sayleford nodded. 'The finding of a wife who best suits you is an important business,' she said, giving him one of those penetrating looks justly famed for making the recipient uncomfortable. 'I was most fortunate in my own choice. I hope yours will be equally wise.'

'It will, if I have anything to do with it,' Miss Dunnfield said.

'Thank you again, Miss Dunnfield. Next time, though, I trust you will save me a dance? Despite what you told Lord Rollesbury, I suspect you do enjoy dancing.'

And I can't get enough of the feel of you in my arms...

'Perhaps. Have you made any progress with Lord Vraux on his list of desirable objects?'

'I have, actually. If you would allow me, I'd like to call at King Street again to discuss it.'

'As you wish. Good evening, Mr Lattimar.'

They'd had so little time together, the importunate Lynch and Trevethen having interrupted when they'd barely begun conversing. But she'd gone from angry to withdrawn, looking not so much physically weary as dispirited and eager to leave the gathering.

Bowing to Lady Sayleford and her, he let her go. And watched as the most enjoyable, briefest part of that long evening walked out of the door, taking with her whatever pleasure could be had in it.

Despite her efforts, he was no closer to finding a lady who would attract him as much as she did. He was becoming increasingly convinced that until her scintillating presence was removed from his life, he wasn't going to.

He recalled what Lady Sayleford had said about choosing a wife, her look more speaking than her words. Had that been meant as much a warning as advice?

How could he make a wise choice, when what his head told him he needed and what everything within him yearned for were in such conflict?

Chapter Eleven

Two afternoons later, Charis stood arranging an assortment of *kilij* and *khanjar* weapons on the table in the salon. Answering a note from Gregory Lattimar, she'd invited him to come and view an assortment of swords and daggers from her father's collection, to see if he could match them to objects Lord Vraux had mentioned he wanted.

She'd asked her father to come down and join the meeting. Not only was his expertise in the matter of weapons greater than hers, she was hoping that consulting with a client would energise him and brighten his mood. She wanted to believe he seemed a little improved, but even after the inclusion of additional meats, spices and vegetables in his diet, he hadn't yet retained his usual vigour.

His skin was still too pale, his strength so limited, she thought, frowning as she recalled his appearance when she'd visited him in his chamber this morning.

However, along with the improvement in his condition she hoped the meeting would produce, her father's presence would guarantee she kept her attraction to Lattimar under control. But for the sudden appearance of Jameson during his last visit, she might have succumbed to kissing him again.

She'd thought that over time, as she grew more accustomed to seeing his handsome face and being near his compelling masculine presence, the intense attraction he aroused in her would fade. That she would continue to appreciate his appearance, as one did any object of beauty, but that the visceral pull that drew her to be with him would lessen and that inconvenient urge to kiss him would dissipate.

That happy prospect had not materialised. If anything, her attraction had deepened and her desire had increased as she'd got to know better the honourable, amusing and intelligent man within the handsome form.

With a smile, she recalled her teasing remark to Grand-Tante about finding a handsome young assistant to pleasure her in old age. If passion were as hard to dismiss or resist as it was turning out to be, perhaps she ought to reconsider her determination not to marry.

Not that she could wed Gregory Lattimar, alas. But if she should encounter an equally compelling man, someone who was interested in learning Father's business and who delighted in travelling as they did…might the promise of pleasure be worth the risk?

But she'd not yet envisioned a way to become a wife and still avoid the possibility of growing too fond of someone whose loss could crush her—or losing her heart to a child of their union whom death could steal from her, as often happened. Probably wiser to redouble her efforts to resist passion instead.

A knock sounded at the door, Jameson stepping in to announce, 'Mr Lattimar is here to see you.'

Warmth filled her…along with keen anticipation and that simmer of attraction deep in her belly. 'Send him in. Did Father say when he would be coming to join us?'

'He said he would be down as soon as he finished dressing. I'll go assist him once I've seen your guest in.'

'Wonderful! I'm so delighted Father decided to make the effort.'

Nodding, Jameson stepped aside, letting Gregory Lattimar enter the room.

She rose to greet him, drinking in his smile of welcome and exulting at the thrilling touch of his lips as he kissed her hand. Which she let him retain a bit too long, staring at him with an intensity that probably made her look as mindless as the vacuous Miss Honington.

No, his effect on her had not diminished one bit.

Belatedly snapping herself free of the spell he cast, she said, 'Thank you for calling today. Please, take a seat.'

'Thank you for letting me call. And for arranging quite a display for me to inspect!' he added, gesturing towards the table. 'I recognise several items that are similar to objects in Vraux's collection.'

'Yes, probably some we obtained for him on previous trips. I shall ring for tea in a bit, but I'm expecting Father to join us shortly. An appreciation for intricately crafted weapons is what first inspired him to begin collecting, and he's far more knowledgeable about them than I am. Although I can give you a general background before he arrives, if you'd like.'

'Please do.'

'These first two are among Father's finest. This one, a *kilij*, is an Ottoman sword. This *khandar* is the Arab version of the same weapon and often, as this one does, features a jewelled hilt. But though grip and hilt are richly decorated, the swords are truly prized for the quality of their blades, made of Damascus steel. Careful!' she warned as Lattimar drew his finger along the sword's edge. 'The barest touch can draw blood.'

'Impressive!'

'The sword masters create a truly beautiful patterning along the blade during the forging process.'

'The blade hardens into those swirling patterns as it cools? Magnificent! They look too fine to be used as weapons.'

'Perhaps, but I have it on good authority that they are viciously efficient in that role.'

The sudden pounding of running footsteps distracted her. A moment later, Jameson burst through the door.

'Miss Charis! You must come at once!'

'What is it? What's happened?'

'When I went in to help your father finish dressing, I found him collapsed on the floor. He cannot seem to get up. I'll need assistance to get him back into bed.'

Shock and fear held her momentarily motionless. Shaking herself free of it, she said, 'I'll come at once.' Turning to Lattimar, she said, 'I'm sorry, but you must excuse me.'

But as she rushed out after the butler, he followed her. 'If Jameson was not able to get your father to his feet, I doubt you are strong enough to be much help. Would you allow me to assist?'

Thoughts raced through her head—the distaste she knew her father would feel at having a stranger witness his helplessness warring with the need to get him off the floor as quickly as possible with the least amount of pulling and tugging on his already weakened body. 'Yes, I'd appreciate your help,' she said, deciding on the moment.

Privacy would have to wait. Her first imperative was to determine whether Father had suffered any injury and then get him back to bed.

Anxiety roiled in her stomach while they hurried up the stairs to his chamber, where the door stood open. She ran in, her heart giving another painful jolt as she saw him on his side pawing ineffectually at the rug as he attempted to turn onto his knees.

'S-sorry to alarm you, my dear,' her father said, panting with effort. 'One moment, I was knotting my cravat… The next, I was on the floor… These old arms…seem damnably useless in getting me back up.'

'You mustn't worry. With Mr Lattimar to assist him, Jameson will be able to help you up and back to bed.'

It was a testament to her father's weakness that he didn't even protest, just nodded tiredly.

'Did you injure yourself? Does anything hurt?' she asked anxiously.

'Only my pride,' he said with a trace of his usual spark.

'Let me run my hands over your arms and legs. Tell me if you feel pain anywhere.'

'My daughter…has done a good bit of rescuing me… on our travels,' her father gasped as she swiftly but gently felt along his limbs.

'Yes, there was that camel who objected to your presence as we were leaving Damascus,' Charis said, hoping the stories would distract her father from any pain or embarrassment. 'Several pack horses along the way and one recalcitrant elephant. Fortunately, you suffered no breaks, but you accumulated an impressive assortment of sprains and bruises. I don't feel anything out of order, Father. I think it will be safe for you to get up.'

'I'd expected…to present a more dignified appearance…upon our first meeting, Mr Lattimar,' her father said between ragged breaths. 'I've had the pleasure… of discussing beautiful objects…with your father over the years.'

'Please, don't exert yourself further. We'll have that conversation once you've recovered,' Lattimar said. After quickly scanning her father's position, he continued, 'Will you allow me to put my hands under your arms and turn you onto your knees? Jameson can then grab your waist and between the two of us, we'll help you stand up and walk you back to the bed.'

'Whatever…you think best,' her father said.

Lattimar nodded to the butler and the two men turned and lifted her father—who, to Charis's further alarm, appeared to be a dead weight, hardly able to assist them at all. After easing him onto his feet, they half-dragged, half-carried him back to the bed and pulled him onto it.

Her father sagged back against the pillows, his breathing still rapid and his hands trembling.

'Can I bring you something?' she asked. 'A sip of wine? Some water?'

He shook his head. 'Just…let me rest.'

Anxious as she was to do *something* to assist his recovery, there didn't appear anything more she could do at the moment, except give him the quiet he'd asked for. Already his eyelids were fluttering shut.

'Rest, then. Jameson will help you back into your dressing gown later. You'll stay with him, Jameson? I'll come back up after I see Mr Lattimar out.'

'Yes, Miss Charis. Don't you worry. I'll keep watch over him.'

She walked towards the door, then paused, still loath

to leave him. He lay with his eyes closed, grey-faced and exhausted. Trying to still the panic in her heart, she said, 'I'll bring you up some soup later.'

He made no attempt to answer.

Walking back down the stairs with Lattimar trailing her, Charis tried to push back her anxiety and distress. She'd ask Lattimar to give her a quick summary of which weapons he thought his father would like them to acquire, send him on his way and then spend the rest of the day tending her father.

After leading him back into the salon, she said, 'Would you like that tea now while we finish our discussion?'

He gave her an incredulous look. 'Surely you know you don't have to entertain me! You must be terribly worried about your father.'

Her anxiety had been building for weeks, and after the shock of her father's collapse, needed only his expression of sympathy to burst free of her ability to contain it. Hot tears stinging her eyes, she admitted, 'I am worried.'

'He's not getting better, is he?' Lattimar asked bluntly.

'I've tried to tell myself he is, but after this... I can't deceive myself any longer. No, he's not getting better. And just now he looked so much *worse*. So...weak and helpless.'

Putting her arms around herself, unable to hold still, she started pacing the room. 'It's this infernal cold and greyness that's preventing his recovery, I just know it! Even when it's not cloudy or raining, everything here— trees, grass, meadows—is so damp and *green*. Oh, I wish we'd never come back to England! Father needs warmth and golden sand and the bright sun of Constantinople. How I long to have him wrapped in his robes, sitting on cushions in a sunny bench in our back garden! But seeing him as he was today… I don't think he could tolerate the journey. I… I don't know what to d-do.'

Her voice broke and she struggled to hold back the sobs.

His intense gaze fixed on her, Lattimar had been watching her pace back and forth. He stepped towards her, hesitated and then, muttering something intelligible, strode over and pulled her into his arms.

She clung to him, her distress keen enough for once to overshadow her sensual response to being in his arms. Burying her head against his shoulder for several moments, she wept tears of fear and frustration. At last, with some difficulty, she was able to pull herself together and step away.

'Sorry! Sorry to burden you with my fears—and my problems.'

'Friends share their burdens—and help each other find answers to problems. You love your father, so of course you are deeply concerned about the slow pace of his recovery.'

'I shall have to figure out something…different. We can't keep on like this. There must be something else I can try. Somewhere else I could take him.'

'Have you a destination in mind?'

She shook her head. 'That's just it. The only places I know that would be better for him are on faraway Mediterranean shores.'

He nodded. 'Travelling to Constantinople is clearly out of the question.' Looking away, he gazed into the distance, frowning, then turned back to her. 'Do you think your father could tolerate a shorter journey?'

'How short? And to where?'

'Our family owns a small property on the South Downs near Eastbourne. It belonged to Vraux's aunt, who never married and left it to him after she died. A distant cousin manages the farm now. As I recall from several visits in childhood, it boasts a simple manor house of Caen stone, surrounded by fields, the house situated close enough to the Channel that one can hear the distant whisper of sea. It wouldn't offer the Mediterranean sun, but that coastal area is the warmest, sunniest part of England and the roads leading there from London are reasonably good.

'A carriage could cover the distance in two days at an easy pace. The journey would involve some inevitable jolting, but once your father arrived, he could have a spacious bed chamber with a distant view of the sea, its windows open to capture the salt breeze. There's a garden terrace in the back where he could sit in the sun, protected from the wind.'

Charis felt her eyes fill with tears again. 'You are inviting us to stay there?'

'For as long as you wish, while your father recovers. I'll escort you there myself, introduce you to the staff and see you settled in. I haven't visited the property for almost a year, so the farms are overdue for an inspection anyway. The manor house hasn't had a full-time occupant since my great-aunt died, but since Mama or my sisters enjoy visiting in the summer, we haven't let the property.'

Warmth. Sun. A place out of the chill and damp and smoke and noise of London. It sounded like the answer to the prayers for healing she delivered every night on her knees. 'It wouldn't be an imposition?'

He shook his head. 'There's just a skeleton staff, whom I wager would love to have someone in residence again. They've been cleaning and polishing a house that no family has lived in since my great-aunt passed away five years ago. The estate manager has a house of his own on the property, so you wouldn't be disturbing him.'

'It sounds…perfect. You are sure you want to do this?'

Lattimar gave a wave of his hand. 'I don't offer something unless I intend to deliver,' he said with a smile.

'Then…yes, thank you. I would love to take Father there.'

"How soon can you make him ready?'

'Give me two days. I'll need to let Grand-Tante know our change in plans, pack up just the essential belongings, hire a carriage—'

'No need for a carriage. Vraux has a travelling carriage, though it hasn't been used for a while as he never goes anywhere. It's old-fashioned—it belonged to my grandmother, who used to travel in style with a full contingent of outriders—but it's large and commodious. We could probably fit it out with a sort of bed, to make it as comfortable as possible for your father. As I recall, there's a hostelry in Little Horsted where we could break the journey. Excellent accommodations, the landlord puts on a fine dinner and your father could have a night in a good bed to recover before the next day's travel. Do you think he could manage that?'

'I think he could manage any two-day journey that would get him out of London. How can I thank you enough?'

Lattimar waved away her gratitude. 'To relieve your anxiety and see your father comfortable and back on the road to recovery will be more than thanks enough.'

A sudden thought broke into her euphoria. 'But…what

about our campaign to find you a wife? We've hardly begun, and are nowhere near achieving our goal.'

Lattimar shrugged. 'I'm not in my dotage yet. There's no urgent need for me to wed immediately. There will never be a shortage of maidens looking to marry a man of wealth and title. If the selection of eligibles has diminished too much by the time your father has recovered enough for you to return to London, I can always look again next year. And if some unforeseen accident should carry me off before then, I have a younger brother who can assume the name and title after Vraux.'

'By next year, I hope we will be far away on our travels.' She sighed. 'I did so want to see you well settled.'

'You mustn't worry about me. I might actually be able to find a wife on my own, you know,' he said, giving her a teasing smile she knew was meant to distract her from her worry.

Sobering, he continued, 'Restoring your father's health is the most immediate concern. Let me know when you are ready, and in the interim, please let me know if there's anything I can do to assist your preparations. I'll send word ahead to Westdean Manor to have the house made ready to receive us.'

'I will of course check with my father, but I cannot imagine he would prefer to remain in London. What can I say then, but to thank you again? For Father as well as for me. Rest assured, it will be our privilege on our next journey to acquire whatever Lord Vraux desires.'

'We'll speak about that later, after the sunshine and warmth and sea air of the Sussex coast coaxes your father back to health again.'

Gratitude and affection swelled in her, making her

chest tight. 'You've relieved me of such anxiety,' she murmured, pressing his hand.

Quickly, before prudence could prohibit it, she went up on tiptoe and kissed his cheek.

Well aware that only the depth of her distress was holding desire in check, she knew she must leave him before she was tempted to do more. 'If you'll excuse me, I'll go check on Father and tell him about our plans. I'll send Jameson down to show you out.'

'No need. I can find my way out. Go tend your father. I'll be prepared to take you to Sussex whenever you're ready.'

'The words are so inadequate—but I must say them again. Thank you. I'll never forget this kindness.'

He caught her hand and placed a brief kiss on her knuckles. 'It's the least I can do.'

'It is hardly little. But I must go now. I will see you soon.'

She walked out, conscious of his concerned gaze following her.

She'd kissed him again from gratitude and relief. But once her father was settled and recovering, she vowed, danger or not, she would give him a kiss of gratitude worthy of the name.

Chapter Twelve

Four days later, Greg waited at Westdean's stables, his gelding tethered beside a mare he thought would be perfect for Charis Dunnfield. Their journey to the Sussex coast had passed without incident, the hostelry where they'd spent the night fortunately living up to the favourable account he'd given her about its superior dining and accommodation. Although her father had been understandably weary, he'd been able to express his fervent appreciation as they'd installed him in his bed chamber when they'd arrived at Westdean yesterday, just before nightfall.

He needed to consult with the distant cousin who served as the estate manager, but on her first day on the coast he wanted to show Miss Dunnfield around the area that was to be her temporary new home.

Having discovered during the journey that, but for the need to tend her father, she would far rather have ridden than travelled by coach, he'd decided to do that tour on horseback. When he'd proposed the excursion last night as they ate a cold collation the cook had saved for them after getting her father to his room, she'd enthusiastically agreed, saying that after being cooped up for two full days, spending several hours on horseback sounded wonderful.

Never having visited Constantinople, Greg didn't know how the Sussex coast would compare. Different, certainly, but he hoped she would find the area as lovely as he did. Fortunately, the day had cooperated by dawning warm, with a brilliant sun and little wind.

He heard footsteps approaching and looked over to find her walking towards him. His heart made that little flip it had taken to doing whenever he first saw her, while he felt an instinctive smile curve his lips.

'Good day,' he called to her. 'How is your father?'

'Much better, thank you. First thing this morning, he had Jameson help him over to sit by the open window. He told me he loves the view of the sea, and asked that you call on him later so he can thank you in person for all your many kindnesses. He already looks so much brighter! Your house is lovely, by the way. Beautiful stone and wood. The windows are larger and the rooms better lighted and airier than I would have expected of an old English manor.'

'The house isn't that old. My great-aunt tore down the Tudor era manor previously on the site, which was practically falling down around her ears when she inherited it. She used the original stone to rebuild the present building. She wanted a house that faced the water and invited in sunshine and sea breezes.'

'It certainly does that.'

'There haven't been any problems between the staff?'

'Not as yet. I went below stairs first thing this morning to thank your staff for making our people feel welcome and explaining I would like Mrs Davenport to continue preparing my father's food, since his illness requires a special diet of foreign herbs and spices I've just finished training her to prepare, and I didn't want to further burden your cook with taking that on when she's just had the lot of us descend upon her. She's not best pleased to share her kitchen, but she agreed.

'Jameson has already served Father as valet, so he will have no problem settling back into that role. My maid is just excited to see something outside London. There may be some friction going forward, but all is well so far.'

'I'm glad to hear it. If there are any problems, let me know. The cook and the butler have been in service here since my childhood. I think I can manage to sweeten things for them.'

'Ah, the charm of the young master, eh?'

'Which I will trade upon shamelessly, if necessary. Are you ready to ride? That's a fetching outfit, by the way,' he added. 'Is it new?'

She twirled around for his inspection, smiling. 'It is. After resigning myself to a longer stay in London than I'd planned, I decided I must begin riding again, and ordered the habit made along with a few dresses. Fortunately, it arrived just before we left.'

'Do you ride much at home in Constantinople?'

'Not in the city, no.' Shaking her head, she said, 'The roads of the old city are very narrow, and as you can imagine, quite congested.'

'So no one attempts to travel by carriage?'

'On the contrary, the *arabas* add to the congestion. Ottoman ladies, who seldom leave the city, don't ride at all, so if they don't wish to travel by foot, they are transported in little wagon-like carriages covered over with cloth, with latticed windows on the sides. Quite comfortable for the occupants—they have coverlet-padded benches and a quantity of pillows. The driver takes the ladies to the markets, or stops in front of shops where he summons an employee to bring for her inspection whatever item the lady is seeking. And the time required for that inspection generally depends on how handsome the employee is.'

'Ah…so they do escape the harem for some flirtation.'

'You would be surprised how much flirting can be done by a veiled lady with just a fine pair of dark eyes.'

'Not at all. I haven't observed veiling, but I have witnessed a very effective use of fine dark eyes.'

She looked up at him inquisitively before comprehension dawned and her face coloured. 'You mean Lynch and Trevethen. I did learn by observing masters of the art. Well, shall we mount up and get started?'

'Allow me.' Leading her to where he'd tethered the mare, he gave her a leg up.

'Ah,' she sighed with pleasure as she adjusted her reins. 'What a joy to ride again! And this little mare seems like a perfect lady.'

A surge of delight filled him. For the first time since he'd watched her gazing in horror at her father sprawled on the floor of his London bed chamber, she looked almost carefree, her eyes alight with energy and enthusiasm.

Greg found it deeply satisfying to know his intervention was responsible for lifting her burdens and bringing that sparkle back to her eyes. He wanted to continue lifting them.

'Since you've not ridden for a while, would you like a good gallop before I show you around the property?

That is, if you think you could handle one. It's your first ride on Sunshine and you don't know her yet.'

Miss Dunnfield gave him an indignant look. 'I'll have you know I've ridden camels, elephants, pack mules, donkeys and the fleetest of Arabian stallions. I can keep my seat galloping on any horse with four legs, even the first time I ride one.'

Grinning, Greg made her an exaggerated obeisance. 'A thousand pardons, O Divine Riding One! I'll race you to the top of the rise, then. You'll have a great view from there.'

In answer, she leaned over her mount and urged her to a gallop. Greg sped his gelding after her, his heart alight just watching her. She was as skilled and graceful on horseback as she was walking. Although he had expected no less.

He pulled his mount up beside hers on the top of rise and had the pleasure of watching her expression change from amusement to amazement as she gazed with awe at the scene spread out below her. From this vantage point, one could see a long line of chalk bluffs leading into the distance, with the sea churning and foaming at their feet, while just below them a sliver of golden beach gleamed in the sunlight.

'It's beautiful!' she breathed. 'Ah, to view the sea again! Can we go down to the water?'

'Of course. We'll need to dismount; the trail is too steep and narrow to ride safely. I'll tether the horses here and you can follow me.'

She hopped down and he took her reins and secured them along with his to some low bushes growing on the crest near some grass where the horses could graze. 'This way,' he said, leading her along a worn trail to the rocky path that led down to the beach.

Though the wind coming off the water was brisk enough for her to have to hang onto her bonnet, the sun-warmed air was mild and fragrant with sea salt. Looking enthralled, she strolled down the beach, then walked to the water's edge, ripped off a glove and leaned down to trail her fingers in the water that lapped at her booted feet. 'It's almost as beautiful a blue as the Bosporus! Even if it is frightfully cold. One would need a long sojourn amid the warm waters of the hammam if one tried to swim in this.' She looked up at him. 'I don't suppose you have a hammam at the manor?'

'No. I'm afraid we make do with a hip bath placed in front of the bed-chamber fire, filled with hot water from the kitchen.'

She sighed. 'A shame. A long afternoon in the hammam would be good for father, too. We have a small one at our house in Constantinople, but usually I go to the large public baths. As I think I mentioned, for ladies especially, it's a gathering place as well as a place of refreshment where one is bathed and groomed. One can eat and chat while servants serve food and drink, have one's hair brushed and styled, get henna applied and conduct whatever business is necessary.'

'Like finding wives for sons?'

'Yes, that, too. The baths are excellent for the skin and one's health in general.'

'If your luminous complexion is any example, it must be excellent indeed.'

She nodded to acknowledge his compliment, then said 'It's so much brighter and warmer here than in London! Do you visit often?'

'Not in recent years. First there was university, and since then I've been responsible for all the Lattimar properties, with Entremer the largest and requiring the most time. But Vraux was not always as reclusive as he's become of late. We spent time here over the summer when we were young. My brother Christopher and I swam, hiked the trail along the cliff line, fished, chased rabbits through fields of clover and pimpernel and rode our ponies all through the fields and pastures, much to my great-aunt's amusement and the annoyance of her estate manager. I remember loving the sun and sea breeze, so different from London and Entremer.'

'That's your estate in Northumberland, isn't it? Far to the north? I imagine the sea water there is never warm enough to swim in.'

He nodded. 'It can be quite cold, especially in winter. You probably wouldn't like it. We're closer to Hadrian's Wall than we are to the sea, and it's often just as cloudy and rainy as London.' He smiled. 'And very *green*! But there's an austere beauty about the broad fields separated by rows of trees and the high, windswept, rocky tors. In such a vast sweep of countryside, one can feel small and insignificant. But also uplifted and inspired.'

'I know what you mean!' she exclaimed, looking at him with surprise. 'I've felt like that crossing the desert. A huge empty expanse of sand and rock as far as the eye can see, shimmering with heat haze during the day, but possessed of a harsh beauty. It does make one feel insignificant...but at the same time, awed and grateful for the privilege of being able to look upon it.'

'Exactly.'

'Perhaps now you understand better why I love travelling. Seeing sights like the edges of the Great Salt Desert outside Tehran, or the spectacular view of Mount Olympus in the distance beyond the sea from the heights of Scutari.'

Yes, she was a born explorer. One who would never be content seeing only the prosaic sameness of a Sussex beach, Greg thought, his high spirits dimming.

Telling himself not to ruin his enjoyment of this moment by recalling how brief his time with her was likely to be, he said, 'Shall we walk back up? There's more to see, including one item which, with your love of sunshine and gold, I'm sure you'll enjoy.'

'Can I come here again?'

'Every day if you wish. This part of the cliff walk and this beach are on Westdean land, so no other permission is needed.'

'Then I suppose I can tear myself away, though I can't imagine viewing anything finer than this.'

Motioning her to go ahead, he walked back up the steep trail behind her, so he might catch her if she stumbled—which, alas, she did not. He did have the pleasure of helping her remount, savouring the feel of her small booted foot in his hands.

After leading her along the cliff path, they reached the farm road that turned inland, away from the sea. She turned to look over her shoulder towards the beach one last time before following him down the farm track that led upward past some grazing land before reaching another hill crest, from which the road descended to an expanse of planted fields.

He reined in as they reached the top of the hill, where a view of farm fields covered in blooming rapeseed spread out below them. And watched with anticipation as once again, an expression of pure delight animated her face.

'What are they—those beautiful yellow blooms that stretch as far as the eye can see?'

'With your aversion to green fields, I thought you would enjoy them. It's rapeseed. The plant has grown here for ever, and is used for cattle feed, but more recently it was discovered that oil made from the crushed seeds makes an excellent lubricant for machinery. Between the power looms now weaving cloth and the engines that drive wagons on the new railways, demand for the oil has quadrupled, so I've had the manager convert many of the barley fields to rapeseed. It blooms in early summer, so I was hoping it would still be flowering when we arrived.' He grinned, sweeping an arm out to indicate the gleaming meadows of gold. 'Just for you.'

She grinned back, then spurred her mount to a trot and rode down the hill to the first meadow, Greg signalling his gelding to follow her. Jumping down from the mare, she tossed the reins around a fence post. 'Can I walk in the field?'

'If you like.'

After dismounting as well, he smiled as he watched her wade into the waist-high blooms, a bonneted barque sailing into a vast sea of yellow. She walked down a row, threading the golden blossoms through her fingers, turning back to him with a look of utter joy.

She reacted that way to everything that pleased her, he realised suddenly, whether it be a sparkling jewel or a pattern in Damascus steel or the sunlight reflecting off a tossing sea. No veneer of bored sophistication tempered her enthusiasm. She embraced what delighted her with the wholehearted, unfettered exuberance of a child.

Just as she'd impulsively and passionately initiated that first kiss.

Absently he touched a finger to his lips, recalling that moment as well as the kiss of thanks she'd planted on his cheek, a touch that fired his response despite its chasteness. He'd held himself under rigid control, knowing it would be unfair to take advantage of her gratitude. With Miss Dunnfield consumed with concern for her father, it hadn't been the place or time to coax her to more.

He shook his head. He mustn't dream about coaxing her to more. He needed to remind himself what a bad idea it was to initiate something that could so easily spiral out of control. Especially now, when it would be an unforgivable breach of his duty as host to try to lure her into intimacy when she was a guest in his house, dependent on him for food and shelter.

If he was going to avoid that temptation, he'd probably better not linger here before returning to London.

'It's like fording a river of sunshine!' she cried as she turned and began walking back towards him. 'You can't imagine how it buoys my soul to be surrounded with golden warmth and sunshine after all that grim, grey darkness. Thank you, dear sir, for my second delight of day.'

She emerged from the field and he helped her pick off blooms that had snagged on her habit, making sure his hands didn't stray to places they shouldn't, even if it meant leaving an errant petal. Her maid could brush the riding habit after she returned.

Even that limited contact had desire humming through him again. Trying to think of some light-hearted remark to distract him, he looked down at her. Shock zinged through him as he recognised an answering desire in her eyes.

He was desperately fighting the urge to lean down

and kiss her when she whispered, 'Now I will have my third delight.' And leaned up to kiss *him*.

She must be a fast study, he thought, for this kiss had none of the awkward hesitancy of her first, inexperienced one. Despite his good intentions, it was impossible not to respond. With a groan, he cupped her head in his hands and kissed her back, nuzzling her lips, tracing them with his tongue.

When she opened to him, touching her tongue to his, an explosion of sensation made him drop his hands and wrap his arms around her, binding her against him. He kissed her harder, deeper, unable to get enough of the taste of her—honey, apricots and sweetness. He felt the swell of her breasts against him, and fought to use the small amount of sanity remaining to him to keep his hands from cupping her bottom and pulling her closer still.

Arms wrapped around her shoulders, he let her kiss him. Insatiable and drowning in sensation, he could have let it go on for ever, ignoring the feeble sense of honour clamouring somewhere at the back of his brain that he should break the kiss. No way was he going to end what she'd begun, until she was ready.

Regrettably, at last, she was, moving her mouth from his and stepping away. Though it was the last thing he wanted, he let her go.

Her expression startled, her eyes still foggy with desire, she gazed up at him, her lips so enticingly reddened that he wanted to pull her right back into his arms and begin again. With a supreme exercise of self-control, he managed to refrain.

Finally gaining control of her erratic breathing, she said. 'Well, that was probably not wise. But I'm so grateful for all you've done, I wanted to let you know just how much.'

A little stung, he said, 'You don't need to kiss me out of gratitude!'

She gave him a beguiling smile. 'I've wanted to kiss you again every time we've met since that first kiss.'

Liking that admission much better, he laughed. 'As you probably could tell, I wanted it just as much. Even though, as you noted, our kissing isn't wise. You might not be concerned about your reputation, but I must be. I couldn't face your father or your great-aunt if I let my... enthusiasm for your charms lead me into compromising you—which I would have just now, had anyone seen us! Your family would insist on a wedding, and I know how much you would hate being forced into marriage.'

'I would be sorry for Grand-Tante to be disappointed in my character, but I'd never let English society's stupid rules compel me to marry.'

Not that he'd want her to wed him under duress, but it still hurt to have her baldly confirm that she wouldn't marry him under any circumstances. Before he could come up with a response that didn't make him sound churlish, she said, 'But I will take no more advantage of you, I promise. Passion should be a gift reserved for your bride and it isn't right for me to steal it. Now, have you any more treasures to show me? If not, I should get back and see how Father is faring.'

'That's all for today.'

'I hope to go to the beach every day. Ride here and enjoy this spectacle every day until the blossoms fade. Will you ride with me if I promise not to attack you again?'

I wish you might attack me as often as you liked, he thought.

But that was not possible. He wasn't made of Damascus steel; his control could shatter. 'I can ride later. But I do need to consult with the estate manager tomorrow.'

'Ah, yes. You'll need to discuss what business he has for you so you can get back to London as quickly as possible, I expect.'

He should. But he found himself deeply reluctant to leave. 'How quickly depends on how much work needs to be done here.'

With luck, it would be a lot. 'Shall I escort you back now?'

'Yes. Thank you again for a wonderful ride.'

'It was my pleasure.'

Touching a finger to his lips, she smiled. 'I think it was mine.'

He sighed. 'I think it was mutual.'

Prudently, she walked over to use a wall as a mounting post. He stood by to assist, if she slipped, but she managed to seat herself with ease.

Taking up his own reins, he remounted as well. He was reluctant to end the magic of this time alone with her, where they were able to talk of whatever they liked with no overhearing ears to disapprove, blessed with a freedom that had allowed her to kiss him.

They'd been trotting their horses along for several minutes in silence when suddenly, she lifted her face up to the sky, sighing. 'Ah, I want to let the sunshine soak into my bones. You were right, it is so much warmer here than London. I can't get enough of it!'

'I'm glad you're enjoying the warmth. Is it never cold in Constantinople?'

'It is, actually. It even snows in winter sometimes.'

'But you find the cold in England less tolerable?'

'It's only cold in winter, not most of the year, like it seems to be here. By now, at home, it would be lovely, sunny, sultry. Even in winter, the house is warmer than those in England. With so little sun and most of the heat going up the chimney, the rooms at King Street never seem to truly warm up. In our Ottoman house, the main chamber has a sofa that runs against two walls, covered with thick carpets, with a large assortment of cushions to recline upon.

'In winter, in the corner where the two walls meet, there's a *tandour*, a table-like frame covered by padded coverlets one can draw up to one's chin, while in the centre of the table there's a copper vessel full of burning charcoal. In the middle of the room stands another copper stove filled with more charcoal. There, instead of a thin worsted gown over even thinner undergarments, I wear long trousers, a long embroidered cloak over a silk gauze blouse, and over that a vest thickly lined with fur. When not going about to supervise household work, I can rest in warm, cushioned comfort to read, write, or study.

'Which reminds me, I was going to ask if it would be permissible for Father and I to don Ottoman attire while in the house and its immediate environs? The loose trousers, vest and fur-lined robe would be much warmer and more comfortable for Father than European dress.'

'Of course. Wear whatever makes you most at ease.' Even as he said the words, curiosity fired as he wondered how she would look in that foreign garb.

'We occasionally wear Ottoman dress in London, so our own servants are familiar with it, but you probably ought to warn your staff here so our appearance doesn't startle them.' She laughed. 'They are doubtless going to think us very odd. But I'm willing to endure their dismay if it helps Father feel better and recover his strength more quickly. I promise, I will don a proper habit when I ride out and a proper walking dress if I go strolling beyond the back garden.'

'You may wear whatever you like and go wherever you wish to go. Westdean is at your disposal for as long as you need it.'

She turned that brilliant smile on him again. 'Once more, I can't thank you enough. And I have one more question.'

Raising an enquiring eyebrow, he said, 'Ask away.'

'As we will be sharing your house—and I've already kissed you several times—it seems rather silly to continue calling you "Mr Lattimar", as if we were distant acquaintances rather than friends. After all you have done to help Father, I think of us almost like family. I would continue to address you formally outside the house or if any neighbours should call, of course, but might we be a little more informal among ourselves? I would prefer for you to call me Charis. When I hear "Miss Dunnfield", I feel you're about to take me to task for something.'

If by 'family', she meant his feelings towards her should be sisterly, Greg didn't think he could manage that. Still, he was pleased that she felt comfortable enough with him to dispense with formality. 'I'd be honoured to be permitted to use your given name. And you are welcome to call me Greg.'

'Good.' She nodded decisively. 'That's settled, then.'

They neared the manor house and took the trail towards the stables. 'Thanks again for the ride, too. And that marvellous walk to the sea! I can't wait to tell

Father about it. It will inspire him to improve, so I can take him down to the beach. I also can't wait to get him out of that stiff coat, trousers and cravat and into a soft robe and his furs!'

Her smile turned tender. 'You couldn't give me home. But you have given me a lovely echo of it.'

That warm feeling tightened his chest again. He wanted to give her whatever she needed. He loved seeing the worried look fade from her face, replaced by the joy in her eyes as she gazed at the sea, the delight as she walked through the golden meadow of waving rapeseed blooms.

'I'm so pleased that you've found Westdean acceptable. It's not the sunny Mediterranean, I know, but I hoped it would be enough.'

'It's far more than enough. It's magical.'

She dismounted, turning her mount over to the groom who came out to receive the mare and Greg's gelding. As they walked back towards the house, she touched his hand.

Though 'touch' didn't begin to convey the full impact of what she did, drawing her fingers slowly along his, an intimate gesture that set all his nerves tingling. 'I know you are tiring of hearing it, but I must thank you again. I'll dine with Father in his room tonight, if that is permissible. It makes me an unappreciative guest, but I didn't want to desert him on his second night here. I hope soon he will feel well enough to come down to the dining room.'

She laughed. 'I will wear European dress when I sit at table, I promise you. I wouldn't want to shock the footman.'

'Of course, stay with your father,' he agreed, conscious of disappointment in knowing he'd not have her company at dinner. 'The whole point of coming to Westdean was to help him recover. I'll need to go over paperwork in the estate office anyway, to be ready for my meeting with the manager tomorrow.'

'I'm grateful for your understanding. I hope your paperwork goes well and you encounter few problems that need fixing. And I'll try not to astound or offend your staff and create any more.'

'Don't worry about that. I'm here to support you.'

'I feel wonderfully supported.' Her smile fading, she swiped at a tear that suddenly appeared at the corner of her eye. 'It's been just Father and I for so long. I shouldn't need any additional assistance…but I'm so grateful for the help you have given me and your truly noble generosity.'

By now they had reached the front entry steps. 'I'm just thankful I had a useful alternative to offer.'

'A marvellous one. I'll see you tomorrow, then.'

He nodded. 'Tomorrow.'

He lingered, letting her enter the manor ahead of him, enjoying the delight of watching that unique, swaying, rhythmic gait as she crossed the entrance and started up the stairs.

He should start running through his mind the usual checklist of items he reviewed each time he inspected a property he'd not seen in some time.

Instead of wondering what she would look like when she traded her gown for trousers, a flowing robe and a fur vest.

Chapter Thirteen

Later that evening, Greg stretched out his back, stiff after several hours of sitting at the desk in the estate office, poring over ledgers while he absently consumed his dinner from the tray the cook had sent up. With his usual determination, he concentrated on mastering the details of acres planted, amount of seed used and the size and increase in the herds of Sussex cattle and flocks of Sussex chickens. He made a reasonable job of focusing on his task, despite the distraction of knowing that Miss Dunnfield was somewhere in the house.

Charis, as he now had permission to call her, he thought, another little eddy of satisfaction adding to the pleasure today of watching her delight at the beach and her joy as she'd waded through the blooming rapeseed in the meadow.

She'd planned to dine with her father, but that gentleman, still recovering from the fatigue of the journey when Greg had stopped by to check on him mid-afternoon, would probably retire early. She might want to rest as well, but after he'd finished reading the last of the reports he should be a good host and seek her out. If she was still up and about, he would propose some entertainment to occupy the rest of her evening. A few hands of cards…or perhaps he'd invite her to read to him or him to her in the library, which as he recalled from his childhood visits contained a good assortment of literature.

It went without saying that being able to spend part of the evening with her would be an excellent cap on a wonderful day for him. He'd just have to remember to keep his distance and make sure they occupied separate chairs a safe distance apart. No sitting beside her on the sofa in the salon or the library.

The prospect of seeing her again raising his spirits, he returned to his reports with increased enthusiasm. Less than an hour later, completing a sheaf of notes and questions he needed to ask the estate manager tomorrow, he closed the ledgers and walked out of the office.

After trotting upstairs to the reception areas of the house, his initial excitement dimmed as he walked through rooms now fading into darkness as the long, nearly midsummer's daylight faded. To his disappointment, he didn't encounter Charis in the grand salon, the library or the small family breakfast room.

Apparently she had retired early.

Coming back into the hallway, he paused, irresolute. He could return to the library, light some candles, pour himself a brandy and choose a book to read. As he didn't play the piano well enough to amuse himself, it would be the most pleasant way to spend the rest of the evening.

He smiled as he recalled Charis's desire to exchange stiff, confining European dress for the freedom of the loose robes of the East. Maybe he'd cast off his own cravat and jacket and don a banyan before finding that book and settling in.

That decided, he took the stairs up to the bed chambers. As he approached the next floor, an odd sound reached his ear. Some sort of music, he realised as he drew closer.

Reaching the bed-chamber hallway, he determined the music was coming from the front room allotted to Mr Dunnfield. Curious, he paused to listen more closely.

The tune was being played on some sort of stringed instrument, the lyrics sung in a language he didn't understand by a pure, sweet feminine voice. *Charis.*

The plaintive melody, very different from European music but haunting and lovely, captivated him. Without being conscious of moving, he walked closer until he found himself standing just outside the door.

It must be some tale of lost love, he thought as the sweet sadness of the music played over him. Listening was a pleasure, despite the fact that he understood not a word.

He ought to move along to his own chamber, not lurk outside Dunnfield's door like a beggar outside the window peering in at a banquet—though, he thought with a wry smile, he felt much like that. Vowing not to disturb them, he made himself turn to walk away.

But with the hallway now in almost complete darkness, he bumped into a side table that had been placed outside the chamber door, knocking to the floor a metal tray the staff must be using to bring meals and necessities up Dunnfield's room.

Before he could catch it, the tray hit the floor with a loud clang that reverberated through the hallway. Cursing under his breath, Greg bent down and retrieved the tray, placing it carefully back on the table. He was about to creep away when the chamber door opened—revealing Charis, standing on the threshold.

'Greg?' she said, her tone surprised. 'I heard a noise and worried one of the servants might have fallen carrying the tray and hurt themselves.'

For a moment, he had no reply... Greg realised that, silhouetted against the candles glowing in the room behind her, Charis was wearing wide, gathered trousers that fell to the floor, a long robe made of some sort of brocade embroidered with glittering metallic thread, soft fur outlining her shoulders and a blouse whose lacy sleeves belled out around her wrists. Her dark hair, lustrous in the candlelight, fell in long braided tresses down her back.

With the jasmine scent wafting from her, the silk of her hair blowing in the soft breeze made by the warm air of the chamber exiting into the colder hallway and the unusual clothing with its glitter of metal and lushness of fur, she looked incredibly lovely.

A treasure from Ottoman lands, he thought, like those she collected for her clients.

He only wished the hallway was in daylight, so he might see her more clearly.

'No, it was just me being clumsy,' he said, finding his voice at last. 'I heard the music as I came up the stairs and was curious. What a lovely song! But excuse me, I didn't mean to intrude upon you and your father.'

'I didn't mean to disturb you,' she replied with a smile. 'Rather than retire early as I expected, Father asked me to play and sing for him. I was so pleased, for it's been quite a while since he's felt well enough to stay up in the evening. I didn't even consider that the sound might penetrate beyond the walls of his chamber.'

'I'm glad to hear he is feeling better, and you didn't disturb me.'

After hesitating for a moment, she said, 'Would you like to join us?'

He bit back an immediate acceptance. 'I wouldn't want to intrude.'

'You wouldn't be intruding. I seem to remember you once saying you'd like to hear some Ottoman music. This is your opportunity, and with this private exhibition, you'd be free to grimace if it doesn't please you without anyone noticing. I know Father would be happy to have you, though I must warn you'll have to suffer receiving his thanks again. He's so delighted with the room, the views, the sea air, he's been singing your praises all evening.'

'If you're certain it wouldn't be an imposition...'

She laughed. 'We're in your house, with your servants taking care of our every need, and you think your visiting us would be an imposition?' She shook her head. 'Not in the least. We'd be pleased to have you join us.'

Delighted to have been granted what he'd yearned for, he said, 'Then I will, and thank you.'

Greg followed her into the pleasant warmth of the room, where a fire burned on the hearth and a number of braces of candles provided a cheery illumination. Dunnfield reclined on a sofa which had been pulled up near the fire, propped on a number of pillows and, like his daughter, was garbed in loose trousers, a long robe and a short jacket whose fur lining warmed him up to his chin, with a coverlet tucked over his feet.

'Father, I saw Mr Lattimar in the hallway when I went to investigate the noise. I've invited him to join us.'

Dunnfield looked over and spied him. After a surprised moment, he said, 'Welcome, Mr Lattimar. You enjoy Ottoman music?'

'I've never experienced it before. If the little I heard while walking down the hallway is any indication, it's beautiful.'

'Hearing my daughter play and sing would be the best introduction you could have to it,' he answered, pride in his voice. 'She rivals her excellent teacher, Bayam Zehra—a dear friend of my late wife and one of most skilled players in Constantinople—on the *tambur*—the guitar-like instrument you see there—and the *kadum*, which is a sort of zither.'

'I'm hardly her equal, but I did have a master instructor,' Charis said, giving her father a fond glance for his praise. 'Would you take a glass of wine before I begin again, Mr Lattimar?'

So they were to maintain formality before her father, he noted. Which was wise. Despite her claims to the contrary, Greg suspected her father would be less opposed to the idea of his daughter's marriage than she was, and would immediately begin observing them much more closely once he had recovered enough to be more observant of what happened around him.

Knowing the intimacy of first names would be shared just between the two of them made the permission she'd given him even more special.

She must have felt him watching her, for after she handed him the glass of wine and waved him to a chair beside the sofa a little farther removed from blaze on hearth, she said, 'This must be your first time viewing Ottoman attire as well as hearing Ottoman music.'

Making a little pirouette for his inspection, she said, 'I assure you, these thick trousers are as warm as they are comfortable and the brocade robe and fur jacket feel wonderful against the night chill. All that we're missing is a *tambour* to snuggle under, but we are making do with this English fire.'

In the brighter illumination of the fire and the candle-light, Greg saw that the trousers, though their bell-like shape echoed her form, were as loosely fitted as she'd described. The fur jacket, however, clung tightly to her torso, while the wide-sleeved blouse was of a gauze so fine as to be transparent, revealing her arms and the loveliness of her throat down the hollow between her breasts before the vest covered them.

'It's very attractive, and it suits you.' In the full shimmering light that played over the red brocade robe richly embroidered with gold thread, the gleaming green silk vest with its soft fur caressing her shoulders, the translucent beauty of the silk blouse beneath, she looked even more like a treasure from the East, he thought.

'Thank you, kind sir. Now, Father, what song would you have next? Shall I play your favourite again for Mr Lattimar?'

'Please do, my dear. I can never hear it too often.'

She took her seat on a stool near the hearth and picked up the instrument—a *tambur*, her father had called it. It looked to him like a gypsy's guitar, but with a much longer neck. Putting the instrument in playing position, she took up a pick made of bone, then turned to him.

'Like so many folk songs, this one is about all-consuming love. The singer describes being ablaze with it, feeling as if he is whirling like the wind, drifting like dust over the plain, flowing like raging rapids of river. Plaintively he asks the listener to "see what love has done to me".'

Bent over the instrument, she began to play. Her voice, clear, sweet, bell-like, drew him in, while the chords she plucked carried the lilting melody. 'Ablaze with love until one felt he was whirling like the wind, swept along like dust, tumbling madly down a rushing river'... The emotions of the song touched an answering chord.

He'd always enjoyed music, but this was *Charis* performing, occasionally looking up to give him a smile, while her voice and her playing captivated him. He stopped thinking, analysing, worrying, and let himself be transported. Privileged to share this private performance, as if he'd been invited into the secret heart of the harem where a beauty played just for him, he would savour it.

Suddenly he recalled her telling him how her mentor had drilled her so she might entertain a husband. Making her perfect movements so graceful, a voice so sweet and beguiling, and playing so skilful that her spouse would be mesmerised and become devoted to her for life. Gazing at her, he thought that her teacher would be quite satisfied with the results.

She certainly mesmerised him.

When she finished the song, he joined her father in enthusiastic applause.

'That was beautiful. You are just as talented as your father claimed.'

'You've never heard Bayam Zehra,' she replied modestly. 'But I do well enough.'

'Will you play another?'

'If you wish.' When he nodded, she said, 'What shall it be next, Father?'

'How about the ballad by Perousse Hanoum?'

Wishing he had one of those fur-lined robes for himself, Greg leaned back in his chair, sipping his wine, letting Charis's honeyed voice flow over him. At his and her father's request, she played several more before declaring it time for them to finish their wine and then for her father to retire.

'I'm so pleased you are feeling better tonight, Father. I don't want you to over-tire yourself on your first evening,' she replied when her parent said he could listen awhile longer. As could Greg.

A short time later, the wine finished, Greg reluctantly rose to leave. He was tempted to wait until Charis bid her father goodnight and walk her to her room, but under the exotic spell of her music and with a moonlight of enchantment streaming through the windows, that was a recipe with too much potential for disaster. He'd had enough trouble restraining himself out in the open field, where at any moment some farm worker might have happened by.

With the two of them alone, at the door to her bed chamber...

Shaking his head to rid it of that beguiling vision, he thanked them both for including him in their evening, bid them goodnight and walked out.

Once outside the closed chamber door, he paused, irresolute. Energised by the music, he wasn't in the least sleepy. He supposed he could go down to the library, find himself that book, return to his chamber, put on a banyan in pale imitation of Mr Dunnfield's luxurious fur-lined robe, and settle in to read.

Though there was no chance he could find a book that would offer as much enchantment as watching Charis's expressive face and graceful hands, or listening to the pure beauty of her voice as she sang and played.

Ottoman garb did suit her. What a creature of contrasts she was! Sometimes, in her proper London riding habit and bonnet, she looked like a quintessentially English maiden. At others, when she walked with that indefinable grace, or moved her hands in that lovely ballet of serving tea, she was definitely the product of an alluring foreign land, doubly so when dressed the part.

A woman of infinite interest and mystery, always surprising one with the unexpected, since it was impossible to predict in any given circumstances whether her conversation and behaviour would feature the English or Ottoman side.

He was glad the questions he needed to ask the estate manager and the projects he'd noted that needed completion had created a considerable list. He hoped they would require him to remain at Westdean for some time.

He only knew for certain that, with her father's improvement moving the day of their departure steadily forward, he wanted to spend as much time as he could with her. Before, like clouds blown on the wind, she was swept away for ever beyond the boundaries of his world.

Chapter Fourteen

After settling her father for the night, Charis walked back to her room, still filled with a heady excitement about what had been a magical evening. Her spirits already buoyed by Father feeling well enough to ask her to stay and play for him, the time had been made even more special by Lattimar's unexpected appearance.

He'd told her earlier that he wanted to hear her play, and she'd been keen to discover whether he would enjoy the music curiosity had led him to request.

By all indications, he had. His gaze never leaving her, his fingers tapping in time with the rhythm of the *tambur*, he'd looked entirely transfixed. So connected had she felt to him that despite the presence of her father on the sofa near him, she had the strongest sense that she was playing for him alone.

How extraordinary was it that this proper English gentleman, who had never left this island's shores and had no previous experience of anything similar, would find her music compelling?

But then, Gregory Lattimar was exceptional. She recalled again the pleasures he'd arranged for her today.

He could have just told her about the proximity of the beach and given her directions on how to get there. Instead, he'd taken time, not just to escort her, but to do so in a manner that had made her first perception of the sea a surprise and delight. And had then surprised her again when he'd revealed the fields of flowers he'd known she would love.

Though she knew he'd accompanied them on the journey to watch over Father, to make sure the trip was as easy as possible for him and to see him safely arrived at Westdean Manor—a concern for which she could never adequately thank him—she also knew he'd come to make an inspection of a property he was responsible for overseeing. Yet, putting off his other tasks on his very first day here, he'd ridden out with her, letting her explore the beach at her leisure and then, like a giddy child, wander through the rapeseed blooms, as if he had all the time in the world and nothing more pressing to attend to.

She couldn't say enough about his compassion, generosity and kindness.

She could also say a great deal about his skill at the game of passion. When she'd been driven to give him the kiss she'd promised herself, he'd responded with desire but also restraint, never losing track of his need to protect her. A less scrupulous man could easily have taken advantage of her, alone and isolated as they'd been, excusing himself with the truth that, having been given such flagrant encouragement, he couldn't be held accountable for his actions.

Instead, Greg had kept himself under rigid control. She'd sensed him holding back, even as he'd tangled his tongue with hers and pressed the hardness of his body against her. His embrace bound her to him, but his hands never strayed where, to be honest, she wished they had… to caress the sensitised breasts yearning for his touch or lower, to bind her tingling centre more tightly against his hardness.

Credit for limiting how far passion was allowed to progress belonged all to him, for she had shown almost no caution. Only the reproach of a conscience that had finally broke through the sensual enchantment to accuse her of stealing a passion not meant for her had finally forced her to step away.

'Pleasure is a gift a husband gives to his bride, a gift she returns to him,' Bayam Zehra had told her.

Did she really want to do without that gift for all her life?

But if she envisioned the giving and taking of that treasure, the face of the bridegroom in her hazy imagining was Gregory Lattimar's. Trying to fit another, unknown man into that role seemed…distasteful…wrong, somehow.

She sighed. An odd but fortunate reaction. It would be a good deal easier to resist passion—and the risks marriage would bring—if no other man ever tempted her as he did.

Still, it was beguiling to daydream about singing and dancing for him, as the Bayam had taught her, and then giving herself to him. Feeding him dates and apricots, entertaining him until he took her hand and led her to his chamber.

She wished she could bring him to Constantinople and let him explore more of the culture she loved. Show him the beauties of the sun rising over the sparkling waters of the Black Sea and setting over distant, snow-capped Mount Olympus. Though he'd never voyaged abroad, he seemed so appreciative of her music and dress, so interested in listening to her stories, she thought he would enjoy travelling and seeing new lands.

But his responsibilities anchored him here, as her life drew her abroad. If she were ever to marry, it couldn't be to him.

If she had to turn away from passion, at least today had given her renewed hope for Father's recovery. He'd tolerated the journey here better than she'd hoped, and his total delight with the house and its surroundings had brought about an amazing improvement in his strength and spirits. She'd want him to take things slowly, so that he didn't over-tire himself by trying to do too much, too soon, but for the first time since his terrifying collapse, she could envision the possibility of returning to their cherished life some time soon, rather than in the far distant future.

A cherished life that would take her far from Gregory Lattimar. Sadness pierced her at the thought but she steeled herself against it. Since parting was inevitable, she would lose no more time repining over the necessity.

Greg had responsibility for managing a number of estates besides Westdean, and probably could not afford to neglect them for very long. In a week, perhaps two at most, he would leave, quite likely not to return before Father recovered. At which time, after so long a delay, they would want to resume their travels as soon as possible.

It might well be years before she saw him again, if ever. And if she did see him when they next returned to England, he would almost certainly be married. Reclaiming the closeness they were sharing now would be impossible.

Rather than regretting what could never be, she resolved to enjoy every minute they had together at Westdean. And redouble her guard against once again trying to purloin what could not be hers.

To her regret, the next day Charis didn't see Greg at all. He was out with the estate manager, Jameson told her when she asked. Father had been tired after staying up for his evening entertainment, as she'd feared he might be, so she had not tried to keep him company, instead letting him sleep away much of the day.

The weather was once again beautiful, fair and sunny, making it a pleasure to venture out of doors. After all the gloomy days in London, she revelled in it, taking her time exploring the kitchen garden, where she checked the plantings for any useful herbs she might add to Father's diet, then proceeded to the walled rose garden the housekeeper told her had been her late mistress's special project. She strolled along the brick pathways, spent a leisurely time seated on a garden bench in the sun under a fragrant curtain of climbing roses and finished by picking bouquets of familiar damask and apothecary varieties to perfume the bed chambers and salon.

Deciding to walk rather than ride, after changing into a London day dress, she hiked back to the cliff walk, then carefully descended the steep rocky path to the beach—missing Greg's hand at her back to steady her if she stumbled. Taking time to do a thorough exploration, she walked the length of the beach to where the thin verge gave way to jagged rocks where the sea crashed and foamed, the sharp, steep chalk cliffs rising at their backs.

She missed being in that lovely place with him. Missed him in general, which was the main reason she chose to walk rather than ride. Going on horseback would be a continual reminder of the companionship they'd shared the day before, the conversations as well as the times they'd ridden in silence, content to be together with only the sounds of the sea, the whistle of the wind and the chatter of bird song between them.

She returned from the shore windblown but refreshed and more than ready to abandon the tight bodice, stays and sweeping skirt for her Ottoman trousers. After checking with Father, who requested a simple soup followed by an early rest, she carried up his meal, hoping Lattimar might return in time to dine with her. But while she sat with Father, Jane brought up a note from him explaining that his return would be further delayed. He'd encountered the Squire on his rounds and had been invited to dinner, a refusal to which would have given offence. As Greg was a responsible neighbour and landlord, she couldn't fault him for that.

After reading to her Father for a while and settling him for the night, she added another cashmere shawl over her robe and jacket and went out onto the sheltered back terrace to breathe in the soft sea breeze and, she admitted, listen for Greg's return. A jolt of excitement and anticipation roused her from drowsy contemplation of the night sky as she heard his voice return the butler's greeting. Jumping up, she hurried back into the hallway to meet him.

'Charis!' he said in surprise, halting. 'I thought you would be abed by now.'

'It was too lovely an evening to waste in sleep. I'm still enchanted by an English night that isn't cold, foggy or raining. Did you have a successful day? I know it was long.'

'Far longer than I expected. I apologise again for being such a poor host.'

'Nonsense. Your sole task was to escort us here, not to entertain us. You may be our host, but you are also a manager with duties to attend. So mild was the air and so gentle the breeze tonight that I couldn't bring myself to sit inside. I've been enjoying a glass of wine and letting the sea air blow the worries from my mind.' She smiled. 'The few worries you haven't already chased away.'

'Would that I might chase all of them away. Do you mind if I join you for a glass?'

'I would be happy for your company. You can tell me all about your day with your estate manager.'

Motioning her to walk with him back to the terrace, he chuckled. 'You truly want to know? I fear you will find it all very dull.'

'I would know more about how you spend your life, as you have always been kind enough to enquire about mine.'

'Ah, but that's different. Your life has been well-travelled and exciting, with you discovering and importing treasures. Mine has dealt with…the prosaic and commonplace.'

'A job well done is always interesting, no matter how commonplace its activities. I'm sure you do yours well. And you must remember, for me, life in England is often strange and different.'

'Very well, if you truly want to hear about it.'

'I do.'

Prudently, he took a chair near the one where she'd been sitting rather than inviting her to sit beside him on the metal garden bench. She resisted the temptation to

move her chair closer, where she might touch his hand
or pat his shoulder.

His mere presence is gift enough, she reproved herself. *You are not entitled to more.*

She contented herself with pouring him a glass of
wine. 'So, tell me everything about today,' she said,
handing him the glass.

'I will,' he said after taking a sip, 'but I shall not be
offended if the recital puts you to sleep.'

As she chuckled at that, he continued, 'I began the
morning in the estate office with the manager, Ben Stillfield. An older gentleman, he's my cousin, another great-
nephew of my great-aunt who served as her estate agent
as well. After reviewing the ledgers, we rode out to inspect the fields, rapeseed in bloom, which you've already
seen, and other fields planted with barley and wheat. The
weather has been fair, with no late rains to delay the ma-
turing of the plants, so he expects a good rapeseed harvest in late summer and the corn to come in a bit later.'

'The rapeseed is harvested after the blossoms turn
to pods?'

'Yes. We're building a production facility to extract
the oil ourselves, rather than selling the pods to a fin-
isher. Then we stopped to visit several tenants; one has
a problem with draining in his wheat field, another has
a cottage in urgent need of thatching. The old gentleman
who lives there, a widower, has farmed the property for
half a century, and remembers me from when I was a
boy. He invited us to share an ale with him.'

'It must be gratifying for him to see what a fine, responsible landlord that boy has become.'

Greg laughed. 'He wasn't as fond of Christopher and
I when we were riding our ponies through his fields! He

allowed that I'd turned out rather well, in spite of my early misdeeds.'

After pausing for another sip, he continued, 'In the afternoon, we rode out to the pastures, to check with the farmers who tend cattle. We ended the afternoon by stopping in the village for a glass of ale, which is where I encountered the Squire, who'd also stopped for a pint before heading home. He invited me to dine and, as he is about to leave for London to visit his married daughter and I wasn't sure how long I will be at Westdean, I felt obliged to accept. He would have felt slighted had I not made time to see him.'

'Of course. As the foremost pasha of this area, you must honour your obligations to the neighbourhood. Are your tasks completed, then?' she asked, unhappy at the idea that he would soon be leaving.

He laughed. 'Indeed, no! They've hardly begun. That was just the inspection tour. The agent and I must go back and meet with the tenant with the soggy wheat field and determine the best way to address the drainage problem. We'll need to arrange for thatch and get some of the neighbours to help redo Claxen's cottage roof. Talk with the farmers about which animals they should add to their herds and where to obtain them. I should probably ride into Eastbourne and Brighton to explore possibilities of where to market the processed oil for the best price. Which mainly entails checking to see whether it is more profitable at the moment to sell the oil to be distributed in England or export it to the continent. All of that will require two more weeks, at least.'

'So you cannot leave for London before then,' she said, relieved to learn she would have his company at least that much longer.

'No, which brings me to what I'd intended to ask when I next saw you. Tomorrow will be the beginning of the Midsummer Fair, long held here and each day ends with the traditional bonfires. I know your father isn't yet strong enough to leave the house, but would you be interested in attending?'

Seeing more of his world, in his company? Delighted by the prospect, she said, 'Of course! What happens during the fair?'

'Do they not have fairs in Constantinople?'

'Not in the city—the streets are much too narrow and crowded. Most events take place at an area called the "Sweet Waters of Asia", an open place where the peninsula meets the sea. On a pleasant day, the greensward there is filled with visitors from the different quarters of the city—Turks, Armenians, Greeks, Europeans. Often there are itinerant musicians and flower sellers going from group to group, tents selling coffee or kabobs of roasted meat, sherbet merchants, occasionally even troops of acrobats or rope dancers to amuse the crowd. Is an English fair similar?'

'In some ways, though an English fair focuses more on the agricultural. There are always exhibitions of livestock, with the Squire judging to determine the prize animals. Farmers gather to evaluate and compare beasts. Itinerant peddlers set up booths, though they are more likely to be selling sundry items of all sorts than food, from mirrors to thimbles to pans to cloth. Servants from the local baker and the public houses circulate among the visitors offering meat pasties and ale. Sometimes gypsy groups looking to buy and sell horses will attend, doing business while their ladies set up booths to tell fortunes. Every night of the fair bonfires are lit along the cliff walk.'

'It sounds fascinating. I'd love to go, if you are sure it won't take you away too long from your duties.'

'Attending, like spending an evening with the Squire, is a part of my duties. Mingling at the fair allows me to meet the tenants away from their work, at a time when they can relax and enjoy themselves. I can buy them a mug of ale, compliment their families, chat about crops and weather and prices. Often, one can gain a better feel for any underlying problems or potential worries when they are away from the labours of the farm.'

'That sounds very wise.'

'I'll be riding out with Mr Stillfield again in the morning and planned to drop by the fair in the afternoon, if that would suit you. I can introduce you to Squire Thursgood and some of our tenants. Take you to the barns where the animal judging will take place. Let you browse through the peddlers' displays.'

He laughed, shaking his head. 'Just listen to me! I can't believe I'm inviting someone who has shopped in the jewel-filled bazaars of Baghdad and Tehran to visit a simple country fair! Please, promise me you'll let me know when you've had all the boredom you can stand and I'll escort you back to Westdean.'

'Nonsense, I will love it. The chief joy of travelling, aside from discovering treasures of course, is meeting a wide variety of people. Some live in palaces, some in mud-walled villages, but they are all fascinating in their own way. All with unique and interesting stories to tell, if one will take the time to share a cup of herb tea or coffee with them and listen.'

He smiled, his teeth gleaming in the flickering light of

the lantern she'd placed on the table. 'Excellent. Knowing you will be there will make it even more enjoyable for me. Now, though, if you'll excuse me, it's been a long day. I need to go up before I fall asleep on this bench. But don't go in yet if you don't want to. It's perfectly safe for you to remain here and enjoy the night breeze for as long as you like.'

She gazed up at the brilliant summer sky bedazzled with stars. 'Yes, I shall remain a while longer.'

'Goodnight, then, Charis. Sleep well. I'll look forward to escorting you to the fair tomorrow.'

'As will I. Thank you for inviting me.'

She watched him go, congratulating herself on resisting the constant urge to kiss him again. How unfair it was that passion must be limited to a husband! she thought with a sigh. But as much as she believed fulfilling one's physical desire was normal and natural, she knew she couldn't succumb to temptation. Getting herself with child would be an embarrassment to both her father and Grand-Tante.

Although there was something oddly appealing about the idea of bearing his child, a realisation that shocked her. She'd never before considered the prospect of having a child even mildly appealing.

A child she might lose, as Bayam Zehra had lost one of her babes. As she had lost her own mother too soon.

No, she wouldn't want that, either. Better to enjoy the novelty of this English fair, the pleasure of being escorted by her handsome, proper Englishman, and look back on this sojourn on the Sussex coast as the highlight of her enforced stay in England.

While keeping her mind firmly focused on her plans for the future.

Chapter Fifteen

The afternoon of the following day, filled with curiosity and anticipation, Charis rode beside Greg Lattimar into Westdean village, around the outskirts of which the Midsummer Fair had been set up.

'We'll leave our horses at the stables at the Jolly Farmer,' he said. 'The animal enclosures and peddler stalls are set up just outside the village, all of them close enough together that we won't need to ride. If you like, we can partake of the landlord's wife's excellent beef stew before we return to Westdean. Although you will probably find English fare rather bland.'

'No cinnamon, cardamom, cloves or cumin in the stew?' she asked.

'Not a bit. I'm afraid you'll have to make do with salt and pepper.'

'It shall be…interesting. And I shall try to remember to walk more stiffly, with as little sway as possible. I don't want your neighbours in Sussex to think I'm something I'm not.'

'Men are sure to admire you, but don't worry. I'll introduce you as the daughter of a diplomat who has lived most of her life abroad. Then they will expect you to be strange.'

She gave him a darkling look that made him laugh.

A short time later, they reached the inn, where Greg turned their horses over to a stable boy.

'Would you like to view the animals first? The judging should be just about completed.'

Charis nodded and followed him into a temporary enclosure set up on the verge just beyond the last cottage. A row of cattle was tied to posts at one end, large draft horses were tethered at the other and, between them, in a penned area, chickens strutted, squawking and pecking at the ground.

A large, bluff man in tweeds and muddy top boots stood by the cattle. 'That's the Squire,' Greg told her. 'Let me present him to you.'

They walked over to halt beside him, exchanging bows and curtseys.

'So who is this lovely stranger, Mr Lattimar?'

'Miss Dunnfield, may I present Squire Thursgood? Miss Dunnfield is the guest I told you about at dinner last night. Her father, a diplomat, is a good friend of Lord Vraux. Sadly, he fell ill after they returned from abroad to London, and has not been improving as quickly as hoped. I knew the fine sea air on the Sussex coast would be just the thing to bring him back to health. Miss Dunnfield came to nurse her father, but I managed to coax her into leaving her duties for the afternoon, so she might take the air and enjoy a bit of the fair.'

'Welcome to Sussex, Miss Dunnfield. I'm sorry to hear of your father's indisposition and hope he improves quickly.'

'How could he not get better in this beautiful fresh air

and sunshine? We are both so grateful to Mr Lattimar for inviting us here.'

'Just so, just so,' the Squire said, nodding. 'Prettiest part of England, if I do say so. Sorry, but you must excuse me, it's time to evaluate the horses. So nice to have met you, Miss Dunnfield.'

'And you, sir,' she said, curtseying again as the Squire strode off.

Gesturing to the line of tethered cattle, Greg said, 'We raise several different breeds here, but the predominant one is the Sussex Red, of which these beasts are fine examples. The story goes that the breed is descended from the red Anglo Saxon cattle who roamed the forests of the High Weald at the time of Norman Conquest.'

'I know nothing of cattle, but they are a handsome colour and look very sturdy.'

'They've been bred for draft work, pulling wagons and timber trugs as well as ploughs. Are you fond of chickens?'

'Yes, especially stuffed with herbs and olives.'

Laughing, Greg gestured towards the penned poultry. 'The hens are another traditional Sussex breed.'

'It's a pretty bird, especially the white ones with silver feathers on neck and tail. I thought you said your principal estate, Entremer, farmed mostly sheep. You seem rather knowledgeable about cattle and poultry as well.'

Lattimar shrugged. 'To be a competent steward of the land, I must be familiar with the animals raised on all our properties.'

She shook her head, smiling. 'Somehow I can't believe Lord Vraux knows much about sheep, hens or cattle.'

'He doesn't,' Greg said, a bitter edge to his voice. 'Which is why I had so much to learn...and so much to restore after his utter neglect forced me to take over management of the Lattimar properties immediately after I left Oxford.'

'You resented it,' Charis observed, noting his tone.

'I resented it at first.' He laughed wryly. 'To see me now, walking fields in muddy boots, talking of hens and cattle and crops, you'd not believe I was once a rather dashing fellow. During university, in the company of my good friend Gifford, now married to my sister, I developed quite a rakish reputation. Until the estate manager at Entremer came to London, telling of an accident in one of the pit mines and begging for assistance. After barely listening to his account, Vraux gave him no assurance he intended to do anything about it. Desperate, the man sought me out. Shocked at the loss of life, I felt compelled to accompany him back to Northumberland.

'Once there, the manager showed me other urgent problems. One thing leading to another, I was pulled from my life of idle dissipation and spent the next six months at Entremer. Though by then the situation had improved enough that I could return to London, I found that lazing at my club, attending scandalous parties and pursuing ladies of questionable virtue had lost its appeal. There was still so much to be done at Entremer, and by this time, suspicious about the state of our other properties, I toured all of them. Most weren't in as bad a condition as Entremer, but they were all in need of attention, as well as a serious infusion of cash.

'I still resented that I had the responsibility thrust upon me without having been given adequate training. And that I'd had to take over the burden of management without the legal right to effect all changes I gradually came to see were needed.'

'Surely Lord Vraux has not contested any policy you recommended?'

'No. But the properties would be in an even better state now if I'd known more about the job when I began. After a few near disasters, I vowed to learn as much as I could about efficiently running an agricultural enterprise, so none of our tenants or properties ever suffered from neglect or bad management again. I regularly attend agricultural meetings, like the ones begun by Coke of Norfolk, read farm journals and try to keep up with the latest innovations in agriculture and animal husbandry. Which is how I learned about the need for rapeseed oil and the desirability of cultivating more of it.'

'You seem to have risen wonderfully to the challenges. And you do seem to enjoy it now.'

'Somewhat to my surprise, I do. I always knew I'd inherit the estate, but growing up, I never thought much about the responsibilities being the owner would entail. Certainly Vraux didn't give me any example to follow. Managing it all is rather like being a puppet master holding a number of strings in one's hand, moving one's fingers adroitly at just the right time so all continues moving forward without any becoming tangled. It's not as exciting as buying diamonds or discovering ancient artefacts, but there's satisfaction in knowing flocks are flourishing and all the land has been brought back into good heart as a direct result of one's efforts.'

'So there should be!' she said, impressed.

'Mr Lattimar, what do you think of the hens?'

Absorbed in their conversation, she hadn't noticed the farmer approach until he stood at Greg's elbow. 'Are those fine birds yours, Thwaite? Miss Dunnfield, let me introduce Mr Henry Thwaite, who manages one of Westdean's largest farms. Miss Dunnfield and her father are my guests as the manor.'

'Honoured, miss,' the farmer said, doffing his cap.

'Mr Thwaite is our local expert on poultry, the man to whom I go when there are any questions about feed, raising or breeding the birds.'

'Chicken Henry, they call me,' the man said with a grin. 'There's just something about them birds. I've loved working with them since I was a lad.'

'Has your bird taken the top prize?' Charis asked.

'Don't know. The Squire's not judged hens yet, but I'd be surprised if Annie here don't rate highly,' he said, pointing towards the white hen with silver feathers she'd found so attractive.

'I'll stand you an ale at the Jolly Farmer later if she wins,' Greg said, clapping the man on the shoulder.

'I'll hold you to that, Mr Lattimar,' Thwaite said, bowing before walking off.

They strolled over next to admire the draft horses, several other tenants coming up to greet Greg, to ask his advice about some ongoing project or to thank him for promising to come by with aid or supplies.

Their review of the judged animals completed, they left the pens and walked to the area where the Romani had set up their enclosure.

'I have a fine horse for the beautiful lady,' one of the men said as they approached. 'On her, you will ride like the wind.'

Charis looked more closely at the animal. She might know nothing about cattle, sheep or chickens, but she did know fine horseflesh. 'Does she have some Arabian blood in her?'

'Ah, so the pretty lady knows her horses! She's a spirited animal, Arabian and Irish. She'll be a fine mount for a lady.'

'I'm sure she would be. But I'm only a visitor here.'

'Tell your handsome Lordship to buy the horse for you, then,' the man coaxed, smiling. 'To ride when you visit.'

Turning to Greg, the Romani said, 'How could you not buy for this charming beauty anything she desires?'

'Perhaps another time,' Greg said dryly.

The man shrugged. 'Then you must at least allow the lovely lady to have her fortune told. Our women will reveal the secrets of her future. Which handsome lover will claim your hand, eh?' he asked, giving Charis a wink.

While Greg rolled his eyes, a laughing Charis let the horse trader lead them to a booth where several Romani ladies in colourful dress were engaged in reading palms.

'This is one endeavour that would very much find favour in the harem,' Charis murmured to Greg. 'The ladies love when fortune-tellers are brought in—predicting, of course, love, riches and happiness for anyone generous enough to cross the seer's palm with the appropriate coin.'

'Are you sure you want to waste your blunt?'

She wrinkled her nose at him. 'Don't be a spoilsport. It's all in good fun.'

She seated herself on the rough cane stool and held out her palm, which the woman took and examined closely. 'I see strength and firm purpose. But clouds on the horizon. There is a threat, which worries you and makes you sad.'

Raising her eyebrows, she exchanged a glance with Lattimar. An awareness of her father's illness?

'A great trial is coming, but happiness waits at the

end of it. Though it may come in a form the lady never expected.'

'I shall await it with anticipation,' Charis said solemnly, handing the woman a coin.

'And you, your worship, will you have your palm read?'

Greg shook his head. 'If bad fortune and trials await me, I'd rather not know in advance. Are you ready to brave the peddlers?' he asked Charis.

'Now that I'm assured of fortune to come, I could spend some of my upcoming windfall,' she said as they walked off.

'You won't need a windfall. Since their customers are generally farmers, labourers and clerks, none of their items are expensive.'

'I might find a bit of colourful ribbon Bayam Zehra would like, or a curiously carved trinket.'

'I imagine your friends and even your servants are used to fine jewels and trinkets of silver and gold. I'm afraid the items carried by the peddlers are not likely to impress them.'

'If I tell them they are special English good luck charms designed to ward off the Evil Eye, they will all be delighted.'

'Yes, you mentioned the ever-present concern about the Evil Eye.'

She nodded. 'Which is why they would be excited to receive new powerful tokens from lands beyond the sea.'

Speaking of the Evil Eye, she'd been receiving it from several of the maidens he'd introduced her to as they walked around the fair, Charis thought. While the Squire's younger, unmarried daughter had given her distinctly unfriendly looks, most of the feminine gazes were just envious. Other than the Squire, none of the local residents were of sufficient stature that their daughters would be considered eligible to marry the son of the rich baron who owned the largest estate in the area.

Lattimar, however, seemed oblivious to the notice he attracted from them, speaking with courtesy to all but not flirting with any, despite the encouragement given him by several of them, including the Squire's daughter.

Once or twice she'd overheard one whisper to a companion as they passed, 'Is she going to be the landlord's wife?'

The question elicited a little thrill, swiftly squelched. The lowliest farm labourer's daughter was more qualified for that role than she was.

Meanwhile, Lattimar stood patiently while she paid for her purchases, then said, 'Are you ready to test the landlady's stew?'

'That sounds delightful.'

'This way then, my lady.' He led her away from the enclosures and the bustle of men and women clustered around stalls, peddlers' carts and meat pasty vendors and back into the village. At the crossroads of the lanes leading to Seaford and Alfriston stood a half-timbered building with a painted sign of a farmer seated on a bench, smoking his pipe, a glass of ale in hand. 'Welcome to the Jolly Farmer.'

As they walked in, the proprietor came from behind the bar to greet them. 'Miss Dunnfield, may I present Michael Laughton,' Greg said. 'He and his wife Nan have run this establishment since they took it over from his parents, who were the proprietors when I was a boy. His mother, lovely lady that she was, always managed to have a bit of sticky bun saved for a hungry lad.'

'Welcome, Miss Dunnfield. Mr Lattimar told me yesterday that your father is a diplomat and you've lived mostly in foreign lands. I hope you enjoy your time in England.'

'Since coming to the Sussex coast, I have very much. I must confess I find London a bit grey and dark.'

'Aye, streets all tumbled over each other and way too many people. The countryside is much finer. Now, with the fair on and all, the missus made up an extra batch of beef stew. Shall I bring you both a bowl?'

'Yes, please, and a mug of ale for me,' Greg said.

As they took a seat at one of the tables, a large, smiling lady emerged from the kitchen and approached them, Lattimar rising to give her hug. 'Nan used to help Christopher and I beg sticky buns from Michael's mother, Betty,' Greg explained, making the woman blush by kissing her roundly on both cheeks.

'Mr Greg weren't above cajoling an extra sweet roll from Mrs Laughton, neither,' Nan said with a grin.

Greg sighed. 'The problem with coming back to a place where you grew up is that people never forget your youthful misdeeds. But I seldom needed to sneak. Old Mistress Laughton never could deny Nan anything—not even the hand of her precious son. Speaking of… How is your strapping boy?'

'Growing like a weed and into everything, though his big sister is hardly better. Good to see you, Mr Greg. And to meet you, miss,' she added, curtseying. 'Best get back to my stove, but I did want to say hello.'

A few minutes later, the landlord brought over steaming bowls of beef, onion and potato in a savoury broth, which Charis found surprisingly tasty despite its lack of spices. While they ate, several more tenants and villagers came over to greet Greg, ask a question, offer a compliment or issue an invitation to stop by their shop or farm. The victorious chicken's owner, Henry, dropped in to claim the promised mug of ale. Greg seemed to know all of them by name, and all seemed to hold him in affection and esteem.

Though the women who came in with their husbands inspected her dress, their menfolk gave her only a brief, respectful glance. She was sure she must look foreign to them, but as Lattimar's guest, she was treated with none of the innuendo that had made her forays into London society so distasteful.

They finished their meal, Lattimar speaking with several more people they encountered as they walked to the stable to collect their horses.

Once remounted, they headed back to Westdean Manor, Charis pensive as they rode away.

It was impossible to have spent the afternoon in his company and not come away impressed by his knowledge, the esteem in which he was held by villagers and tenants and his genuine interest and pleasure in dealing with them.

Though she'd tried to squelch such daydreams, lately, as they spent more time together and she discovered his appreciation for the beautiful objects in which her father traded, his interest in and openness to experiencing new things, she'd been tempted to try to entice him into a closer relationship. See if he might be beguiled into becoming her lover, husband and fellow wanderer.

With the knowledge he already had about fine objects, it would be easy to teach him to recognise the type of articles they sought for their clients. She believed he would enjoy the novelty and challenges of travelling in foreign lands, meeting citizens of different cultures who spoke diverse languages. He had a true gift for dealing with people.

And she knew the passion between them would be incomparable.

But after seeing him here, on his land, among the tenants and villagers, she realised what he'd deprecatingly referred to as a 'prosaic' and 'commonplace' life was in fact rich and full. As they rode away, the last vestiges of that gossamer daydream of a life together disintegrated like a fragile cobweb in the wind.

He belonged here like the rocks and hedges, the cattle grazing on the hills, the crops in the fields. He would be as lost and desolated to be ripped from this place as she felt marooned in England.

Despite how much she'd enjoyed the afternoon, as they rode back, a deep melancholy settled over her. Sadness at the death of a dream she hadn't known until this moment just how much she'd begun to cherish.

After they turned their horses over to the groom at the Westdean stables, Greg walked with her to the manor. 'Would you like to come with me at dusk and see the lighting of the bonfire? We won't stay long. I know after being gone all afternoon you will want to spend the evening with your father.'

She tried to rally herself to some enthusiasm. He was seeking to be a good host, and she should appreciate his efforts. 'Yes, I would like to see it. I've heard about the custom of midsummer bonfires from the Russian diplomats in Constantinople, but I've never witnessed one. Does the ancient tradition hold that the fire was to repel witches and evil spirits?'

Greg grinned. 'In England, it was to repel dragons.'

Charis laughed. 'I would certainly feel better knowing there are no dragons on the prowl.'

'Wear your warmest gown and bring an extra shawl. It may be chilly on the cliff heights once the sun goes down.'

So it was, just at dusk, Greg knocked at the door to her father's rooms, where she'd been keeping him company until dinner. 'I've come to claim your daughter, Mr Dunnfield,' he said. 'I promise to bring her back shortly and safely.'

'Yes, do let her go enjoy the spectacle. When you return, will you join us? I'm feeling much recovered tonight and have prevailed upon Charis to play for me again.'

'I've agreed, but for a shorter time, Father. I don't want you becoming over-tired again.'

'I shall humbly submit to your guidance,' Dunnfield said. 'Off with you, now! Thank you, Mr Lattimar, for persuading her to get out and see something of the countryside while we are your guests. Otherwise, I fear she would make herself a martyr, unwilling to leave my side.'

Charis felt a twinge of guilt at how eager she'd been to leave his side for Lattimar's. She'd make it up to him on their subsequent journeys, she promised herself.

'I'll get my pelisse and shawl and meet you downstairs.'

A few minutes later, sturdily garbed, she met Greg in the hallway and walked out with him.

'We won't ride this time. The nearest of the fires is only a short distance, and the horses can be spooked by the size of the conflagration.'

She nodded. 'Do all the local people come to the bonfire?'

'Yes. Men, women, children. All participate in the lighting, and some remain until dawn. There will be some singing and fiddlers for dancing, along with a good deal of drinking and merriment. Though I'll escort you back well before the revelry gets too out of hand.'

As they approached the crest of the hill, Charis saw the large pyramid of wood silhouetted against the darkening sky. As soon as the last ray of sun faded behind the western hills, several men with lighted brands walked forward, firing the tinder and hay underneath the structure of logs. The dry wood caught quickly, and soon the whole edifice was burning brightly.

Then the fiddle struck up, men and women claiming partners as a lively jig began.

'Dance with your pretty guest, Mr Lattimar,' said one of farmers he'd talked with at the inn.

'Go on, now, don't be shy,' another said, laughing, as both men pushed Greg towards her.

'I think we've been commanded to perform,' he murmured. 'Do you mind?'

'I don't know the steps,' she protested.

'It's mostly like a polka or mazurka. I imagine you've danced something similar at the Russian embassy in Constantinople. See?' He gestured towards several couples who'd already begun, laughing and whirling around by the firelight. 'Ready?'

'I suppose,' she said, blowing out a sigh. 'I'll try not to tread on your toes.'

He held out his hand and she took it—eager for that part of the dance, at any rate. But she found her trepidation unfounded. The bouncing, two-step moves of the jig were simple enough that she soon lost her hesitation.

Even better, like a waltz, the dance required Greg to put one hand on her shoulder and the other on her waist while he swung her round and round. As he looked down at her, smiling, tightening his grip as he whirled her past the other dancers, her melancholy faded and she threw herself into enjoying the rhythm of the lively fiddle and the clapping hands, the roar of the blazing fire, the warmth of his body pressed against hers.

When the tune ended, she was breathing hard. She looked up at Greg, the urge to kiss him welling up again, and saw the same desire mirrored in his eyes.

Abruptly he released her and stepped back. 'Thank heaven for a crowd full of chaperones,' he muttered.

'Yes. Something to hold one's foot to the narrow path, lest one might…slip.'

'All too easily. I'd better get you back. Your father is waiting, and we don't want to keep him up too late this time.'

The group protested their early departure, until Greg explained to those not already aware of her situation that her father, recovering from illness, hadn't wanted her to miss viewing the bonfire, but that she felt she must get back and resume tending him.

With well-wishes echoing in their ears, they headed back towards Westdean Manor, walking in silence as they listened to the sounds of music and clapping, the crackle and roar of the fire fading behind them.

'Will you join us in Father's room?' Charis asked as they arrived back at the house.

'If I'm not imposing.'

'I thought we already answered that question.'

'Then yes, I'd be delighted. Let me wash and change, and I'll meet you in your father's chamber.'

'Before you do, I have something for you—with his blessing.'

Beckoning him with a fingertip, she led him up the stairs to the floor where the bed chambers were located. 'Wait here for a minute.'

Raising his eyebrows in enquiry, he nonetheless nodded.

She sped into her own chamber, retrieved the folded parcel she'd made up and walked back, handing it to him.

'What's this?'

'Open it and see.'

So he did, removing the paper wrapping to discover full trousers and a richly embroidered damask robe. 'Wear these, if they please you. You can be entertained like a real pasha.'

'I should like to try that. Thank you for entrusting these to me.'

'I'll see you shortly, then.'

She watched him walk to his room, smiling.

How bittersweet the day had been! The delight of his company, but also the deeper insight she'd gained into the character of the man that had provided irrefutable evidence of the place where he belonged.

Leaving her with no recourse but to enjoy being part of his world for the short time she would have with him, making memories to treasure once she travelled back to her own sphere...fond remembrances of the only man who had ever tempted her to contemplate marriage and motherhood.

Chapter Sixteen

Ten days later, Greg rode back towards Westdean Manor in late afternoon, muddy and tired. He'd just finished helping shovel rock to complete the drainage improvement in Farmer Halton's eastern field, the last of the major projects he needed to supervise on the estate.

Claxen's cottage had been re-thatched and he'd concluded the consultations with farmers about herds and the progress of crops towards harvest. He'd spent a day each in Eastbourne and Brighton to explore marketing possibilities and then set up tentative agreements for the sale of the rapeseed oil that would be produced on Westdean land.

It was past time to make plans for his stopover in London and return to Entremer.

And yet he lingered, those plans not even begun. One, for the delight of Charis's company. Initially he'd been worried how he might keep her entertained when he needed to be gone all day working at the farms and knew her father would spend most of the time resting. He soon discovered she was quite self-sufficient, needing little tending. She was perfectly content, she reported to him in the evenings, occupying herself in the gardens, reading, writing to friends and suppliers or walking, with the beach still her favourite destination.

Their days at Westdean Manor had assumed a pleasant pattern. He would ride out early and spend most of the day supervising the ongoing projects in the farms, fields and the manufactory under construction. Then return in late afternoon, eagerly looking forward to sharing the evening with Charis and her father. After washing and changing out of muddy riding attire, he would dine, Charis eating with him on some nights, while on others she took her meal with her father in his rooms.

Though it seemed to him that Mr Dunnfield's colour was better and he had more energy when Greg visited him, he had not yet recovered enough to join them in the dining room. Or for that matter, to leave his chamber for anywhere in the house except the back terrace, where Jameson and his daughter helped him to spend the warmest, sunniest part of any day he felt well enough to be assisted down the stairs. But even those limited excursions resulted in him spending the following day or two in his room, recovering from the exertion.

Which led to Greg's other reason for hesitating to depart—concern for Charis. Initially exuberant about the possibility of her father's swift recovery, he knew she had begun to worry again when that improvement seemed to stall. Frustrated that he was powerless to do much else to promote her father's return to health, he tried in their evenings to amuse and divert her, plying her with questions about the stories behind the songs she sang and played, the cities in which she'd lived, and every detail of her travels. Not only did he find her answers—indeed, everything about her life—fascinating, for a time he had the pleasure of chasing from her lovely face the worried frown that all too often crept over her features.

Though to be fair, she probably diverted him much more than he amused her. Wearing the Ottoman garb borrowed from her father, lounging at his ease in a chair while her father reclined on his couch, listening to her sing, play or tell her stories...

Close his eyes, and he could hear the music of her voice, beguiling as a siren's. It needed only the long couch set against the wall padded with carpets and festooned with embroidered cushions, the fragrance of sandalwood burning in censors, to imagine himself a guest in her house in Constantinople.

Part of him wished he could wash his hands of all the duties that held him here, pack her up with her father and take her to the home that the plaintive longing in her voice told him she missed with every song she sang. There with her, in the gardens and the flower-filled terraces, beside the trickling fountains she'd so vividly described, he might remain for ever, bewitched by his own personal Scheherazade.

But his duties here couldn't be shirked. His fanciful daydream of being with her in the land of sultans, pashas and Effendis was only a phantom that disappeared each morning as he walked out in corduroys and riding boots to tend his farms. Whatever reality that dream possessed would be lived out here, in a small stone manor house on the Sussex coast, before vanishing for ever.

And so he lingered.

And wondered with anticipation what delights would be in store for him tonight.

* * *

After leaving his horse at the stable, before entering the manor, he walked by the back terrace, the place he often found her in the late afternoons if she was not in her father's room. His spirits lifting with that automatic rise of warmth and joy, he saw that she was indeed seated on the garden bench, bent over a book, reading. Looking, he thought, enchanting in her trousers, jacket and long robe, one foot dangling a heelless leather slipper.

'The story must be interesting.'

Looking up, she smiled at him and he felt his chest expand with happiness. 'One of Sir Walter Scott's. Very diverting. I read a few chapters aloud to Father, then left him to nap before dinner.' Her smile faded. 'If you don't mind, I'll dine with him in his room again tonight.'

There was worry—even a touch of fear in her tone—he thought as he walked over and studied her face. Which she averted, gazing out towards the distant sea.

'Is there anything I can do to help?' he asked quietly.

She didn't pretend to misunderstand. 'You've done so much already. Brought us to this wonderful place, arranged everything for his comfort. I had such hopes...' Her voice trailed away. 'But after his initial improvement, he seems...just suspended at the same level. Not getting worse, praise heaven. But not making much progress. One day he seems better and we sit here together, playing chess and carrying on animated conversations about what we need to acquire on our next journey and the friends we will visit. Then the next, he's too drained to leave his bed. He tries his best to cheer me, telling me how much better he feels. But I don't really see any evidence of that, and it...worries me.'

'I know.' Greg sat down on the bench beside her. Then,

unable to help himself, he pulled her into his arms. She huddled against him, her slender shoulders shaking with the sobs she was trying to suppress, as his heart twisted again in sympathy and frustration.

So he did the only thing he could…he held her as she battled her demons of fear and uncertainty, allowing himself to do no more than press a kiss on the top of her silken braids. He might forbid his hands to caress, but he couldn't stop his mind from imagining unplaiting the strands, running his fingers through their satin lushness, burying his face in her ebony tresses as he bound her against him.

Keeping desire under rigid control, he murmured, 'Summer has hardly begun. The good weather will continue for months yet. Just be patient and try not to worry so much. Is there anything else I could find for his diet? I could ride into Eastbourne or Brighton, check the markets, send to London if they don't have what you need.'

With a shuddering sigh, she pulled away. Regretting her loss, he let her go. 'You've been so wonderful. How can I ever thank you for all you have done?'

I'd do anything, everything *for you,* he thought, wishing he could remove all her burdens and just cherish her for life.

And with a jolt, he suddenly realised in that moment that he did indeed want to cherish her *for life.* That he had long ago lost his heart, probably from that first moment he'd stood on the doorstep in King Street, dumbstruck by a dark-eyed beauty in an outdated gown.

That certainty didn't produce as much panic as he would have expected, just resonated deep within him with the solid ring of truth. He *loved* Charis Dunnfield. Though he couldn't marry her, would never possess her and, but for father's lingering ill-health, would already have lost her.

All he could do for this woman he'd come to care for so deeply was to remove every obstacle he could to her father's recovery—so Dunnfield could take her away from him.

While Greg sat immobile, struck to the core by his sudden insight, Charis was shaking her head. 'I gathered up a large supply of the necessary spices before we left London. In any event, I doubt if you could obtain cardamom or turmeric in any of the local markets, though I thank you for the offer.'

Leaning back, she swiped at her eyes. 'Sorry. You've been toiling all day and have returned ready to rest and be refreshed, and I give you a gloomy face and gloomier thoughts. Will you join us after you dine? I promise to offer much more sparkling wit and conversation.'

'How about I share the meal with you and your father tonight? If you don't think that would be too much for him.'

He had the satisfaction of catching her by surprise, chasing away for the moment her expression of anxiety. 'Are you growing to like our spiced dishes?'

'I have to admit, I've beguiled Mrs Davenport into letting me taste some of the things she prepares for your father. I especially like the rice and chicken dish she's preparing for tonight. I already asked her to make enough for me too—much to the distress of my own cook! I had to take her aside, explain I wanted to honour our guest by partaking of his meal, strange and foreign though it was. Reassured, she promised to have a cold collation ready to send up to my chamber, so after doing my duty, I might look forward to some solid English fare.'

'What a thoughtful master you are!' she said, smiling. 'After going to so much trouble, including risking the rebellion of your cook, how could we not include you?'

Her smile fading, she lifted a finger and ran it slowly along his bottom lip. 'I wish... How I wish I might do more for *you*.'

He froze, even breathing suspended as every sense focused on the sizzling pleasure that barely perceptible touch rocketed to every part of his body. He gazed into her eyes...and understood exactly what unspoken gift she meant.

'As I would like to do...so much more for you,' he replied. 'Sadly, sweeting, doing that is not possible—for either of us.'

Then, before his control shattered completely, he rose and left her.

Fortunately, he had time to rein in his desire and recover from his shocking insights before he joined them for dinner, after which Charis demonstrated how to prepare Turkish coffee. Sipping the dark brew, thicker and much stronger than any coffee he'd previously tasted, he said, 'What other diversions occupy your evenings over this excellent coffee?'

'As you've already seen, playing and singing. But especially story telling. The ladies of the harem are always excited when the senior lady invites a *massaljhe* to entertain them.'

'Does she relate myths and fables? Or make up the stories as she goes along?'

'Some of both. There are many wonderful legends from the area around Constantinople.'

'Tell him about the Maiden's Tower,' Dunnfield suggested.

'Please do,' Greg said, eager to get her to forget the present and immerse herself in a story.

'If you insist. Very well. On a small rocky islet in the Bosporus, just off the Asian shores of Scutari, rises a dwelling called the Maiden's Tower. Legend says the tower was built by a sultan with a beloved daughter who, astrologers predicted, would be killed by a serpent before her eighteenth birthday. He clapped her up there, forbidding any guests, only to discover the fruit he brought her to celebrate her eighteenth birthday concealed an asp, which bit and killed her.'

'A sad story.'

'Aren't so many legends sad? Star-crossed lovers, men attempting the impossible who almost but do not quite succeed, basically good men tempted to bad deeds in hopes of a better end.'

'Romeo and Juliet, Macbeth and the like,' Greg agreed.

'Any there any legends connected to this place?' Charis asked. 'Other than the midsummer bonfires kindled to drive away dragons.'

A memory recurred, making Greg smile. 'No actual legends, but my brother Christopher and I once invented one to try to frighten our sisters. We told them they must not stir from their rooms at night, for the ghost of a smuggler who'd hidden in the cellar and been trapped and killed by revenue agents came out at midnight to prowl his prison, railing against his fate. My sister Pru took care to lock her door, but her twin, Temperance...'

Greg laughed. 'We should have known such a tale would only intrigue madcap Temper. She waited until everyone was abed, snuck off with one of Vraux's jewelled daggers and stationed herself in the cellar, ready to confront the spectre. Then condemned us loudly in the morning when nothing appeared, while her maid despaired over her muddy gown and ruined slippers. Mama just laughed and scolded us for deceiving her.'

Charis smiled but, when Greg glanced over at her father, he noted Dunnfield had started to nod. 'It's getting late. I'd better leave you and let us all get some rest.'

Rousing, her father protested, 'Not quite yet. You haven't played anything for us, Charis. I would have at least one song.'

'Very well. But only one.'

'"See What Love Has Done to Me"?' Greg suggested.

Their gazes met. She gave him a bittersweet smile.

'Father always enjoys that one, don't you, Father?'

'Always.'

A reminder of the wife Dunnfield had lost? Greg wondered.

Charis picked up the *tambur*, sat on her stool, bent her head and began.

'I am ablaze with love,' she sang. 'Feeling as if whirling like the wind, tumbling like dust over the plain, flowing like the raging rapids of a river...'

The lyrics continued. Greg felt the emotions as well. Did Charis's sad smile say she did, too?

Might they be two hearts attuned, driven apart by separate destinies?

It always came back to that. He couldn't wander with her. He couldn't ask her to stay. And he was only beginning to realise how bereft he would feel after she went away.

There was a special poignancy in listening to the

sweetness of her voice tonight, knowing that the lyrics might define them both.

He went to sleep with the song playing over and over in his head.

The next afternoon, driven by the imperative of knowing he could not put off his departure much longer, Greg finished his work early and headed back to Westdean Manor just after noon. With the day sunny and fair, he hoped to lure Charis to a picnic on the beach, if her father was doing well enough that she was comfortable leaving him.

She loved the beach, no other outing bringing as bright a smile to her face when she related to him in the evenings what she'd done during the day. He wanted to seize this chance to walk there with her, to let the sea air blow away, at least for a while, all the worries that plagued her, as she often said, and watch her joy as she gazed over the water and talked to him of the distant lands to which she hoped soon to travel.

Where he would be able to accompany her only in spirit.

He arrived at the stables to find a commotion of footmen and grooms milling about while a coachman in livery supervised pulling a large, elegant travelling carriage into the coach house, a crest he didn't recognise blazoned on the door panel.

'Who's arrived?' he asked a Westdean groom.

'Some great lady from London. Lady Sayleford, I think her coachman said. A relation of your guests, Master Greg,' the groom replied.

Greg frowned. As far as he knew, Lady Sayleford had sent no notice of her intention to pay them a visit, though she was certainly welcome, uncomfortable as it made him to remember her penetrating glance fixed on him. He'd just as soon not have her study him while in the same room as Charis, lest she suspect how he felt about her great-niece. Besides, if Charis had been notified of her relative's visit, she would certainly have warned him.

So she must not have known either.

What would bring a 'great lady from London' to the Sussex coast?

Although the season hadn't yet ended, she might be on her way to visit friends or family. She had relatives and connections all over England, and there were several aristocrats with fine properties in Sussex.

She'd come to visit her great-niece, not him, of course. Still, it would be prudent for him to slip up to his chamber and make himself presentable before he encountered her, as he certainly would at some point.

He'd nip below stairs before he went up, to make sure Cook had enough provisions to offer a dinner worthy of a great London lady and warn the housekeeper to have accommodations made ready for her and her staff.

Still, the idea of her arriving unannounced while visiting in the area didn't quite wash. With a feeling of unease in the pit of his stomach, Greg headed to the house.

Chapter Seventeen

Meanwhile, in the grand salon, Charis sat with Lady Sayleford sipping tea, having retreated there with her guest after that lady had surprised her by appearing at the door to her father's bed chamber. Not wanting to tire Father, their visitor said, she'd chatted with him for just a short while before following Charis to the salon to take their refreshment.

'I'm so pleased you diverted from your route to visit friends to stop by and see us,' Charis told her, refreshing her tea cup. 'Though I am surprised you decided to leave London. The season is still going on, isn't it?'

'It hasn't ended yet, no. They are able to conduct it without me, you know,' her aunt added with a smile.

'Ah, but a great deal of style and dash is missing if you are not there to participate.'

Lady Sayleford tapped her hand. 'Saucy chit! I'm always glad of an excuse to come to Eastbourne. Such delightful weather here! You've been most kind to keep me updated, but I wanted to see for myself how you and your father were getting on.' She paused for a moment. 'How would you assess his current condition?'

Charis sighed. 'I want to tell myself he's getting better. And he did improve shortly after we arrived. I wrote to you how worried I was when he collapsed in London. Lately, he's seemed much more like his former self, and his spirits are brighter. But…he just doesn't seem able to recover his old strength and stamina.'

Lady Sayleford nodded. 'After I got your note, I made some enquiries. In fact, I called on Viscount Hasterley, your father's older brother. He doesn't attend the social events of the season, but he does come to London to attend Parliament.'

'You spoke to the viscount? May I ask why?'

'Your account of your father's condition tickled a vague memory in the back of my consciousness. Something about the late Lady Hasterley, your father's mother. I talked with Hasterley, who confirmed what I suspected.'

Dread gathered in Charis's stomach. 'Confirmed what? Tell me at once, please.'

She hesitated a moment. 'You will find this news distressing, but I believe it is always best to know the truth and face it squarely. Lady Hasterley suffered in her later years from a weak heart. The condition displayed itself, her son said, in a lack of appetite, decreasing strength and fatigue suffered after the least exertion. Hasterley himself hasn't developed the malady, but his sister has begun showing signs. Apparently it runs in the family.'

Charis stared for a moment, trying to take in the enormity of what Grand-Tante had just related.

'You are trying to tell me my father is suffering from some sort of…congenital malady?' she said slowly. 'One from which he will not recover?'

'Sending you out of the room to fetch me a shawl while I visited your father was just a ruse to allow me to talk privately with him. He tried at first to evade my questions, but after I pointed out to him rather sharply that the state of his health has a direct and very serious effect on your future, he admitted that he hasn't felt truly well for years. That he has hidden the extent of his suffering from you, so as not to alarm you. But thinking back, don't you remember instances in the past where he has seemed ill, exhausted and needed an extended period of rest?'

Charis tried to force down the panic rising up so she could think. And after her great-aunt gave those thoughts direction, she found an alarming number of memories crowd in to confirm that suspicion.

'He did seem to have…more episodes of illness these last two years. We always laughed about it, passing it off as him having drunk some bad water or eaten something that had gone off, as the traders and sellers with whom we dealt would always offer tea or some kind of refreshment. It would have been most impolite to refuse, so he always accepted whatever was offered.'

'Were you also present at these meetings?'

'Quite often.'

'And were you, too, taken ill afterwards?'

'Not very often,' she said, stricken by the contrast. 'We always joked that I had a constitution made of Damascus steel.'

'Lady Hasterley lived for a good many years, despite her weakened condition. But Charis, my dear, I think you must face the strong possibility that your father will never fully recover. Certainly not recover enough to be able to travel and conduct his business in the way you have for the last decade. In case that prediction turns out to be correct, you need to take a hard look now and consider what you will do about your future.'

Charis felt ill, struggling to get her brain to function. Father...unable to travel? Their beloved business suspended?

Trying to make sense of it, she said, 'I suppose I could carry on without Father. I've done all the planning and provisioning the last few years anyway. I could travel on my own to meet our contacts. Admittedly, there are some men who would probably choose not to do business with a woman, but I already handle most of the trade in jewels with women of the harems, and many of the other dealers do know and trust me.'

'Charis, you cannot travel from England to Constantinople to Baghdad to Tehran on your own. Without being under the protection of your father, you would need to engage a considerable escort. The bald fact is that most of your father's wealth is tied up in his collections. I'm sorry, my dear, but you simply don't have the resources to hire the assistance you would need. Nor do I think your father would feel comfortable having you travel about on your own.'

'Are you suggesting I should just...give it all up?' she spat out bitterly, trying not to be angry with the messenger. Grand-Tante wouldn't have brought her such distressing news just to upset her. Clearly, she was concerned about Charis's safety and future.

Trying to quell her agitation and come up with some alternative, she said, 'I could return Father to London and try to sell our house in Constantinople to generate enough funds to allow me to travel safely.'

'It might take a long time to sell the house or as much of his collection as you could stand to part with to secure the necessary resources. I admit, you could return to Constantinople. You have your mother's friend there, I know. But both she and Ottoman society would be concerned and scandalised if you were to reside there, to say nothing of doing business from there, with no male relative to act as your protector. I would suggest another alternative. One safer and more easily achieved, though it would have to be acted upon much sooner.'

'So what do you suggest?' she asked, exasperated and wary.

'I propose that you return to London, where you have me to watch out for you. Be realistic, give up the slim chance that you might be able to carry on your father's business alone and make the best of life here in England. Find a good man to marry who will care for and protect you after I'm gone.'

Her addled brain hadn't had enough time to dredge up all the possible options—but this would never have been one of them.

'Stay in England...for ever?' she whispered, horrified. She wasn't sure which prospect was more anguishing—being trapped on this island permanently, or being trapped into marriage with an Englishman. Stripped of what few assets she had, no longer even considered an independent person under the law.

'Both prospects seem intolerable,' she said at last.

'If you remain in England and marry someone suitable, you'll be able to take proper care of your father. Your husband might even agree to escort you abroad from time to time, so you might visit your friends in Constantinople.'

Lady Sayleford's expression turned tender. 'Dear child, it pains me to distress you so. But I wouldn't be doing my duty to protect you if I didn't alert you to the danger of your situation and offer my best advice for safeguarding your future. Think long and carefully, my dear. I will return to London shortly and hope you will come back as well. There is still some time left in this season. I know you spent your few forays into society looking for a bride for Lattimar. I think you should come back and look instead, quite seriously, for a husband.'

Unable to make her shocked brain form words, Charis stared at her numbly.

Lady Sayleford sighed. 'Now, I have delivered my terrible news and will plague you no longer. There's no need to finish your tea. I doubt even your Damascus steel constitution has any stomach for it now. Lattimar's housekeeper will show me to a room where I can rest for an hour or so, and then I will be off to my friends in Eastbourne.'

Lady Sayleford leaned over to kiss Charis on the forehead. 'Things are not as dire as you may now think. I know you were treated with vulgar speculation when you entered society, but I promise—with you seriously looking for a mate, I will monitor events much more closely. London contains many more eligible gentlemen than you have yet met who could be charmed by such a well-travelled, lovely, accomplished bride.'

Her great-aunt stood, Charis rising as well, her body automatically following the rituals of courtesy. 'I do appreciate you telling me what you learned from Lord Hasterley, unpalatable as it is. I… I must walk, so I can wrap my mind around the news and think about my options. I don't like your solution at all, but I promise to consider it carefully. Thank you for making me aware of the reality of my situation.'

'I am so sorry, my dear,' Lady Sayleford said, her compassionate gaze following her as Charis hurried from the room.

She felt nauseated, her heart pounding in her chest, hardly able to breathe, as if the manor walls were closing in around her. She needed to confront Father and confirm what Lady Sayleford had told her. Though her great-aunt had no reason to lie to her about what they'd discussed.

Still, she must have a frank conversation with him about their future. She just couldn't face it right now.

She had to get outside, she thought, clawing at a throat that didn't seem to be able to pull in enough air. Go to a place where she could breathe and think.

Hard as it was going to be to think clearly with the agony of disbelief and anguish burning in her chest.

A few minutes later, washed and dressed in more formal attire, Greg was coming down the stairs when he met Lady Sayleford coming up them, escorted by his housekeeper. They both halted, exchanging bows and curtseys.

'Thank you, Mrs Jennings,' Lady Sayleford said. 'Mr Lattimar can show me to the blue bedchamber.'

'Yes, my lady,' the housekeeper said, dropping a curtsey. Looking grateful to escape the countess's intimidating presence, Mrs Jennings hurried back down the stairs.

'Welcome to Westdean Manor, Lady Sayleford,' Greg said. 'Kind of you to pay us a visit. I take it you've already seen the Dunnfields, and wish to rest before dinner?'

'I'm afraid the visit hasn't been kind, although it was essential. Yes, I've spoken to Charis. I fear I had to deliver some rather distressing news. I'll let her tell you as much of it as she wishes when you see her later.'

Immediately, worry for her consumed him. 'Where did you leave her? I'll seek her out at once. That is, after I escort you to your chamber,' he added, belatedly remembering he couldn't just run off and abandon a guest in the middle of the stairway. 'I hope you can stay for some time. I'm sure Miss Dunnfield and her father would enjoy your company. Cook is already arranging dinner for tonight.'

Lady Sayleford shook her head. 'I'm afraid I can't stay. I've let your housekeeper know I will be departing as soon as I've rested. I'm promised to a friend in Eastbourne tonight in any event, and Charis...will not feel like entertaining me, I am certain.'

Charis not wanting to be with her beloved Grand-Tante? Had it been anyone else, Greg would have discounted the remark, but Lady Sayleford was not one to make such a comment lightly, especially about the girl of whom she was so fond. Still, he shook his head. 'That I could not believe.'

Looking up at him, she studied his face. 'I trust you will know better than I what to do to help her.'

Wondering what dire calamity could have happened, he said, 'I will do everything in my power.'

'You have a great fondness for her, do you not?'

Greg swallowed hard, not sure how much that famously prescient lady was able to read in his face. 'I do,' he replied, limiting it to that.

'Then see that you truly do all in your power. She was going for a walk, she told me.'

'I'll find her.'

She put a hand on his arm. 'Be gentle with her. She's had a shock.'

So impatient was he to seek out Charis, he almost

brushed Lady Sayleford's hand off his sleeve. Instead, he made himself walk her to the door of her bed chamber. 'If I don't see you again before you leave, have a safe journey. I promise you, I will take care of Miss Dunnfield.'

She studied him for a minute. 'See that you do.' Then she walked into the bed chamber and closed the door.

Greg set off down the stairs at a run. If Charis was upset and had gone outside to walk, he knew where she would be.

A short time later, panting from having raced all the way, Greg started down the rocky path to the beach. After spying Charis in the distance, he picked up his pace, several times skidding and almost falling, so impatient was he to reach her and discover the reason for her distress. Then do whatever was necessary to alleviate it.

Her great-aunt must have surprised her, for as he drew closer he realised she was still garbed in her Ottoman dress, something she normally wore only in the house or the walled garden. She was walking in the opposite direction from the path he'd just descended, and with the whistle of the wind and sound of the waves unfolding on the beach, didn't hear him approach.

Not wanting to startle her, as he drew near, he called out, 'Charis! It's Greg. Lady Sayleford told me you'd gone walking after receiving some…upsetting news. What can I do to help?'

Even forewarned, the deathly pallor of her face and the absolute desolation in her eyes alarmed him. Barely able to keep himself from hauling her into his arms, consumed with the need to protect her from whatever threatened, he added, 'I don't want to pry. Only tell me if you choose. But I would do whatever I could to help.'

'There's nothing you can do,' she said, not even glancing at him, her voice lifeless. 'Nothing anyone can do. I'm still mulling over how I might make it work. But Grand-Tante was right, as of course I knew in my heart she was, even as I resisted what she was advising me. Everything has changed, and it will never be the same again.'

'Can you at least tell me what's gone wrong?' He took her hand, which thankfully she didn't pull away, and found it cold, despite the warmth of the sun. 'You left without a shawl and you're cold. Come here now, out of the wind.'

Listless, she let him lead her behind an irregular wall of large rocks at the bend of the cove, a sheltered spot where he and his siblings used to go climbing when he was a boy. 'Sit here,' he said, ripping off his coat to lay it on one of the rocks, then chaffing her cold hands. 'Tell me, please. You're alarming me.'

She shook her head tiredly. 'Sorry, I don't mean to. My mind is still racing, everything is so muddled.'

'Lady Sayleford said the news was terrible.' A sudden thought occurred. 'It wasn't… It's not bad news about your dear friend, Bayam Zehra, is it?'

She frowned for a moment, as if those words had no meaning, before comprehension dawned. 'No, nothing to do with Bayam. So far as I'm aware, she is in perfect health.'

'Someone in your Constantinople household, then? I know how fond you are of all of them, they being more like friends than servants.'

She shook her head. 'The news wasn't about anything in Constantinople. The trouble is much closer to home. Lady Sayleford told me that when I wrote to her about Father's collapse, it triggered a vague memory. She sought out father's elder brother, who confirmed what she remembered—that their mother, the late Lady Hasterley, suffered from a heart ailment that saw her confined to her house and nearly bedridden for the last years of her life. A condition that one of Father's sisters now suffers. Lady Sayleford believes that same condition is what is afflicting Father. A condition from which he will never truly recover.'

Angry with the countess for upsetting Charis, Greg demanded, 'Did she uncover any proof before coming to distress you with such news—some vague "condition of the heart" suffered by a lady whom no one can now question? How could she be sure?'

'After sending me out of the room on an errand, she talked with Father. She persuaded him to admit that he hasn't felt truly well for years. That he took elaborate pains to hide from me how ill he was. Now that she set me to thinking back on it, I can see the signs were all there. The extended time we had to spend at the sharif's encampment two summers ago, for instance.'

'When you had to talk the sharif out of marrying you?'

That earned him a brief smile. 'Yes. There were a number of other times he fell ill and needed to rest for several days before we went on, which he always passed off as the result of eating or drinking something that didn't agree with him. But the symptoms...lack of appetite, slowly decreasing strength, fatigue after just a short exertion...they were all there, exactly as Lady Sayleford described about his mother.'

She shook her head sadly. 'All that time, I thought the problem was with his stomach. When apparently, it was his heart.'

'Can you not return to London and consult doctors? See if perhaps now they have discovered some remedy?'

'Consult English doctors?' She gave a contemptuous huff. 'Who would recommend bleeding or ingesting noxious substances? I fear their remedies would be worse than the disease. Grand-Tante says despite the illness, he is likely to live for years. But he will probably never be well enough to travel again.'

'I see.' Greg could think of nothing to add. Their wandering business, meeting new people, learning their stories, offering sellers the coin that would make their lives easier while the treasures they parted with would delight appreciative connoisseurs... She lived for that. How was she to exist without it?

'I've been trying to work out how I could carry on alone. But Grand-Tante reminded me that Father doesn't have much in the way of cash. The small sum he inherited upon the death of his mother and what he earned in India was invested in his collection, as are most of the profits not needed to fund subsequent trips.

'If I did try to carry on, as a lone woman travelling alone I would have to hire a larger escort than we usually have. I could try to sell the house in Constantinople to raise the funds, although I would then have to rent accommodations there. Though I handle the trading with ladies wanting to sell jewels, all our other business contacts are Father's. Most know me and are courteous, but I don't know if they would deal with me as they did with him.

'In the same way, collectors have accepted me as my father's assistant, but would they trust a woman to handle their purchases? They might well be right not to trust me. In Ottoman lands as well as here, it's not considered suitable for a woman to carry out activities normally performed by men.'

She sighed. 'I've done nothing but run all the possibilities through my head since I left the house but, much as I want to continue the business, the chances are very good that I could not run it successfully. Not to mention that if I were to try, I would have to leave Father on his own here in England for months at a time.'

Greg stood silently, nearly as overwhelmed by the shocking news as Charis. Until one bit of what she'd recounted recurred to him.

'You mentioned that Lady Sayleford had a suggestion,' he said, feeling a bit better. That lady's wisdom was legendary.

'Just one.' Charis laughed mirthlessly. 'Resign myself to my fate, give up the impractical idea of continuing the business, and settle in England. Re-enter society and find a husband to take care of me.'

Find a husband... Excitement, hesitation, concern, compassion and anxiety a roiling mix in his belly, Greg said slowly, 'Are you inclined to do that?'

'No... Yes... Oh, I don't know! One might describe my time in society as sensational, but one could not term it successful.'

'Not all the gentlemen you encountered were clueless dolts. Although I admit, many were.' Much as he hated to remind her, Greg made himself say, 'There was at least one you might consider. Lord Rollesbury seemed very interested, and you certainly had a lot in common.'

'Who?' she asked with a frown.

Relieved the man he'd thought would appeal most to her had made so little impression, he said, 'Rollesbury. The widowed diplomat.'

'Ah, him.' She made a little round motion with her hand. 'Yes, I suppose Grand-Tante might consider him suitable. He would take me abroad, but his specialty isn't in the lands I love. Besides, were I to marry him, it would be worse than carrying on the business. I could be away from Father for years, rather than months. If he truly has only a limited time left, I don't want to miss most of it.'

'Have you talked with your father about all this?'

She shook her head. 'Not yet. He's bound to still be distressed after Grand-Tante made him reveal what he has hidden for so long. Worried about what will happen to me, guilty that he waited so long to let me know the truth. He knows how much I've loved the life we shared—which, I'm sure, is why he hasn't been able to bring himself to tell me that it might have to end. I don't want to cause him further anguish. So I wanted to decide what I should do and present him the solution with a cheerful face, not weeping and repining over what we've lost.'

It was probably premature to make her an offer, maybe ill-advised when she'd just been dealt such a life-changing blow and was struggling to decide what to do about it. Nevertheless, Greg felt compelled to speak.

Almost dizzy from emotion swinging wildly from anxiety to hope, he said, 'If you truly must give up travelling and can resign yourself to the prospect of marriage, marry me. Surely you've guessed how I feel about you? I suppose I've loved you for weeks, though I have only fully realised how much during the time we've spent at Westdean. It would be the joy of my heart to make you my wife. I would do everything in my power to make the life in England you do not want as happy for you as I could.'

'You would truly offer for me?' Her shocked eyes rising to meet his gaze, she gave him a wan smile. 'My dear Greg. Truly the only man in England I could imagine marrying.'

'Then...you will marry me?'

Sighing, she opened her lips, then shut them abruptly, her eyes widening. 'But no, I cannot! I am not at all the wife you need! I won't let my problems ruin your chance to re-establish your family and redeem your lady mother.'

'It's different now. It was one thing to be set on finding a respectable bride to redeem the family's reputation when I had no strong feelings about anyone. But Mama would be the first to tell me to follow my heart, if I think that road gives me the best chance for happiness. She, who was forced to marry for the sake of her family and unable to marry the man she loved, would never forgive herself if I gave up the one *I* loved to try to buy her respectability. Her feelings are the only ones that concern me; otherwise, what society thinks of our family matters not at all.

'If the choice is between society's approval or winning your hand?' He shook his head. 'Always and for ever, I would choose you.'

She studied his face while his heartbeat thundered in his ears and he held on with both hands to the joy trying to soar within him, lest he exult prematurely. 'Are you sure?' she said at last.

'Absolutely sure. I've never been more sure of anything in my life.'

Sighing, she gave him a sad smile. 'Then yes, Gregory Lattimar, I will marry you.'

Releasing that pent-up joy in a wild rush, he ached to kiss her to seal their bargain, giving her a foretaste of the passion with which he would worship her for the rest of their lives. But her eyes were still blank, her face shocked and drained. He might be exulting, but she was numb and hurting, reeling from the loss of everything she'd expected her life would be.

He took both her hands instead. 'Come along to the manor and warm up by the fire. We'll talk more about this later.'

'Tomorrow? I think I will go directly to my own chamber and have Jane tell father I'm feeling tired. That may increase his anxiety for the moment, but I don't want to speak with him until I am totally sure of my plans. When I can address him calmly and cheerfully.'

Greg offered her his arm, and silently she took it. As he walked back, his effervescent euphoria began to dissipate, overshadowed by worry and a deepening concern.

He'd never imagined that when he finally made an offer of marriage, he'd receive so tepid a reply. Was he taking advantage of her dire circumstances to press her into something she'd regret? Was marrying him really the best solution to her dilemma?

They truly did need to discuss this further.

But looking down at her weary, shattered face, tenderness curled around his heart. She'd just watched the life she'd always wanted explode into tiny pieces all around her. He only knew he couldn't press her more today.

Chapter Eighteen

Greg passed a long, sleepless night. At first, he lay wide awake in his bed, mesmerised by thoughts of lying here with Charis in his arms. Able to release, finally, all the aching passion he'd had to restrain for so long. Taking long, leisurely hours to caress every inch of her body, discover where touches, kisses, nibbles gave her the most pleasure. He'd not have to proceed cautiously; unlike an English virgin, who might know nothing at all about the business of love-making, she had been raised where a man and wife's physical enjoyment of each other was considered normal and natural.

A titillating thought, but he was just as excited at the prospect of sharing life outside the bed chamber. It wouldn't be like touring eastern lands, but he'd take her to visit all the Lattimar properties, from vast open fields of Entremer to the small valley manor in Devon, along with several other larger properties brought into the family over generations through purchase or inheritance. They could visit Alex and Jocelyn at Edge Hall, maybe even take a railway journey with Crispin and his engineer wife, Marcella.

At each property, he would introduce her to neighbours, like the Squire, and farmers of expertise like Chicken Henry. Let her meet and chat with other landowners and farmers at the annual agricultural meetings. Introduce her to the hefted sheep at Entremer, that passed the knowledge of their territory from generation to generation without the need of sheep dogs to direct them. Interested as she was in everything, he knew he could awaken her curiosity to explore all things English and agricultural.

In the evenings, he'd encourage her to share more of her songs and stories. Both of them in Ottoman garb, lounging by the fire, drunk on warmth and pleasure.

But after the initial euphoria of envisioning her as his wife, doubts began to creep back. The most unanswerable was the recognition that it hadn't been fair to spring his offer on her virtually out of the blue. Even though after hearing Lady Sayleford's advice, the words virtually burst out of his impetuous heart, the need to express them too strong to be able to keep silent. It was too soon for her to make so important a decision, still in shock from the abrupt upheaval in her life.

At the very least, though he detested the idea, he should let her return to society under Lady Sayleford's more scrupulous sponsorship and be presented to other men. She'd not given a thought to choosing a husband before, but now the quest would be serious. With time to meet other gentlemen and consider them carefully, she might find someone she would prefer to him.

Though he was absolutely convinced she would never find another man who would treasure her or love her more than he did. The very idea of other men ogling her, sizing her up as a potential wife, made him want to wall her up in Westdean Manor like the sultan's daughter in the Maiden's Tower and never let her go.

But she couldn't be coerced and shouldn't be forced. If she did marry him, he wanted it to be her own choice, freely made after considering all possibilities, chosen because she was convinced marrying him would make her happy.

Which was the heart of the matter in every way. *Could he make her happy?* Or, despite his best efforts, would she always pine for the life she'd lost? Perhaps later, resent or even hate him for wedding her, feeling he'd forced her into taking that step before she'd had time to fully explore the feasibility of other options, such as selling the Constantinople house to maintain her father's business?

The thought of making her unhappy was even more intolerable than the possibility that she might come to resent him.

What did he think made her most happy?

When he considered the answer to that question, his spirits sank even lower. Touring properties in misty, rainy England would be a far cry from her jaunts skirting the edges of blazing deserts, sharing mint tea in the tents of sharifs and thick, bitter coffee in the glittering harems of great ladies. He knew she cared for him, but did she care enough to make up for losing the exotic people, scenery, cities and activities of her former life?

In the depths of the night, another possibility occurred. He liked it only marginally better than sending her off to the Marriage Mart to shop for potential husbands, but instinctively he felt it might offer the best chance of letting her retain what she loved most about life with her father.

In any event, he must offer up that option and gauge

her reaction. If she truly wanted to marry him, she'd reject it. And if it tempted her...then it would probably be better that she did not marry him after all.

Knowing he would get no sleep until after he talked with her again, he got up, threw on some clothes and went out to walk along the moonlit beach.

Greg gave Charis until after mid-morning of the following day, when he could stand the waiting no longer. He sent a note up to her with Jane, asking if she would meet him for a walk along the beach. To his relief, desperate for a resolution to stop his ragged nerves swinging from excitement to hope to resignation and back, she sent back a reply saying she would meet him on the back terrace.

He rushed there to meet her, arriving first. She arrived a few minutes later, wearing an English walking dress, bonnet and pelisse. A bonnet shadowed tired eyes that, he thought, said she had got as little rest through the long night as he had.

He held up a hand as she walked onto the terrace, motioning her to silence. 'Let's go to the beach before we begin the conversation.'

Nodding assent, she followed him out. Neither, he noted with a stab of anxiety, holding out a hand to clasp his arm or asking him to offer it. Vanished was the heady sense of attraction that had always hummed between them. The woman walking at his side was as shuttered and withdrawn as if already imprisoned behind the walls of the Maiden's Tower.

To his relief, for he was aching to touch her, when they reached the steep beach path, she reached out—her motion tentative, as if she wasn't sure, with the unsettled state between them, whether she should ask for assistance or not. Gratefully he took it, guiding her down the pathway, making sure not to alarm her by crowding in to take whatever familiarities she might think he expected from a woman who had last night agreed to become his wife.

The sky was cloudy today, the wind stronger, the breakers larger, crashing against the rocks beneath the cliffs or rolling onto the shore in a volley of mist and spray.

'Let's sit on the rocks where we talked yesterday, where it's quieter,' he said over the rush of wind and unfolding of the breakers.

She nodded, then followed him into the sheltered spot. 'You don't need to sacrifice your coat today,' she told him, the first bit of humour she'd attempted since Lady Sayleford's arrival with her shocking news. 'I wore my warmest walking dress.'

She seated herself on the rock, letting him perch beside her. 'So, what was it that you wanted to discuss?'

'You may rightly chide me for being inconstant, but I want to withdraw my offer of marriage—temporarily, at any rate. I'm sure it was Lady Sayleford's intention to have you return to society and meet more gentlemen, so you had a broader acquaintance from among whom to choose a husband. It's not really fair for me to snatch you away before you've had a chance to do that.'

'You really think I'd find someone who suited me better? Or are you just regretting having made a hasty offer?' she asked, her neutral tone giving him no real clue to how she felt. Although she hadn't, he thought ruefully, gasped in alarm or protested the withdrawal of his proposal.

'I don't know,' he said frankly. 'I don't think you will

find anyone who would love you more. But it takes two hearts united to create real happiness.'

Tears glimmering in her eyes, she clutched his hand, the first sign of affection she'd given him—though the trembling of her fingers indicated how shaky and uncertain she was still feeling. 'I will do so if you and Lady Sayleford think it wise, but if I must marry, I don't think I could find an Englishman who would understand and appreciate me more than you. Or one for whom I feel more affection.'

It was hardly a passionate declaration, Greg thought, her lack of enthusiasm painful. Rather sure he now knew how this conversation would end, he made himself press on.

'I'm honoured that you think I understand and appreciate you. I hope I do. And since last night, I've been trying to think of a different solution to your dilemma which might please you more than being forced to marry.' *Much as I might rejoice at that solution*, he added silently.

Her listlessness fading, she looked up sharply at him. 'A different solution?' She attempted a smile. 'You would spend some of Vraux's assets to fund my continuing Father's business?'

'That would be one possibility, but that wouldn't answer the problem of how—or whether—your father's contacts would be willing to continue trading with you. A daughter assisting her father is one thing. A woman working on her own is quite another. What I'm suggesting, though, would overcome that problem, as well as the ones of funding and escort.'

'And you are suggesting…?' She watched him avidly, the tiny spark of enthusiasm generated by his initial comment now grown to real interest. Which pretty much answered the question about whether or not she truly wanted to marry him.

Forcing down the pain of that realisation, he continued, 'I think you spoke with Mama about the business run by my sister Pru and her husband Johnnie. It's the same sort of trading enterprise you and your father have operated but, having been posted with the army in India, Johnnie's expertise is in the lands farther east. Whereas you and your father have done most of your trading in Armenia, Persia, Mesopotamia and the Levant.

'If you were to join forces, with your experience dealing with the ladies of the harem, expertise in jewels and your father's contacts in the areas he has traded—he could give Johnnie letters of introduction to the dealers he recommends—you could combine your strengths. Expand the trading empire from India to Constantinople and all the areas in between, making it a larger and even more successful enterprise than the one your father established.

'It would allow you to continue travelling, visiting the cities, harems and friends you love, and applying the expertise you've gained working with your father to continue turning a seller's treasures into the money they need while finding new owners who will appreciate the objects as much as their original owners.'

She nodded, her eyes even brighter now as he continued, 'Your father would remain in England, of course, but you could visit him between each journey, regaling him with stories of your travels, which would be certain to entertain him. Even skip one or two trips if you wished to spend more time with him. He would probably feel much better if he felt his ill health had not forced you to accept an alternative you've always resisted. That you had found instead the means to continue the sort of life you've shared with him.

'By the way, he's welcome to continue living at Westdean for as long as he likes. I promise to check on him frequently. I've become quite fond of him, you know. So…what do you think?'

An expression of wonder on her face, she wiped tears from the corners of her eyes. 'You would do that for me?' she whispered.

'Of course. We said we would look at all the possibilities for your future today and choose the best one, didn't we?'

'You think your brother-in-law and sister would agree?'

'I don't see why they wouldn't. Pru is a sweetheart, Johnnie a fine fellow. Also very astute. He'll realise in an instant what an asset it would be to have a partner fluent in Armenian, Persian, Greek…' He looked up.

'Italian, Arabic and several Baltic languages,' she supplied.

'All those languages, along with a network of traders with proven records of providing exceptional goods to add to the sources he already has. You're a seasoned traveller, too, who has no need to be coddled or watched over. You'd be a full, contributing partner who offers only advantages. I can't see why it wouldn't be an excellent arrangement for you both. The only drawback is that you'd not have your father with you.'

She sat silently for a long moment, obviously mulling over all that he'd said. 'You would release me from my promise, set me up as a trading partner, and let me go? Even though, much as I hate the thought, you cannot but help feeling hurt that I would prefer continuing life as I have always known it to accepting your hand?'

'It...stings,' he admitted. He wasn't about to tell her the extent of the devastation he felt, the brief interlude of euphoria he'd spent dreaming she might be his making the idea of losing her now even more bitter. 'Nothing would hurt more than rushing you into a marriage you later regretted. Or even worse, know that by selfishly claiming what made me happy, I'd made you *un*happy.'

He touched her soft cheek. 'I never want to see those eyes dimmed by tears. When I meet you in the future, I want to see the same joy, exuberance and delight in life I've seen in you every day until Lady Sayleford's arrival. Knowing you were happy would make me happy, too. So...would you like to explore that option?'

'I would, but...'

He held up a hand. 'No repining or apologising. How can I not feel satisfied at knowing I can offer you your heart's desire?'

'Let me mull this over a while longer. I must go and see Father soon, and I want to have firm plans in mind by the time I see him.'

Greg nodded. 'I'll leave you here to think. Let me know when you've decided.' In the meantime, he'd start writing a letter to Johnnie and Pru, he thought. Since he felt the chances of her deciding to remain in England and marry him instead of taking up her wandering life again were next to zero.

It was hard to turn and leave her sitting on the rocks, gazing into the distance as she contemplated her future. But he'd better get used to it. Since he was by now pretty sure the best way to express the love he felt would be to walk away and leave her free…

Tramping through the ashes of his brief, brilliant dreams, he headed back to Westdean Manor.

Chapter Nineteen

Sitting on the rock, staring out to sea, Charis hugged
herself—as if to contain all the ragged emotions that had
pulled at her over the last twenty-four hours until she felt
the core of her must unravel like a plucked string on the
hem of a garment.

Disbelief, concern, horror at learning what might be
responsible for her father's inability to recover his health.
Grief at the idea that they would lose the business that
had meant so much to them both. Anger and frustration
that continuing it on her own would be difficult, if not
impossible. Resistance, then sadness and dull resignation
at the idea that she might be forced to marry and remain
for ever in England.

Shock when Greg Lattimar had offered for her hand.

Although she wasn't completely shocked. They had
both danced around a heady mutual attraction since the
first moment they'd met. She knew he desired her as she
desired him. One thing about which she was certain was
that the passion they shared was incomparable.

But marriage?

She'd spoken truly when she'd told him he was the

only man she had ever contemplated wedding. But being tempted to marry him didn't mean that all her objections to marriage had suddenly disappeared. Lack of independence. Lack of independent income. Imprisonment in cold, cloudy, rainy England for the rest of her days. Worst of all, the possibility of losing someone whom she'd allowed to become the centre of her universe.

She'd deliberately held her emotions under tight control, freely acknowledging her desire but doing all she could not to fall in love with Gregory Lattimar. Troubled, uncertain, on the one hand, the drive to get away consumed her. On the other, the wonder of what they'd shared tempted her to stay and marry him.

But if that turned out to be a mistake, in England there would be no remedy. She knew she'd wounded him by not enthusiastically accepting his proposal, would wound him further by leaving, and that knowledge tore at her heart. But better to leave him as a grieving friend than ruin his life as an unhappy wife.

She'd already made him unhappy today. She'd read the hurt on his face when she hadn't immediately rejected the idea of letting him withdraw his offer. An even deeper hurt when she hadn't been able to conceal her enthusiasm for the idea of taking up trading again.

She hadn't wanted to hurt him. Regretted she'd let him get close enough for her to be able to hurt him. If she left him, he would grieve, but it wouldn't be the horrible grief her father had suffered when he'd lost her mother. She would grieve, too, for being naïve enough to think she could refuse his offer of marriage and recover the easy, teasing, sensually intense friendship they had been sharing.

The price of salvaging the life she loved would be the loss of closeness with Lattimar.

If she did take up trading, he'd pledged to watch out for her father, so she would probably see him again—and how could she ever adequately thank him for the care and concern he'd shown for her beloved parent? But when she met him again after her travels, he might well be married.

Silly, when she was so conflicted about accepting his offer, to feel unhappy about the idea of his wedding another.

If he hadn't already married by the time she got back, perhaps she could re-join society and continue the search for a wife worthy of him. She certainly hadn't found anyone yet who even came close to deserving such an honour.

It was a stark choice, and she need to make it right now. Pick up the mantle of the trading world she so loved…or accept Gregory Lattimar's proposal with its potential for heartache if she couldn't reconcile herself to life in England, making them both miserable. Or the deeper heartache of letting go her caution, opening her heart to him and losing him as her father had lost her mother.

One was clearly the easier, safer choice. She'd just have to steel herself to inform him.

He was strong, brave and fine. In time, he would find someone else to help heal the hurt she'd done him. Someone much better suited than she was to become the wife of an English country gentleman.

Now she must go and speak with her father.

Once her decision was made, and she confirmed her choice with Gregory and discussed it with her father, events moved quickly. Greg dispatched a letter to his sister, secured her father's agreement to remain at West-dean Manor indefinitely and informed them he probably wouldn't be at the manor very often over the next several days, as he needed to finish up the last of the work on the farms and factory so he could return to London.

Still, Charis listened for his return, sometimes not hearing his step on the stairs until late at night. He didn't eat in the dining room. He didn't visit her father's room to listen to her sing and play. He didn't seek her out on the back terrace or walking on the beach.

But what had she expected? Despite hurting and disappointing him, he had put her happiness above his own and done all he could to arrange a future more to her liking. Even he was not saint enough to want to spend time with a woman for whom he'd declared his love—and who had then rejected him.

Her heart ached that she had been forced to turn him down. But she saw no other safe option. So it was just as well that he avoided her before he left.

Like the sudden, unexpected end of her travelling life with her father, the end of her idyll with Greg at West-dean had been abrupt and unforeseen.

Despite her choosing a different life, she was too honest not to admit she mourned losing the closeness they had shared. A closeness they were unlikely ever to recapture.

Two nights later, in the dark of a star-spangled evening, Charis sat out on the back terrace. Greg was in the house somewhere, she knew, having heard him come in an hour or so ago. Peering down in the flickering light of the lantern she'd brought outside, she read again the note from him that Jane had delivered this morning.

Everything was in readiness for her to meet with Pru and Johnnie Trethwell as soon as she arrived in London, he'd written. Lady Vraux would be delighted to host the meeting, perform introductions and do whatever was necessary to help them launch their new coalition.

He would be leaving Westdean in two days' time and would stop by her father's room after dinner tomorrow to say his goodbyes.

She'd known he would be leaving, but having a note in hand pinpointing the date made it somehow final, stirring an odd mix of anguish, regret and sadness. There would be no private farewells; he was delivering his goodbye in Father's room to keep them friendly and casual, avoiding the risk of strong emotions or any messy, tearful apologies.

Could she let him go in such an impersonal fashion?

She ought to. Being the injured party, he should have right to determine how much interaction they had.

But her aching heart couldn't quite accept that. No, before she saw him for what might be the last time she vowed to give him one last gift to remember her by.

The following evening, Charis could hardly consume a morsel during dinner, knowing Greg would be stopping by at some time during the night to say his goodbyes.

Apparently she was not as successful at concealing her agitation as she'd hoped, for when they'd finished their meal and Charis had made her father coffee, he said quietly, 'Are you concerned about travelling with someone else?'

'Nervous, of course. But if Lattimar's sister and

brother-in-law are as amiable as they seem in the note I received from Prudence Trethwell, we should rub along together quite well. The arrangement is not set in stone, she assured me. If I decide it doesn't suit me, I may end it at any time, with no ill will on either side.'

'I did you a great disservice,' he said sadly. 'I should have warned you long ago about my failing health. Made plans for you.'

'I have plans now, which I think will work out just as well if not better than any we could have devised. I probably would have wanted to continue the business after you decided to retire anyway, and we don't know anyone else I could have joined up with.'

'No, which makes me even more grateful to Lattimar. I wouldn't be comfortable with you travelling alone, with only a hired escort.'

'Don't worry, all is arranged. I just need you to concentrate on getting as well as you can. I do feel guilty about…abandoning you.'

He shook his head. 'You mustn't! I'm grateful for the wonderful experiences we had travelling together, but you are young, with your whole life before you. I would never want to hold you back or tie you down. You must follow your heart and do what will make you happy, love.'

Was she doing what would make her truly happy? Shutting out the image of Greg Lattimar's face, she hoped so.

'Thank you, Father. I intend to.'

He nodded. 'I'm afraid I've done you another disservice, perhaps an even graver one.'

She angled her head at him, puzzled. 'What do you mean?'

'I won't deny it, losing your mother was the greatest tragedy of my life. There's not a day I don't mourn her and miss her. But there's also not a day that I regret loving her, and I treasure every moment we shared. I fear you have perhaps shied away from giving your heart, afraid that loving is not worth the risk of pain. I tell you now that it is worth everything. I've bought and sold costly gems and valuable treasures, so I tell you with assurance that love is the only treasure that is truly priceless.'

He took her hand. 'If you should meet someone who inspires that depth of devotion, don't fear love. I wouldn't have you miss what I had with your mother.'

His words stuck home, penetrating to the depths of her. Conflicted, she knew it wasn't just the enormity of leaving her father soon that was producing such anxiety in her soul.

'But I'm weary now, child. As soon as Mr Lattimar bids me goodnight, I must sleep.'

But if her father wished to rest, how would she be able to dance for Greg, the one last gift she'd promised herself to offer him? Before she could sort out her alarm and confusion, a knock sounded at the door. 'May I come in?' Lattimar's voice called.

Charis went over and opened the door. For the first time since the devastation of her interview with Lady Sayleford, she felt the full force of attraction to him hit her again. Even though he didn't look at her, holding himself aloof, although the voice with which he greeted her father was as warm as always. But though he might not look at her, she knew he felt it too, that invisible ribbon of desire and attraction binding them together.

She hardly remembered the conversation, only half-listening to the exchange between him and her father while she tried to work out how she would still manage to dance for Greg after her father retired. Her attention seized by his bidding her father goodbye, she looked up as he turned to her.

'Miss Dunnfield, I hope your travels are exciting and profitable and the new partnership becomes everything you've dreamed. I'll bid you goodnight, Mr Dunnfield, and both of you goodbye.

'I'm weary, too, Father,' Charis inserted quickly. 'I think I will retire as well.'

'Of course, my dear. Safe travels, Mr Lattimar. I can never sufficiently express my gratitude for all you've done for us.'

Greg held up a self-deprecating hand. 'I'm just pleased to be in a position to be able to arrange things to your satisfaction.'

After giving her father a bow, Greg walked over to open the door and held it politely, letting her go out ahead of him. Once in the hallway, the door closed behind them, he gazed at her, pausing as if to speak, then shook his head. 'Goodbye, my very dear Charis.'

Before he could walk away, she seized his hand.

'One last time, let me express my appreciation for all you've done for Father and me.'

'No need. As I assured your father, it has been my pleasure.'

'It hasn't been all pleasure. I hope you know how deeply I care for you. How I never meant to cause you pain—'

'Hush,' he said, reaching out to stop her lips, sending a jolt of sensation through her as his thumb touched her mouth. 'Again, no need. You must do what is best for you. I'd not be happy if you didn't, just to avoid causing me pain.'

'Would you do one more thing for me?'

'Whatever you want.'

'Will you let me dance for you? I've sung and played for you and Father, but haven't taken the opportunity to dance, which Bayam Zerah always felt was my best talent.'

He flinched, some emotion passing over his face. 'It really would be better—'

'Please!' she cried, panicked that he was going to refuse and she would lose this one last chance to be with him. 'Please,' she repeated softly. 'There's little else I could give you as a parting gift—I know you wouldn't accept a gem or relic, even if I had one to give. But I hope I could give you a glimpse of beauty.'

He gave her a strained smile. 'Very well. You know I could never refuse you anything.'

'Then you'll follow me?'

He sighed, but nodded.

He walked after her. But when she opened the door and beckoned him into her own bed chamber, he halted, shaking his head.

Knowing he was about to refuse, she said in an urgent undertone, 'Father is exhausted and needs to sleep, or I would have performed in his chamber. I can't dance for you in the salon or the library where some servant might interrupt. It must be here. Please?'

Muttering something about idiocy and madness, he followed her in. Filling her with relief that just this once, before their close association ended for ever, she could perform so gracefully, so beautifully, that he would never forget the dance...or her.

She gestured for him to sit on the couch, which had been drawn close to the hearth on which a cheery fire burned, chasing away the chill of the evening. She took a brand from the hearth, lit a censor and within moments the air began to fill with the sweet scent of sandalwood.

Now for the dance. She would call upon all her skill to make it the most exceptional she had ever performed.

Taking up a tambourine from beside the hearth, she began the slow dip and sway of the steps, arms outstretched and shaking the tambourine as she sang the song of Ismail's passion for his beloved.

Though he would not understand the words, the graceful motions of the dance as she undulated towards him and away, towards him and away, would convey the misery and heartache of the pasha who longed to claim a beautiful maiden who belonged to another.

Did she love him too? Might he steal her away? The plaintive melody continued. Then she stopped suddenly, shaking the tambourine violently. Yes, the maiden returned his love, and wanted nothing more than to belong to her beloved.

She'd intended to end the dance here, on that chaste and melancholy note—but when she turned to look at Greg, the unmistakable desire she saw in his eyes inflamed hers too. Perhaps she would perform just one more verse.

From mournful, the song became vibrant, passionate, the movements of her body correspondingly more seductive. Completely swept away now by the erotic mood of the song, she sang the final verse, in which the maiden gave herself joyously to her beloved.

She simply couldn't let Greg go without touching him, feeling his touch, just one more time.

Dropping her tambourine after the final note, she sank down to straddle his lap, pulled his face towards hers and captured his lips.

He jerked in surprise, then opened willingly to her tongue. He kissed her back deeply, and she exulted as his hands went to her breasts, his thumbs stroking the rigid nipples aching for his touch. Gasping at the rush of sensation, she wrapped her legs around his back and pressed herself closer to the rigid hardness in his trousers.

He changed position to roll her onto the couch, shifting him beneath her. She welcomed his weight over her, his hands caressing her breasts as his mouth plundered hers. Far beyond worrying about the consequences, she fumbled at the fastening of her trousers, loosening the silken cords that bound them, opening herself to him.

He slipped a finger into her aching wetness, kissing her harder and deeper while he slid it in and out, up over the tight, throbbing nub and back into her passage, until an explosion of pleasure rocketed through her, stealing breath and sight and consciousness.

She returned to her senses to find him smiling down at her tenderly. 'But now you must let me give you pleasure, too,' she protested.

'You already gave me the unparalleled gift of witnessing yours.'

'Pleasure should be mutual.'

But when she tried to undo the flap of his trousers, the front stretched rigid under the pressure of his erection, he caught her hand and moved it away. 'No, my darling, you mustn't.'

'You mean so much to me,' she whispered. 'I would give you everything, all of me.'

To her dismay, instead of helping her, he sat up and

moved away. Breathing hard, his hands trembling, he said, 'I would give my soul to accept the gift you are offering. But I cannot. Your *kismet*, my love, will take you to the far reaches of the world. How could I let you go, knowing there was a chance you might be carrying my child?'

Abruptly, he stood and paced towards the fire, facing away from her. Anguished and bereft, she jumped up from the couch and ran to him, wrapping her arms around him.

'So you would leave me with no memory of your pleasure?'

He turned round, pulled her back into his arms and kissed her deeply, drawing her tongue into his mouth, tangling it with his, until her just-sated senses began clamouring again.

'To watch you sing and dance is pleasure,' he whispered. 'To touch you is pleasure. To kiss you is to approach the divine. All of paradise I ever hope to merit. But that must be all. This blade of Damascus steel has flaws. I must leave before it cracks, and my resolve splinters into dishonour.'

Backing away, he took her hand and kissed it. 'Goodbye, my love. My life.'

She clutched his fingers, tears dripping down her cheeks. 'I'm so sorry I couldn't be what you need me to be.'

Cupping her face, he kissed her again, tenderly this time. 'Shh, don't weep,' he whispered, wiping away her tears with his thumb. 'I only ever need you to be exactly what you are. Perfection.'

Then, with one last soft kiss, he turned and strode out through the door.

Well, she'd given him her dance and a memory. And discovered more about passion than she'd ever hoped to learn.

How was she now to live without it—and him?

Walking back to the couch, Charis sank down on it, put her face in her hands and wept.

Chapter Twenty

After a brief stop in London, Greg headed to Entremer, determined to bury himself in work. The weather turned, Northumberland having a stream of cold, steady rain which perfectly matched his mood of desolation.

He tried to dull his mind to the anguish, empty his brain of all thought and use the exhaustion produced by hard physical work to keep the memories at bay. He didn't always assist with the tasks needing to be done on the estate, but he was experienced, so the tenants seemed only mildly surprised when he joined in the job of repairing stone walls, thatching cottages and sheep shelters and helping with the shearing. He came back to the manor after long midsummer days to wash off the dirt of his endeavours, force himself to eat food he didn't taste and fall into bed, hoping for dreamless sleep.

He didn't always get his wish. All too often, his unconscious mind replayed the image of Charis dancing for him, then drawing him close. Giving him a passionate kiss that had melted what was left of his heart and fired his passion, only his deep love for her and desire to protect her from harm holding him back from taking what she'd freely offered.

At least he'd been able to offer her a first taste of pleasure.

He'd awake in the depths of the night, aflame with need for her, his body cursing him for not availing himself of her generosity. Staring bleary-eyed into the darkness, he'd remind himself that had he done so, he would feel even worse now. Because of that restraint, he didn't have to worry about her being out somewhere in harsh, difficult or dangerous circumstances, growing heavy with his child with him too far away to watch over her. Blessed with her normal health and vigour, she would be fine. Pru and Johnnie would look out for her.

Then he'd try to blot all thought from his mind and go back to recapture sleep. Usually instead tossing and turning until pale morning light crept into his chamber, and he got up to start the process all over again.

In the early evening two months after his arrival at Entremer, Greg walked wearily into the entrance hall, mulling over whether to clean up and come back down to dine in the small family room, or have a tray sent up to his chamber. As he walked past the blue parlour, the soft lift of a feminine voice sent his pulse rate spiking.

Despite knowing it wasn't her, it couldn't be her, he practically ran into the salon, skidding to a halt on the carpet, as the lady seated on the sofa looked up at him.

His mother, Lady Vraux.

'Mama!' he exclaimed, shocked. 'What brings you to Entremer?'

Closing the book she'd been reading aloud, she studied him, sympathy in her gaze. 'I'm not the lady you hoped to see, I know. But I was worried about you. I needed to see for myself how you were doing.'

'I'm fine, Mama.' She must have been worried indeed to come to Entremer, a place she'd never liked and avoided if at all possible. 'But I'm forgetting my manners. Have you just arrived? Are you settled in?'

'We arrived this morning. I brought Overton and some of the staff and told them to have tea ready when you got back.' She gave him a quick inspection. 'I expect you will want to refresh yourself first.'

'Yes. Give me a few minutes to scrape off the mud and I'll re-join you here in the salon.'

'I'll have the tea ready when you return. Shall I have Cook prepare a plate for you as well? I've already dined myself.'

'Yes, please. I'll be back in a minute.'

Greg trotted up the stairs, wondering about her arrival as he did a hasty wash, brush-off and put on more suitable clothing. He must have looked even worse than he thought when he'd stopped in London after leaving Westdean to tell her his plans before heading north. Mama seldom left London. Although she was invited to very few entertainments, she enjoyed the theatre, opera, concerts by the Philharmonic Society, musical evenings and card parties with friends. The only activity worth doing at Entremer, she always said, was riding, and the parks of London provided ample opportunity for that.

Was she going to query him about Charis? Probably. What should he say? No point trying to avoid the subject; she was too perceptive not to notice the depth of his despair and too perceptive not to know the reason for it. He still found it painful to talk about it. He'd ask at least that the discussion be kept short. With one final look at his hair in the mirror to make sure he'd brushed out all the dirt, he blew out a breath. If there was no avoiding it, he might as well go down and get it over with.

He walked into the parlour to find a fire burning in the hearth, its cheery glow and welcome warmth making him smile and think of Charis. She should be in the sultry warmth of the East she loved by now, probably giving Johnnie instruction on where to obtain the best gems. Perhaps visiting her Ottoman lady friends to discover if some denizen of a harem had jewels she needed to sell. Taking coffee, listening to their stories, enjoying their music.

Loneliness and loss echoed again in the barren desert of his heart.

Suddenly he came to himself, realising he had just been standing there, gazing into the far distance. The look of concern on his mother's face had deepened, but she said pleasantly, 'Come by the fire and let me pour you some tea. Cook will have your dinner for you shortly. I swear, it's like winter here even in late summer. You must be chilled through.'

'I don't particularly notice the cold,' he said. How could he, when the chill that penetrated to the marrow of him had nothing to do with temperature and everything to do with the loss of the one who was all sunlight and warmth and joy? He expected to be grey and chill the rest of his life.

She shivered. 'Well, I do. Come sit beside me.' She patted the sofa.

He took the seat indicated, sipped the warm tea she poured as she chatted about what was happening in London, the latest news from Temper and her husband Giff, who were expecting their first child, and his brother Christopher's current efforts in Parliament.

'All the family is doing well,' she concluded. 'But you, my dear son, are not doing well.'

'No,' he admitted.

Lady Vraux sighed. 'I had great hopes that you would make a match of it with Charis Dunnfield. Lady Sayleford expected it, too. Surely you did not let her go because of concern…for me? My standing in society? I'd be devastated if I thought you'd sacrificed your happiness to try to rectify a situation I've long since made peace with.'

She looked so distraught, he squeezed her hand. 'No, Mama. Actually, I did offer for her—even though marrying a woman who scandalised society would throw away any chance to redeem your and the family's reputation. Initially she accepted me…but I could see she wasn't really happy about it. So I released her. I couldn't bear the thought that I was taking advantage of the misfortune of her father's ill-health to press her to do something that would never make her happy.' He smiled sadly. 'Like the clouds in the sky, she needs to drift where inclination takes her. I'm mired in the English soil; she is the spirit of wind and sun. It would never have worked.'

'You do love her, then.'

'Completely and absolutely.' He swallowed hard. 'Otherwise, I could never have let her go. I think she loves me too. Just not enough. But that's harsh. We are who we are; we cannot remake ourselves to fit a mould that is outside our character just to please someone else, even if we want to. Eventually, ill-fitting restrictions will chafe, until we must destroy the mould or it destroys us.'

'Lady Sayleford told me how devastated Charis and her father were when they lost her mother. She suspects

Charis fears giving her heart and suffering similar loss.' She smiled. 'I expect she's going to find that one doesn't have control over the giving away of one's heart. Love has a mind of its own.'

'That's the bitter truth.'

'You honoured your love by doing what you could to give her what she thinks will make her happy. One can't do more than that. Though that is little enough consolation. I don't want to offer you false cheer or tell you to buck up and endure. But one can survive loss, even loss as painful as this. I did. But then, I had something to cling to. I had you.'

'It was still bad of Vraux not to release you.'

'That's not quite an accurate picture of what happened, you know. At the end, Vraux agreed to a divorce. But if I left, he wouldn't have let me take you with me. I caused Sir Julian so much anguish.' She shook her head. 'I should never have let him fall in love with me to begin with. And then, when the choice became life with him or life with you, I chose my son.'

Shocked to silence, Greg sat stunned, a rapid succession of memories racing through his brain. All the many times he'd failed her, been impertinent, ungrateful, resentful. Amazed at all she'd given up for him.

'It wasn't easy, I admit, but I never regretted my choice. A mother is a poor substitute for the lady you long for, but if I can help, please let me. I wish for you to weather this sadness better than I did my loss.'

'I'm not a beautiful, despairing woman whom a clever and unprincipled scoundrel decided would be a challenge to seduce, as you were after you lost your great love.'

'Well, that should get you off to a better start,' she said wryly, making him laugh.

Sobering, he said, 'You can help most by returning to London, instead of staying here bored and cold while I… work through this. I'm not very good company at present, and I'd like to know you are safe, sheltered and as happy as you can be.'

'I want the same for you. Are you sure there is no chance for…reconsideration?'

'I don't see how. For the first time, I'm truly grateful Vraux has no interest in managing his properties. After I finish here, which may take the rest of the summer, I shall make a tour of all the others, with brief stops in London to see family and in Westdean to check on Mr Dunnfield. So I should stay on the road and busy for the foreseeable future. I appreciate you coming to check on me, though.'

'I hope to encourage you to follow your heart. Happiness is too precious to give up if one has any chance of obtaining it, much more important than society's approval. Family is everything. I pray that you will be able to resolve this. But now, here is your dinner, and we'll talk of other things.'

In the end, Lady Vraux stayed for several more days, the Northumberland weather even grudgingly according them a day of sunshine and warm temperatures that prompted him to abandon his projects and ride out with her. An outing he enjoyed, as she was a capital horsewoman and an amusing companion.

Greg sent her back to London with hugs, urging her to spend some of the money he was earning from the increasing wool yields on some fetching new gowns.

And he settled back to work. In another two weeks, he should finish up repairs on the walls and buildings, check on the production of the iron works, then head south. First to the manor in Kent, checking on the hops and making sure the farmers had all the supplies for beer production, then down to the property in Devon. Then to Westdean on his way back north to check on Mr Dunnfield.

Seeing the man again would be both a pleasure and a wrenching reminder, but he'd promised Charis take good care of her father and he meant to honour his word. And when he was around her father, he could catch a glimmer of her essence, the wisp of an echo of her laughter, memories as painful as they were sweet.

I pray that you will be able to resolve this. At the time Charis had left, he'd believed it impossible. But might there be a way?

He'd explore this new idea, see if it was feasible. Then bide his time, keeping hope in check, until Charis returned again.

Two weeks later, Greg trudged in from the fields, grimy and sore after another day of building rock walls. As he walked in, apologising as usual for the terrible state of his boots and the mud he was tracking in, the butler gave him an odd smile, but he was too weary to wonder at the reason for it.

Until, passing the blue salon on his way to the stairs, he noticed the candles had been lit—and spied a figure seated on the couch. Shock then delight rushed through him. But, no, it couldn't be.

He stood frozen to the spot as the visitor, who must have heard him come in, rose and turned to him.

'It is me,' Charis said, refuting his unspoken statement. 'I realise you are tired and longing for a bath. But would you come speak with me first?'

The fatigue and aching in his back disappeared in the joy of seeing her again, drinking in the beloved lines of her face, appreciating the glory of her hair...which, he realised, another shock running through him, was unbound, flowing down her back in a long silken curtain. She was wearing Ottoman dress.

The same trousers, vest and blouse she'd worn when she'd danced for him at Westdean Manor...

With no memory of moving, he found himself at her side.

'I'm afraid your butler thought me very strange. He almost turned me away for being a wandering Romani, before I assured him I was a guest you would be happy to receive.'

'And so I am. But what brings you to Entremer? Was your journey successful?'

'It was. Successful in a number of ways. I was able to introduce Pru and Johnnie to my friends and contacts in Constantinople. Have a joyful reunion with Bayam Zehra and relate the sad fact of Father's illness. Arrange to purchase some quite magnificent jewels.'

'Are Pru and Johnnie back in London? I thought they intended to continue on to India.'

'They did. But I decided to return to England. The greatest success of the journey was discovering, at long last, who I am and what I was meant to do. Seeing your sister and her husband together reminded me of something Father told me before I left. That I shouldn't fear to love, because nothing else on earth was more important, more rewarding, more lasting. A treasure more precious than diamonds or the most costly pearls.'

She reached up to touch his face. 'Once, you offered me such a gift and, afraid and confused, I backed away. In your great love, you set me free to do what I thought I was meant to do. Only to discover, as I travelled, that apart from you even the sun and brilliant blue skies of Constantinople had lost their lustre. That apart from you, I can never be truly happy. That my true *kismet* is to be by your side.'

'Does that mean...' he said slowly, trying not to let joy outpace a clear confirmation and set himself up once again for painful loss, 'That you are reconsidering forming the partnership with Johnnie?'

'The partnership is already dissolved. I won't let fear and doubt restrain me any longer. The one and only treasure I would like to collect now is your love...and a life together. In cloudy, cold, rainy, impossibly *green* England. If you still want me.'

He pulled her into his arms, his throat too tight for words. Running his fingers through her glorious hair, he kissed the top of her head. 'Of course I still want you. I'll never want anyone else.'

'Then I am yours. As lover, odalisque, wife—whatever you want me to be. As long as I can be with you.'

'As my wife. And as soon as possible. But I wouldn't have you moulder in England for ever. I'd actually come up with another scheme I was going to propose to you when you returned from your travels. Having worked so hard to bring all the Lattimar properties into good heart, I realised these last few weeks that I can spare time to travel periodically. To your beloved Constantinople, so I may meet your friends, tour the bazaars and markets, stay in the house overlooking the Bosporus about which I've heard so much. Let you dance for me again in a chamber with a flowing fountain, scented by jasmine and amber-gris. I thought that prospect might make you reconsider whether or not you could marry me. Be my one and only wife, for ever. So, will you marry me, my love?'

'Willingly, *aziz-e delam*, dearest of my heart! But on one condition.'

Holding her at arm's length, Greg said, 'What would that be?'

'You must allow me to perform another dance for you this very night. But this time, it must be the full, complete, unabridged version—with nothing omitted. I've wasted too much time being careful and cautious. Now I want to embrace every particle of joy from loving you. Are you agreed?'

'As always, I can deny you nothing,' he whispered, lifting her in his arms and carrying her to the stairs.

Epilogue

Three weeks later, his heart at peace and filled with joy, Greg walked into the library at Westdean Manor. He'd arrived at the Sussex seaside earlier that day, accompanied from London by Charis, his mother and Lady Sayleford. While the Countess and Lady Vraux were resting from the journey, Charis had gone immediately to Mr Dunnfield's chamber to spend the afternoon catching up with her father.

Smiling, he put the special licence he'd procured before leaving the city in the estate papers strongbox. Some time later today, he expected the arrival of his best friends and family, who'd been summoned from their respective locations in various parts of England. While Charis had indicated her willingness to marry him anywhere, Greg felt it was most fitting for them to pledge their vows to each other in the place where they had both first admitted their love.

Where Charis had first performed her dance of devotion.

Where he'd steeled himself to send away the woman he loved in order to ensure her happiness.

He still felt awed to the depth of his soul that she'd ultimately decided she could only claim that happiness with him at her side, as her husband.

He'd just relocked the strongbox when a knock sounded at the door, followed by the entry of his two best friends. Delighted, he strode over to clasp the hand of each. 'Alex, Crispin! So glad you've arrived.'

'Good to see you, too,' Alex said. 'And I must say, you look a good deal happier than when I last saw you at Dellamont's wedding.'

'How can one not be happy, after going from uncertainty and loneliness to the astounding miracle of meeting someone who fills your life with joy? As you both should know well. Did you arrive together?'

'Yes,' Dellamont said. 'It took almost a week for your letter to track us down in the north, where Marcella and I were travelling the proposed route of another railway venture. Once I received it, I wrote at once to Alex and suggested we travel together, knowing he was currently in London with Jocelyn, attending the duke.'

'Have any of the others arrived yet?'

'Another carriage was driving up as we walked in,' Alex said. 'I believe it was Giff, arriving with Temper. Your mother said they'd had to travel a little slower, as Temper is with child and not feeling well.'

Greg laughed and shook his head. 'I don't envy the nursemaids they hire. Offspring of a rapscallion like Giff and a wild chit like Temper? The child is going to be a hellion.'

'We left our wives to settle in and pay a call on your bride, then checked with the butler to find you,' Crispin said. 'Will the wedding be tomorrow?'

'Yes. Christopher had one last meeting with some associates in Parliament, but I expect him to arrive with Ellie today. That will make the immediate family complete, except for Pru and Johnnie. But much as I'd love to have my other sister here, I don't want to wait another month for them to return from India before I claim my bride.'

His two friends exchanged glances. 'We completely understand your impatience.'

'I appreciate the two of you making haste to get here in time.'

'There's no way we would miss witnessing your wedding,' Alex said. 'To such an unusual lady, too.'

'We all ended up finding unusual ladies, didn't we? Alex's future duchess a Greek scholar, Crispin's future countess an engineer and my future baroness a world traveller fluent in six languages.'

Alex laughed. 'How did we get to be so lucky?'

'We were incredibly lucky, weren't we?' Greg observed. 'One of us—' he nodded towards Alex '—discovering a gem who'd been hiding in plain sight right in front of him. Another—' he gestured at Crispin '—unexpectedly meeting an engineer's daughter who, in the normal scheme of things, he would never have encountered. And me, who if my father had kept better records, wouldn't have called on an intrepid antiquities trader.'

'Cupid's divine intervention to be sure,' Alex said.

'You would know, with a wife who's a classics scholar,' Crispin said.

'I think it's time for us to toast to your health, your upcoming marriage and our incredible good luck,' Alex proposed.

'I'm fine with that,' Greg said, going to the sideboard to fetch a decanter and glasses. 'Just don't expect me to stay up all night toasting our good luck.'

'He wants to be in the best of health and vigour for *tomorrow* night,' Alex said to Crispin.

'Do you blame him?' Crispin answered.

'Not a bit.'

'Well, before any other guests wander in, I do think a toast is in order,' Greg said. 'To our friendship—long may it endure. To our marriages—may they bring us all the joy and happiness we anticipate. And to our beautiful ladies—the greatest gift chance has ever given us.'

'Hear, hear,' his friends said as they all raised their glasses.

Dinner proceeded later, full of warmth and gaiety, his friends, their wives, his brother and sister and their honoured guest Lady Sayleford kept the witty conversation flowing. But impatient for the morrow, Gregg had a hard time concentrating. Delighted as he was to have his friends and family close, the crowd made it almost impossible to exchange any private words with Charis.

He had to content himself with smiles and longing glances at her where she sat at the other end of the dinner table beside Lady Sayleford.

However, after the party adjourned for tea, skipping the ritual of the gentlemen remaining at table for brandy, Charis, walking by in conversation with his mother, surprised him by pressing a note into his hand. He read it.

Meet me at the cliff walk when your guests go to bed.

Smiling, he caught her eye and nodded. The night was mild and clear, the dark sky spangled with stars and illumined by a full moon.

The beach would be magical.

* * *

An hour later, loitering along the cliff walk, waiting, Greg saw Charis approaching, wrapped in her cloak. Spotting him, she ran towards him, jumping into his arms as he picked her up and whirled her round, then kissed her long and lingeringly. Breaking the kiss at last, he took her hand and led her down to the beach, where moonlight was turning the foam of the breaking waves to silver lace against the pale gleaming sand.

Wrapping his arms around her, he stood behind her as she looked out to the sea she'd once gazed at longingly, pining to leave England. 'Happy?'

'Delirious! Or rather, I will be tomorrow, when I can openly go back to your chamber after the wedding. I cannot wait to lie in your arms as your wife. Until then,' she said with a sigh, 'I'm having to be quite respectable. Lady Sayleford even helped me choose a beautiful, modest gown for the event.'

'What, no Ottoman dress?' he teased.

She turned in his arms to give him a reproving glance. 'Lady Sayleford said as I'm to be a proper English wife, I must be married in a proper English gown. Ottoman dress and the veils are for...later.'

'To wear privately in our chamber, and openly next year when we stay at your house on the Bosporus. We need to finalise plans to visit Bayam Zehra and your other friends in Constantinople.'

'The Bayam will be sorry to have missed our wedding. But she will be so proud of me for snaring as my husband a grand pasha who'll one day be the wealthiest baron in England.'

'I'm the wealthiest man in England right this minute. Because I have your love.'

'As I have yours. As Father said, it is the only jewel truly without price.'

Raising her head, she sealed those words with her kiss.

* * * * *

If you enjoyed this story, be sure to read the first two books in Julia Justiss's Heirs in Waiting miniseries

The Bluestocking Duchess
The Railway Countess

And why not check out her other miniseries
The Cinderella Spinsters

The Awakening of Miss Henley
The Tempting of the Governess
The Enticing of Miss Standish